**The Second in a Series of Jess Williams Novels**

# Brother's Keeper

**By
Robert J. Thomas**

This is a work of fiction. Names, characters, places and incidents are products of the author's imagination or are used fictitiously and are not to be construed as real. Any resemblance to actual events, locales, organizations or persons, living or dead, is entirely coincidental.

All rights reserved. No part of this book may be reproduced or transmitted in any form or by any means, including photocopying, recording, or by any information storage and retrieval system, without the written permission of the publisher. For information contact Boji Books d/b/a R & T Enterprise, Inc., 7474 N. Hix Road, Westland, Michigan 48185

Copyright © 2005 by Robert J. Thomas
Publication Date: January 2006
Published by: boji books d/b/a R & T Enterprise, Inc.
Cover Illustration by Dave Hile, Hile Illustration and Design LLC, Ann Arbor, Michigan

Publisher's Cataloging-In-Publication Data
(Prepared by The Donohue Group, Inc.)


Thomas, Robert J., 1950-
 Brother's keeper / Robert J. Thomas.

 p. ; cm. -- (Jess Williams novels ; 2)
 Sequel to: The reckoning.
 Summary: Jess returns to his hometown of Black Creek, Kansas, to continue on his chosen path of being a professional bounty hunter. His new mission is to locate the brother he never knew he had until recently -- a brother who may have had something to do with one of the murderers of Jess' family.
 ISBN: 0-9668304-3-1

1. Brothers--Fiction. 2. Bounty hunters--Fiction. 3. Western stories. I. Title.

PS3620.H66 B76 2006
813.6                                                    2005902657

In memory of Bernice V. Dopkowski (October 28, 1913~August 29, 1993) In this book I have depicted Bernice as Wanda Dopkowski, a polish immigrant who came out west and worked as a cook in the town of Baxter. I wanted to do something different from the usual dedication page and knowing the impact she had and still has on my wife's life and family, I thought a letter from me to her would be appropriate.

*Dear Wanda:*

*When I first met you, I was dating your granddaughter, Jill. I know that you wondered if our relationship would work. After all, there was a 17 year age difference. I was the Mayor of Westland, Michigan, and politics pretty much ruled every aspect of my life at that time. I know that you wondered what the future held for us and that you only wanted the best for Jill.*

*I want you to know that we got married a few years after you passed away and your granddaughter is very happy. I will make sure that she will always be cared for and loved unconditionally by me. She was the best thing that ever happened to me and I believe that if she could tell you, she would say the same. I wanted you to know that.*

*I am sorry that our time together on this earth was not longer as I feel as though I have missed out on a great relationship. Jill talks about you often. She told me that you had a love for fishing. I have always loved fishing myself and regret not being able to do this together. I plan to take Jill fishing on the lake you loved, Lake Mindemoya, and when we do, I know she will call on you to help her catch the biggest fish.*

*Wanda, your entire family still remembers you, talks about you and still loves you very much. I know that Jill certainly does and I'm sure that wherever you are, you are on a lake, still catching fish. Save a few for me. We all love you and we will always remember you.*

## AUTHOR'S NOTE

For those of you who read THE RECKONING, you know the whole story behind the unique pistol and holster that is depicted on the front cover. For those of you who didn't read THE RECKONING, the pistol and holster on the cover of BROTHER'S KEEPER is the type of pistol and holster used in today's fast draw competitions. I had this pistol custom built as well as the holster.

In THE RECKONING, this pistol is somehow, with no real explanation as to how or why, transported back in time from 2002 to 1876, where young Jess Williams finds it hanging on a peg under his father's hat. Dave Walters, the man who had the pistol and holster custom built for himself in 2002, mysteriously loses them after locking them up in his gun locker. He then finds the pistol and holster in a small basement museum and is so astonished at the discovery; he decides to accept the discovery as if it were fate or destiny.

In SINS OF THE FATHER, the third in the series of Jess Williams Novels, Dave Walters will make another discovery which will somewhat explain why Jess Williams received this unique pistol and holster and it will tie Dave Walters and Jess Williams together for the first time.

# Chapter One

**J**ESS WOKE AT DAYBREAK AND ate a breakfast of salt pork and pan bread. He had learned to make pretty good pan bread and he made it several different ways. Sometimes he made it with just flour and water, mixing it up good and pouring it into the skillet after frying up the salt pork. When it got brown on one side, he would flip it over until brown and then he would cover it and let it bake a few minutes more. Sometimes he added a little corn meal and he had even taken to adding some beef or salt pork crumpled up in it. Sometimes he would make some extra so that he could eat it on the trail during the afternoon when he got hungry.

He ate his breakfast right there under the big oak tree that graciously shaded the family cemetery. He had spent last night sleeping under the big oak tree after returning from a long and very bloody hunt to track down and dispense justice to the three men who had viciously murdered his entire family. His hunt had been very successful. As he ate, he looked around the old home-site and wondered what might have been. He tried to imagine that nothing had happened and he was still working the ranch with his pa. He took a deep breath and he could smell the richness of the soil that had led his pa to this place. He tried to imagine sitting down to supper with his family and enjoying a good home cooked meal that his ma had prepared. He tried to imagine his sister Samantha and whether or not she would ever quit causing him more work and trouble. He tried, but he couldn't. His life had been so drastically changed that there was no going back, even if just for a moment in his thoughts. He had seen too many bad things and killed too many bad men to think much of anything else.

He finished up his breakfast, washing it down with a final cup of hot coffee and said another good-bye to his family. He saddled up Gray and headed into Black Creek, Kansas. As he rode down the trail to the main road leading to town, Jess felt a slight twinge of sorrow slowly creeping into him. The sorrow was like a weight on his shoulders. It was the sorrow of knowing that he would miss most of what people would consider a normal life. Normal was something that he would most likely never get to experience during his lifetime. A tear started to puddle in the corner of his eye but he brushed it away defiantly.

Much, but not all of the rage that still burned deeply within his heart, had been tempered by the knowledge that he had brutally killed all three of the men responsible for the brutal deaths of his family. He also felt the burden of the knowledge that he had killed many men, even though they were all bad men. Well, most of them. Nevada Jackson wasn't a bad man. He was simply a bounty hunter who was very fast with a pistol but also had made a deadly miscalculation. He had thought that he was faster with a pistol than Jess and that had cost him his life. Jess couldn't feel bad about it; it had not been his decision to draw against Nevada. And yet, knowing all of this, something deep within him knew that some of that rage would never leave him. That rage would stay with him to his grave. That was probably a good thing.

The thought of crying for his family didn't enter his mind now. He had promised himself that he had cried for the last time last night. From now on, he would do what he could do to right any wrong or injustice that he saw. He would bring justice to the killers and rapists of innocents just as he had brought justice to the three men responsible for the murder of his pa and the murder and rape of his ma and his little seven-year-old sister, Samantha. It was his own brutal style of justice that he had been forced to learn at such an early age from dealing with other brutal men. It had not been his choice in the beginning but he had now fully accepted it. And in many cases, he would get paid for dispensing such justice. That would be his life's work, and he was already quite good at it. He was now a hunter of men, or as some people called it, a man-killer. And he had just the right tool to help him. That tool was the very unique pistol and holster that had somehow found its way to him a few years ago. He never figured where it came from or why it found its way to him. He was simply grateful for it.

He had spent the last several months using that unique pistol and holster to kill the three men responsible for the murder of his family and quite a few more that made the fatal mistake of getting in his way. He had not wanted to kill those other men but they had forced him to and he could not, or more so, would not allow himself to feel any remorse for it. It had been their choice and he had tried to talk some of them out of it, but he had learned very quickly that mean and stupid seemed to go together hand in hand most of the time for hard cases.

He had not quite turned seventeen yet and he had killed more men than most would kill in a lifetime. He was now a professional bounty hunter with a rapidly rising reputation. A reputation that would cause other men to track him down just to challenge his skill with a pistol and he knew he had to live with that. But he would keep his promise to himself. He would not hunt men for crimes like bank robbery or cattle rustling. He would leave such things to men like Frank Reedy and Sheriff Mark Steele. He would not hire his gun out to some rich rancher to enforce his will on others. He would only hunt men who were responsible for the killing of innocent men, women and children. He would come to the defense of those less able to protect themselves or their families against the brutal treatment that some men inflicted on others. As for those who would challenge him just to prove they were faster than he was, he figured that was their choice to do so and the rest of the world would be far better off without them anyway.

He stopped at the big boulder in the bend of the creek where he had met those three men that fateful day. He let Gray drink his fill as he thought of his trips into town and how he used to stop at the boulder and strip down and jump into the creek. Those were good memories. He would not have many of those in his lifetime and he would have to hold onto them. He would keep the memories stored in the back of his mind and call on them when he needed them. He would keep those memories right next to the place where he kept the rage inside of him to call on when he needed that.

Gray finished his long drink and Jess gently nudged him towards town. He hadn't been back to Black Creek in over four months and the last time he had been there, he had killed his first man, in his first gunfight. That man was Red Carter and as far as Jess was concerned, Red deserved to die that day. He knew that Dick Carter, Red's father, was still offering a three thousand-dollar blood bounty on his head for killing Red. He had second thoughts about riding into Black Creek knowing that Dick Carter was still after him but he had friends there and it was his home after all. Dick Carter could make his own decisions and Jess would make his and Jess figured that whatever happened

happened, and that was that. That was one lesson Jess had learned from his pa. There were times that you could not control events and you simply had to play the cards that life dealt you.

As he rode into Black Creek, the town looked as if it hadn't changed much except for a new building that he noticed, but he could sense that something was different somehow. He couldn't put his finger on it, but it was there nonetheless. He had developed somewhat of a sixth sense about such things. There were people on the street and the boardwalk, but there was something different about the way they acted. He reined up in front of Smythe's General Store and wrapped the reins around the post a few times. It had been a long time since he had seen Jim or Sara Smythe and he was anxious to see a friend. He walked into the store and when he saw that there was no one behind the counter, he called out.

"Hey, doesn't anybody work here anymore!" Jess heard some footsteps and a few seconds later Jim Smythe came out from the back and when he reached the counter he just stood there a moment or two with his mouth agape.

"Oh my Lord! Jess? Is that you? By the love of God, it is you." Jim came around the counter and gave Jess a big bear hug. Jess was somewhat startled by that. He wasn't sure how to react to it. On one hand, he was unsure about letting any man that close to his gun and yet this was someone he would entrust his life to. "Damn good to see you, Jess," Jim added, as he turned his head in the direction of the door going into the kitchen and hollered for Sara. "Sara, you won't believe who's here. Come on out here and see who finally dragged his sorry ass back to see us."

Sara came shuffling quickly out of the back and she almost screamed when she saw Jess standing there. "Jess," she exclaimed, as she ran to him and gave him a hug and a kiss on the cheek and Jess was much more comfortable with that. As she did, she could see the butt of the shotgun strapped to his back.

Jim interrupted. "Come on into the kitchen Jess. Sara will put on a pot of coffee and I'll bet she can whip up a few biscuits for you."

"That's sounds mighty good right about now."

They walked into the kitchen, Sara still clutching Jess' right arm as if she would never let it go. She couldn't help but notice the same unique gun and holster Jess had been wearing when he had left town several months ago. She wondered to herself how many men Jess might have killed so far. Jess sat down with Jim and Sara hastily went about making coffee and some fresh biscuits. She threw in some milk gravy for good measure. Sara served up the coffee and biscuits and they sat around talking small talk for a few minutes before the conversation turned in the direction that he knew it eventually would.

"Well Jess," asked Jim, "did you finally make things right and finish the job you set out to do? Did you catch up with all three of those bastards you were looking for?" Jim already knew the answer; it was simply a question to get the conversation going.

Jess took another long drink of coffee and sat his cup down. He looked at Jim for a moment before he answered. He noticed that Sara had stopped what she was doing and turned to hear the answer. He wondered for a moment if they would think less of him for what he had done. He figured that he needed to be truthful with them since that's how it's supposed to be with good friends. Good friends stick through thick and thin and good or bad. His answer was slow and deliberate.

"I hunted every one of them down and made sure they paid with their life for what they did. I don't feel bad about it either. Those men deserved to die and any others like them." Sara hung her head a little as she fetched some more butter.

Jim nodded at Jess as if he understood and agreed with Jess. "You're already getting quite a reputation, Jess. We've heard about some of it back here. Most people know about some of your gunfights, especially the gunfights with Blake Taggert and Nevada Jackson. Those two were as fast as they come. People also heard about Blake Taggert being the one who murdered that family just outside of Red Rock. Most people like what you did about it."

Sara was watching Jess all the time Jim was talking to him. She could see the dramatic difference in him. He looked ten years older even though she knew he had only been gone about four months. And she could see the coldness and the darkness that lay just below the surface of his eyes. It was a strange look. It was a cold, hard unnerving look and yet she could still see the good deep down and almost hidden unless you looked for it. She could also see the death in his eyes. He knew she was looking him over. He knew that she was sad about the change in his life but there was nothing that he or anyone else could do about it. He wasn't sure that he even wanted to do anything about it. He was what he was—a man-killer. In his mind, someone had to do it. In his mind, it was right.

"Jess," Sara asked, "how many men have you killed so far?"

At first, Jess thought that to be a strange question, but the more he thought about it, he realized it was a question that she had to ask. There was no point in dodging the question, but Jess also figured that there was no point in giving exact numbers or details.

"Let's just say that I've killed more men than most men twice my age. But I will tell you that every single one of them deserved to die. I never started a fight except for Red Carter and two of the three who murdered my family and I never drew first on anyone except for Hank Beard and that was because he tried to ambush me in my room like a coward in the middle of the night."

Sara put her head down and looked at her plate. She had prayed that Jess might be able to have some kind of normal life and she knew now that it would never happen.

Jim broke the awkward silence. "We heard you went into the bounty hunting business. Is that true?"

"Yes. A man has to make a living somehow and it seems to be what I'm good at. And I found out that it pays pretty well too. Besides that, I promised myself that I would only hunt the worst of the lot. I will only hunt down men who have murdered and raped innocent people who have done nothing to deserve it. I won't stand for that. If I run into a man who had done something as terrible as the three men who murdered my family, I would call him out and kill him whether there's a bounty on him or not. Men like that don't deserve to live among the rest of us."

"It's hard to argue that one," Jim said.

"Well, enough about me," Jess said, trying to change the subject. "How are you two doing? How has business been? I noticed no one has come in since I arrived. Is it a slow day or what?"

Jim shook his head in disgust. "Every day is a slow day since that jackass of a new sheriff took over."

"I'm glad to hear that you finally got a new sheriff in town but what does the new sheriff have to do with your business?"

Jim acted like he didn't want to answer. Sara looked at Jim with that look that most men should understand right away but never do and said, "You might as well tell him. He's going to find out anyway and he is going to need to know."

"Need to know what?" Jess asked.

"Oh hell, Sara's right. I might as well tell you. I don't guess that it will come as any surprise that Dick Carter is still after you for killing his son Red. When that one bounty hunter came back—what was his name—oh yeah, Frank Reedy. Well, Reedy came back and gave Carter his money back and told him he wouldn't have anything more to do with hunting you down. Carter was madder than a peeled rattler and I don't think he's cooled off one bit yet."

"I already know that," replied Jess. "What I don't know is what all that has to do with your business?"

"Well, I'm-a-gettin' to that part if you'll let me finish." Jess smiled and picked up his coffee cup and let Jim go on.

"Now, Dick Carter, being the rich son of a bitch that he is, puts up a new general store right down the street and then he uses his money and influence to get a new mayor elected here in town. Then, after he has the mayor in his pocket, he tells the mayor who he wants for the new sheriff in town and it just happens to be one of Carter's men. Now Carter has threatened everyone in town to use the new general store and he's using the sheriff to enforce it. Anytime one of my old customers comes in here, the sheriff comes in and scares them off. Hell, Carter's got the whole town terrified and as nervous as a whore in church and the worst part of it is I think he kind of likes it. And to make matters worse, Carter is using his money to discount everything below my cost just to put me out of business. Hell, he doesn't care about losing a few dollars."

"But why? What does Dick Carter have against the two of you? You've never done anything to him that I'm aware of."

"It's because we're friends of yours. He knows we're like family and when he tried to get us to say something bad about you when he first came into the store after what happened, we wouldn't. Well, that pissed him off and I told him to get the hell out of my store! The rest is history and damn if we ain't just about done in. I don't think we can hold out much longer. He's a mean old cuss, that Carter."

Jess sat his coffee cup down on the table and looked at the coffee in the cup as if he was looking for some answer but he already knew what the answer would be. "The apple doesn't fall far from the tree. His son, Red was the same way. If anyone is at fault in his son's death, it's Dick Carter himself. Sure, I shot Red, but Red deserved it and Dick Carter raised him to be a bad one."

"Jess," said Sara, "why don't you leave town now before Carter finds out you've come back. He has a gang of hired killers and as soon as he knows you're here, they will surely be coming after you. Some of his hired guns are in town right now and I'll bet they already know. You have nothing to prove here. Why not ride out of here while you still can?"

Jess thought about what Sara had just said but he didn't have to think long about it. He knew what he had to do and he made his decision right then and there. That's the way it was with Jess. He set his mind to something and there was no changing it after the decision was made. "I'm not here to prove anything, Sara. But the fact is neither of you abandoned me when times got tough and I don't plan to abandon you either. You both took me in and helped me at a time that I needed it the most. You fed me and left food on my doorstep while I was learning how to fend for myself. You helped bury my family and stuck with me through some tough times. My pa taught me to never forget such things. You were there for me, and now I'm here for you. Jim, you always told me that you always find out who your real friends are when the chips are down and you've always practiced what you preach. Well, so do I.

Here's what we're going to do. First, I have more money in the bank already than I need with my simple lifestyle. I'm going to have Mr. Jameson deposit two hundred dollars into your bank account today."

Jim interrupted quickly. "No, Jess. We don't want you handing out money for our problems."

"Well, who's not letting someone finish what they're trying to say now?"

"Sorry," Jim replied, sheepishly.

"As I was saying, after I have the money deposited into your account, I will pay a visit on the new sheriff and let him know that I won't stand for any more interference with your business from this day forward from him or anyone else."

"You know he's going to ride out and tell Carter five minutes after you see him, don't you?" Jim asked.

Jess smiled a slight but devious smile. "Hell, I wouldn't have it any other way."

Jess gave Sara another hug and shook Jim's hand. Before he let go of Jim's hand he said, "You should have sent for me."

"I figured you were a little busy," replied Jim.

"Well, I was, but I have plenty of time now."

Jess walked out heading straight for the sheriff's office.

"Oh God, Jim," said Sara, shaking her head nervously, "he's going to get himself killed for sure and we are going to be the cause of it."

Now Jim had the devious smile beginning to form across his lips.

"Better men than Dick Carter and his bunch have tried—and failed."

The new sheriff in town was a man by the name of Dan Newcomb. He was one of Carter's hired guns, but he certainly wasn't the best of the lot. Sure, he was fast, but not all that fast and those who really knew him knew that he had a yellow streak down his back wide enough to fill the space between two fence-posts. He would face off with someone but only if he was fairly certain that he could take him. Newcomb did what he was paid to do, which was whatever Dick Carter told him to do. When Jess reached the sheriff's office, the sheriff was just walking down the boardwalk from the opposite direction. He noticed Jess standing in front of the office, staring at him.

"Looking for someone?" Newcomb asked, nonchalantly.

"Actually, I think I just found him, unless you're going to tell me that you found that sheriff's badge and pinned it on for fun."

"No, it's my badge, and I am the Sheriff here. Now, just who the hell are you?"

"My name is Jess Williams."

The name struck Newcomb instantly. The truth was there wasn't one man on Dick Carter's payroll who didn't know the whole story about Jess Williams and how he had killed Dick's only son, Red. Newcomb knew all about Jess and his reputation. He tried to stay calm but Jess was reading Newcomb like a book and he could tell that he was as nervous as a titmouse watching a circling hawk.

"So you're the Jess Williams everyone is talking about. You've got quite a reputation for such a young man. Did you also know that Mr. Carter still has a personal bounty on your head in the amount of three thousand dollars?"

"You plan on collecting it?" asked Jess, staring deep into Newcomb's eyes, unnerving him even more, if that was at all possible.

"Well, I am the Sheriff. I suppose I should lock you up and let Judge Hollingsworth decide what to do with you."

Newcomb hadn't said it with very much conviction and even if he had, it wouldn't have meant much to Jess anyway. "Let's get something straight right up front, Newcomb. You're no sheriff regardless of what that badge you've got pinned on your shirt says. You're nothing more than a hired gun for Carter and that's exactly how I plan to treat you. Now, if you plan to do anything more than flap your gums together, let's get on with it. If not, get the crack of your sorry ass up on your horse and run on out and tell Dick Carter that Jess Williams is back in town and that he doesn't plan on leaving anytime soon."

Newcomb thought momentarily about going for his gun. It would be such a feather in his hat to take out Jess Williams. He would be considered a deadly gunslinger if he did that. He thought about that for a half of a second, and then his senses returned to him. He touched the brim of his hat and nodded. "Well then, I'll let Mr. Carter know that you're in town. Any other message you want me to give to him?"

"As a matter-of-fact, yes. Tell him the next person that does anything to hurt Jim or Sara Smythe, or their business for that matter, will answer to me, and that includes you too, Newcomb."

Newcomb tipped his hat and as he walked away he said, "I'll be sure to give him your message. I don't think he's going to like it though."

"I wouldn't have it any other way," replied Jess, with that same devious smile.

Well, that was that. The gauntlet had been thrown down and Jess was smart enough to know that it meant war. He knew Carter would come to town in a day or so but not before having some of his hired guns take a crack at him first. It was the way rich men did things and Jess understood it, even though he didn't agree with it. Jess knew that when Carter finally did come to town, all hell would break loose and he knew that he had to be prepared for it. He knew many of the townsfolk in Black Creek and many of them had helped him in his time of need. He was not about to walk away from them now, any more than he could walk away from Jim and Sara. Besides, it just wasn't right for one man to run a town like it was his own private domain. People had rights and no one man had the right to take them away. He would take on Carter and everyone else Carter threw at him. He couldn't help himself; it was just his nature.

Jess walked over to the new general store. As he did, he noticed Newcomb riding out of town. Jess didn't have to wonder for a minute as to where he was headed but he did wonder to himself where the comment crack of your sorry ass had come from. Maybe he had heard it somewhere and it just got stuck in his head, waiting for the right moment to be blurted out. He shook his head and smiled. What he didn't know was that Newcomb had already spread the word to some of Carter's hired guns that were in town. Newcomb knew that before he reached the Carter 'D' ranch, every gunslinger and hired gun working for Carter would know that a young man by the name of Jess Williams was in town and that Carter would pay the sum of three thousand dollars to the man who killed him.

The new general store was just about the nicest store he had ever seen. And of course, it was called Carter's General Store. He noticed that it was quite busy with several people milling around the store. Some were buying and some were just milling about. Jess walked into the store and looked around. He recognized some of the people in the store. He was sure that a few of them recognized him, but if they did, they were afraid to say anything or even acknowledge him. Jess walked right up to the counter and picked up a hammer that was laying on it and pounded the counter three times. "I'd like everyone's attention for a moment please."

"Hey, hold on there, Mister," said the clerk behind the counter, "you can't come in here and bang on my counter like that. What the hell d'ya think you're doing?"

"I'm just trying to make an announcement."

"Well, you can't do that," said the clerk.

"Why not?"

"Well, 'cause I say so."

"Really? Well, I say I can."

"Yeah, well, who the hell are you anyway? You work for Carter?"

"No, I don't work for anyone and I wouldn't work for Carter for any amount of money. Now listen up everyone," said Jess, turning his back on the clerk as if he didn't even exist. All of the customers were just standing around in surprise, shocked at what was taking place, but they were paying attention.

"I know some of you people and I know that you used to be loyal customers of Jim and Sara Smythe. I'm here to tell you that Jim not only will match Carter's price, but his service is much better and you all know that. As for being intimidated by the sheriff or Dick Carter, you don't have to put up with that anymore. Most of you people used to get credit from Jim back when you couldn't afford what you needed and he let you pay him back whenever you could. You don't turn your backs on a man like that. Those are the kind of people who make a town what it is. If anyone bothers you for shopping at Smythe's General Store, they'll have to answer directly to me."

There was an awkward moment of silence as all the customers looked at one another and then back at Jess. Then a strange thing happened. Every single one of them quickly walked straight out of the store as if they really hadn't wanted to be in there in the first place. As they were walking out, one older lady spoke very quietly as she walked by Jess. "It sure is nice to see you again, young Mr. Williams." Most of the customers walked into other establishments but three of them went straight across the street to Smythe's General Store. Jess threw the hammer back down on the counter.

The clerk stared at Jess as if somehow the stare would bore a hole in him. "Mr. Carter ain't going to like this one damn bit. You're in a whole heap of trouble, Mister. You'll be lucky to still be alive by tomorrow night. What name shall I tell the undertaker to put on your headstone?"

"Jess Williams is the name but I wouldn't be ordering any headstones yet, unless you want to order one for Carter ahead of time. I have a hunch he might be needing one soon." Jess walked out of the store and the only thing he heard from the clerk was: "Holy shit, things are gonna get wild around here!"

Newcomb's horse was plumb tuckered out when he arrived at the Carter 'D' ranch. He reined up in front of the huge ranch house and quickly scurried inside. He found Dick Carter sitting in the dining room with four of his best hired guns. Carter motioned for him to take a seat and have something to eat. Newcomb sat and picked a warm roll out of a basket on the table and started to pinch off little pieces one at a time and eating them, chewing very slowly. Carter watched him for a minute and knew that Newcomb was just busting at the seams to tell him something but Newcomb knew better than to say anything until he was asked. That was the way it was with Dick Carter. You just didn't run in and start talking to him. He would call you down hard for that. You just had to sit there and act like you had something to tell him and wait for him to ask. That was the way Carter liked it. He liked to control the situation every time. Carter finally put down the chicken leg that he was gnawing on and began to wipe his hands.

"All right, Newcomb. You look like you've swallowed a cat and waiting to spit out a hair ball so tell me what the hell you rode out here to tell me and it better be good since you interrupted my lunch here with my best men."

"Sorry Mr. Carter, but I knew that you would want to know right away."

"Know what?"

"That kid you been looking for, Jess Williams? Well, he rode into town this morning."

Carter fell absolutely silent and he stayed that way for almost a full minute, which is quite a long time when you think about. He looked down at his plate of food of which he had lost all interest in now. His mind wasn't on the food anymore. He was thinking about his only son, Red, and how Jess Williams had killed him in a gunfight. It may have been a fair fight but that didn't matter at all to Dick Carter. Red was just as dead, fair or not. He thought about the discussion he had just had last week with his friend, Cal Hardin, who owned the ranch abutting his. He thought about the note he had just wrote out and sealed in an envelope that he was going to give to a rider tomorrow. He thought about how he had put up three thousand dollars and offered to pay the money to anyone who killed Jess Williams. He thought about how he had sent Frank Reedy and Todd Spicer to hunt Jess down and how Spicer had gotten himself killed. He remembered how Reedy came back to the ranch and returned the money to Carter because refused to go after Jess. And now, here he was, right back in town not more than five miles away. An evil grin began to form on Carter's face and it didn't go unnoticed by anyone in the room. "Did you see him yourself? You're certain it's him?"

"Yes sir. I talked to him myself."

"You talked to him? What the hell did he have to say?"

"He said to tell you that he was back in town and he didn't plan on leaving real soon. He also said he wasn't going to put up with anyone bothering Jim or Sara Smythe or their store."

Carter mumbled something as he hung his head but no one in the room could make out what it was and then he looked back up at Newcomb. "He said that?"

"Yes sir."

"Well, you go back to town and you tell that no good son of a bitch that he's a dead man whether he stays in town or travels to the far ends of the earth. I'm going to see him dead one way or another. You tell him when it's over I'll drag his dead body back here and bury him next to my son's grave so my son can watch me piss on his grave every God-damned morning! You tell him he can count on that and you tell him that I swear by it on my only son's grave!"

"Yes sir. I'll tell him." Newcomb stood up and almost got to the doorway to leave when Carter stopped him.

"Tell me something, Newcomb? Why didn't you kill him when you had the chance? Three thousand dollars ain't enough money for you?"

Newcomb shrank from Carter's cold glare and he put his eyes to the floor as he spoke. He did it partially out of shame but mostly out of fear for Carter's wrath. "Mr. Carter, you know I ain't that good with a pistol. I wouldn't stand a chance against that kid and you know it. I ain't half as fast as any of these men in the room with a gun, sir. I figured I'd just get plugged trying and decided instead to ride out here pronto and let you know."

Normally, Carter would have stood up and punched Newcomb for failing him but he was too consumed with the fact that Jess Williams was right here under his nose.

He was within his grasp. Newcomb sidled out of the room and that left Carter with his four best men. He looked up at the four of them who had been silent all this time. "Well, boys, seems like it's time to earn your pay."

All four of them nodded, still silent. These four were professionals and the best that Carter's money could buy. They understood what that meant and while not one of them was in a hurry to die, every one of them was in a hurry to collect the three thousand. They all went back to finishing their meals, except for Dick Carter. He was thinking about Jess Williams and he felt like the cat that had chased a mouse around the room and finally had it cornered. He was, however, forgetting one small fact. Not all cats have nine lives.

# Chapter Two

**T**ERRENCE HANLEY WAS A RUN of the mill ranch hand and his pistol skills were definitely short of spectacular, which is exactly why Dick Carter had picked him. Carter knew he would need his best hired guns with him when he went into town, which would most likely be tomorrow. Carter had something else he had to attend to though, just in case everything that could go wrong did go wrong, and that's why he had sent for Hanley.

Hanley was grumbling to himself as he walked up to the ranch house to see Carter. He figured maybe he was getting fired for losing a few extra head of cattle to rustlers the last few weeks or even worse, maybe Carter had picked him for one of several men who would ride into town tomorrow and kill this kid named Jess Williams. Hanley had heard the whole story about how Red was killed and how fast the kid was that shot him and the strange looking pistol and holster and all, and he didn't want any part of it. Truth was, neither did most of the men at Carter's ranch, except for the crazy ones. That's exactly what Hanley called men who stood out in the middle of a street, skinned leather, and shot it out for things as little as a cheap whore or a two-bit poker hand.

Carter was waiting for him in the large room that he had always thought of as his study room. It was the room that Carter did all of his heavy thinking about such things as which rancher he would run off next week or which ranch he would buy out or force out if his offer was rejected. Those were big decisions and he needed a place of solitude to do such planning. It was a large room with heavy wood trim all stained in a dark blood red color. It almost looked black until you looked a little closer. He probably chose that color because it matched his mood most of the time, which was usually dark and moody. He was just pouring himself some very expensive brandy into a nice crystal glass when Hanley tapped ever so slightly on the door to the study, which was partially open. "Mr. Carter, sir? You sent for me?"

Hanley was nervous and Carter could sense that right away and knowing what he was going to ask Hanley to do, he wanted to put him at ease right away. "Yes I did, and don't worry, you're not in any trouble. I've lost cattle before and I'll lose cattle again. Some of the other boys are taking care of that little problem." Hanley knew exactly what that meant and he suddenly had a vision of men hanging from tall oak trees with their tongues all swollen and hanging out. "Anyway," continued Carter, "that ain't why I called you in here. Would you like a glass of this fine brandy? It's really quite good."

Hanley went to ease right off. "Yes I would, sir, and thanks for letting me know right away about not being in trouble. I need this job and I was thinking that maybe I'd lost it. I appreciate you going easy on me." Carter poured him a full glass of brandy and Hanley took a nice sip of it and it went down really smooth. "Damn, I don't get this kind of stuff often. I think this is just about the best brandy I've ever had the pleasure of sipping."

"I have that brandy shipped in by the case all the way from New York. It's expensive brandy for sure but it's worth every damn penny."

"Too rich for my blood," said Hanley, taking another slow sip.

Carter smiled. He always enjoyed showing off that he had more money than most men could count. Hanley sat there for a minute or two slowly sipping the fine brandy and then, his curiosity finally got the better of him. "So, why did you call me in here, sir?"

Carter sat down in a plush leather chair and motioned for Hanley to do the same. Hanley sat in the chair and the leather seemed to wrap itself around him with a comfort he had not felt before. "I have a very important job I'd like you to do for me," said Carter, his smile now turning towards a more serious look. "It pays a nice bonus, along with your normal pay, and its easier work than busting your ass herding cattle all day."

"Sounds interesting, but will I live through it to get my bonus?" Hanley asked, wondering if Carter was going to ask him to go into Black Creek for the big showdown.

"Hell yes you'll live through it. I'm not talking about tomorrow when I kill that little no-good son of a bitch of a kid that murdered my only boy. I'm talking about you taking a letter personally to a man for me."

"What letter, and who do I deliver it to?"

"It's a sealed letter and it's only to be read by the person you're going to deliver it to. Only he can open the letter, understand?"

"What if I can't find this man you're talking about?"

"Then bring the message back here to me. And if for some reason you can't do that, I want you to destroy the message. Burn it."

"Who is this person you want me to deliver it to?"

Carter poured them both another glass of the fine brandy. "His name is Tim Sloan." Hanley looked at Carter as though he recognized the name. "Did you say his last name was Sloan?"

"Yes. Why, do you know him?"

"I've heard of Eddie Sloan. He's one mean son of a bitch and they say he's damn quick with a side iron. I heard he outdrew two men at the same time in a bar over in Abilene. The way I hear it, he's one of the best."

"You're right on both counts, but the man I'm sending you to see is his son, Tim Sloan. They say he's just as fast as his old man, and probably faster since he's got youth on his side."

"Never knew Sloan had a kid. Where do I find this Tim Sloan?"

"The last place he was seen was in a town called Holten; about three days ride south of here. That was about two weeks ago. I wired the sheriff there and asked him that if Sloan was still in town, to give him a message to wait there and that a man was coming to hand-deliver him a letter."

"What makes you think that this Tim Sloan will wait around that long?"

"Because I told the sheriff to tell Sloan that the man coming to see him would pay him five hundred dollars just to wait for the letter."

"Not bad pay just for waiting around."

"That's why I figure he'll still be waiting there when you show up."

"So, how much do I get paid for delivering the letter?"

"Same as I'm paying him to wait, five hundred dollars. That's on top of your normal pay. But you have to make sure you hand the letter to him personally and no one else, and you make sure that he reads it before you give him the money, understand?"

"Sir, for five hundred dollars, a man can understand a whole lot."

"Good. I knew I picked the right man for this job." Carter walked over to the counter where the brandy was and picked up a small envelope, which was sealed in wax with Carter's personal stamp in the wax. He walked over to Hanley and handed him the envelope. Then Carter pulled another envelope out of his back pocket. "The sealed envelope is the one you hand personally to Tim Sloan. The other envelope has one thousand dollars in it, five hundred for you, and the other five hundred for Sloan. Hand him the five hundred but only after he reads the letter."

"I don't suppose you're going to tell me what the letter says, are you?"

"No, but it's pretty important to me. I trust you to make sure that you get it to him."

Hanley finished his brandy and stood up. "Consider it done, Mr. Carter."

"I already did."

Hanley walked out and headed for the barn to get his things and saddle up his horse. His horse was a liver chestnut, which was close to the same color of the wood in Carter's study room. He took exceptional care of the horse and the truth was he liked the horse more than he liked most people. Hanley realized that a good horse could mean the difference between life and death sometimes especially on the trail. It was early in the day yet so Hanley figured he might as well get a head start to Holten. He didn't really care what was in the envelope he was to give to Tim Sloan. Hanley was a simple man and he knew how to follow orders. He had a job to do, and he would simply do it without question. He did, however, figure it must be pretty important since Carter was paying a whole lot of money just to have it delivered. And paying a man five hundred dollars just to wait around for a letter was pretty much unheard of. Hanley saddled up and headed out.

Carter sat down in one of his big leather chairs and sipped on his fine brandy. He had a grin forming across his lips that only he and his innermost dark side could really understand. He hadn't told Hanley what the letter to Tim Sloan said in the envelope although he could remember it by heart. He recited it again in his head and the evil grin grew a little wider.

| | |

Jess left Carter's store and walked back to Smythe's General Store. Jim had just finished waiting on the customers that Jess had steered over to him. Jim had a smile on his face for the customers, but as soon as they left, the smile quickly evaporated. "Are you out of your mind? Carter's going to be pissin' blood an' shittin' nails when he hears about this."

"You leave Carter to me."

"And how about his two dozen or so hired guns?"

"I'll deal with them also. Here's all you need to worry about. Have Tony from the livery come over and get my horse and tell him to take good care of him." Jim nodded.

"Good. Now, I need to buy some shotgun shells and I also want a couple boxes of .45 cartridges. I have a feeling that I'm going to need them before this is all over."

"I got lots of ammo. I haven't been selling much lately."

"I'm going to take a little look around town and maybe pay a visit to the saloon." Jess pulled the shotgun

# Brother's Keeper

out of its back sling, checked it to make sure both barrels were loaded, checked his pa's Colt .45 Peacemaker in the front of his belt along with his pistol and headed out the door.

"You watch your back, Jess," said Jim, "they'll be gunnin' for you and before the day is through Carter will know you're here, if he doesn't already." Jess looked back at Jim with a grin and replied in a very low voice, "I'm counting on it."

Jess walked out and stayed on the boardwalk. He walked the entire length of the town on both sides of the street and behind every building in town. He checked for any ambush points including ones that he himself might be forced to use. He stopped in at Tony's Livery. Tony was a big strapping hunk of a man. Some said he was so strong that he could bend the shoes for horses with his bare hands. Yet he was a gentle man and it was hard to rile him but once you did, you'd wish you had riled a grizzly bear watching over a new cub instead. Tony had been the one who had made the grave markers for Jess' family and checked all the stock at the ranch the day his family was buried. Jess had worked for Tony before leaving Black Creek the last time and Tony had taught him some hand-to-hand fighting techniques, which Jess had not forgotten. Tony was a good man and Jess considered him a good friend and more importantly, a man you could count on when things got tough.

"Well, well, look who comes to visit me," Tony said as he looked up and saw Jess standing in his doorway. Tony was in the middle of fitting a horse with some shoes and had been pounding out some metal and hadn't heard Jess walk up. Jess shook his hand and Tony's grip was like a vise.

"Hello, Tony. How have you been?"

"Just fine, but we sure have missed you, Jess. I know it's been a while now but not a day goes by that I don't think about…" Tony's voice trailed off as he realized that it wasn't all that long since that day. "I really miss your pa. He used to stop by and talk some with me whenever he came to town."

"He told me you were the best smithy he'd ever met. He said you could do things with metal that most men couldn't."

"Well, I've heard that you can do things with that fancy pistol of yours that most men can't," Tony said, glancing down at Jess' rig. "Sure is a pretty thing."

"I'm not sure yet whether it's a blessing or a curse though."

"The way things are shaping up here in town, I'd call it a blessing."

"I guess so. I trust you'll take good care of Gray?"

"I'll take care of him like he was my own. Jim brought him over about ten minutes ago. I already brushed him down and put him in a stall with some of my best feed. That's one damn fine horse. I'm the one who sold him to your pa."

Jess thanked Tony again and headed for the saloon. There had been several men who had been eyeing him up and down while he had strolled around town. He knew they were trouble and he knew that before the day ended he would be facing some of them and it wouldn't be over a deck of cards in a friendly game of poker. He figured that he might as well get things started. He knew that most of these men wondered about his reputation and his plan was to capitalize on that. They wanted to test him and he was going to give them the chance to do exactly that. Afterwards, he would either be dead, or they would fear him more than the grim reaper himself. It might even cause some of Carter's hired guns to just leave town rather than have to face him. It was one thing to walk away from a challenge and be labeled a coward forever. It was quite another to simply get on your horse for no particular reason and head out to the next town. Jess' real problem though was that the best of the lot would stay. They were being paid the most and you get what you pay for. Jess figured that he would deal with that later. For now, it was time to thin out the herd.

Two men were standing across from the saloon when Jess walked through the doors. They stood there silently, watching him. Jess knew they were there and that they were watching every move that he made. He was watching them also although he wasn't sure they knew it. He had already made a mental note of what they were carrying. Each of the two men wore a single six-shooter tied down tight and both had a full cartridge belt. The man on the left had a small knife tucked in his left boot. Jess had learned to notice such things quickly. The name of the saloon was Andy's Saloon and there were at least a dozen men inside. Jess sized up the room quickly and calculated that there were about four men that he might have to deal with. Two of them were at the far right end of the bar, and two more sitting in a corner table with a bottle of whiskey and two glasses in front of them on the table. The place went silent for a moment when Jess walked in. He had already pulled the double-barrel 12-gauge out from its holster and had it in his left hand. He walked up to the left end of the bar, placed the shotgun on the bar, and ordered a beer. The chatter in the saloon slowly began to pick up again. He had the barrel of the shotgun pointed straight down the length of the bar towards the two men and he still had his left hand on it. He figured that if he needed to, he could use his left hand to trigger the double-barrel in their direction and still leave his right hand free to use his pistol on the two men at the table. The bartender, Andy, knew Jess and got him a glass of beer and placed it on the bar in front of Jess. Jess threw a dollar on the bar and Andy refused to take it.

"Beer's on me, Jess. I used to serve your pa whenever he came in. He was a damn good man. He stood up for me one time when a couple of cowboys tried to give me a beatin'. I don't forget things like that. I wasn't here the day you shot Red, but I'm glad ya did it. I liked Sheriff Diggs. He was a fair man."

"Thanks, Andy. I appreciate it, especially what you said about my pa. So, how much trouble do you think I'm really in here?"

Andy shook his head. "A whole lot more trouble than I'd care to be in. Old man Carter wants you dead real bad and the hired guns he's got working for him want a piece of that reputation you seem to be building up so early in your life. I'd say that you've got at least six men in town right now who would plug you if they got the chance, and a couple of them are here right now, and at least eight or ten more out at Carter's place that will eventually come for you. Hell, you give them half a chance and some of them would shoot you in the back when ya ain't lookin'. If you've got a lick of sense in you, you'd get on your horse and ride out of town now while you're still standing upright."

"Can't."

"Why not?"

"My horse is tired."

"Well, I'd shoot the damn horse and get me a new one," replied Andy, a disgusted yet somewhat proud look on his face. "But since you're stayin', I'll back ya with my double-barrel I keep down here under the bar. And if I can serve you a cup of coffee in the morning, I'll consider you a lucky man."

"Luck's got nothing to do with it." Jess leaned towards Andy and said in a real soft voice, "I'll tell you what, Andy, I have the two at the end of the bar and the two over in the corner covered. If you need to use that double-barrel, cover anyone else in the place that has a mind to throw in, but I don't think anyone else will."

"You got it my friend."

Jess sipped his beer and waited, knowing he wouldn't have to wait very long. The two men at the bar were staring at him and they were talking quietly back and forth and laughing. Jess figured this was as good a time as any to get the show on the road and that's exactly what this was going to be. He turned to the two men at the bar. They were both grungy looking men who looked like they had been on the trail for awhile, but neither of them looked to be real gunslingers. Jess still had the scattergun lying on the bar pointed in their direction and set for his left hand to grab it and trigger it, if needed. "You boy's sure seem to be having a good time over there. Why don't you let me in on the joke?" Both men turned to face Jess.

"Hell kid, you are the joke!" the larger of the two men said.

"Really? Me? Why, whatever do you mean?" Jess asked innocently.

"Hell," the larger man spoke again, "Carter's put up three thousand dollars on your head. Shit, my maggot-riddled grandma would crawl her ugly ass out of her grave and back-shoot you to collect that kind of money. If that ain't enough, there's a few men in town who would shoot you just for your reputation and then there's about a dozen more getting paid to shoot you and the first one to do it still gets the three thousand dollars of bounty on top of that. Now, I don't know about you, Mister, but I find that funny. You're going to be lucky to live till tomorrow."

Jess took another sip of his beer and purposely took a minute before he replied, and when he did, he used his left hand to cock both barrels of the shotgun and looked straight into the eyes of the two men. "I have a question for the both of you. Do either of you want to try to collect that money?"

Everyone in the room stiffened. Jess figured that there was not a man alive that liked the sound of a 12-gauge scattergun being cocked and they liked it even less when it was being pointed in their direction. The two men certainly didn't like it and the look on both of their faces told Jess everything he needed to know. They didn't want any part of this. One of the two men who were sitting at the table slammed his glass down on the table. Not because he was done with it, and not because he wanted the bartender's attention, he did it to attract Jess' attention. Jess had been watching both of them out of the corner of his eyes. They didn't want to be left out of this deal. After all, three thousand dollars was a whole lot of money just to kill one man.

"I know you two are there," said Jess not even looking directly at them, which was somewhat of an insult in itself, "and if you want in, that's entirely up to you."

One of the two men sitting at the table stood up. The other man stayed in his seat. He was quiet and never looked up at Jess. Jess knew that this man was the more dangerous of the two and the one he had to worry about if he threw in. The way a man acted spoke the loudest and always said more than mere words ever could. "Just because you're Jess Williams you think you can take four men at once?"

"The only thing better than killing two assholes in a saloon, is killing four assholes in a saloon at the same time. And, by the way, it wouldn't be the first time."

Jess could see the nervousness heighten in the two men at the bar. They could see that Jess was as calm as ever and they didn't want any part of this no matter how much money it paid. They had heard of Jess' reputation and while they weren't the smartest two men in town, they were smart enough to know that dead men couldn't spend money. Andy had his double-barrel cocked under the bar. He would throw in with Jess if it came to that.

"We ain't having anything to do with this, Mister. You can count us out. We'll be leaving town soon as we finish our beers." Two men out, Jess thought to himself.

That left the two men at the table. The one was still standing and the other one, who was still seated, was now looking up at Jess. He seemed a little agitated at Jess' remarks. "Mister, did you just call me an asshole?" he asked.

Jess took a drink of his beer and turned to face them directly. He let go of the shotgun on the bar. "I guess I did. However, if you're not trying to collect the blood money on my head, then maybe I'm wrong."

The man slowly stood up. This man was a gunslinger for sure. He had a six-gun in a low cut holster and tied down tight. Jess could sense this man was a killer. He spoke real quiet and sounded sure of himself. He was a confident man and that made him a very dangerous man. "I guess that makes me an asshole then, but I'll be one with half of three thousand dollars."

"No, you'll be one with half of nothing," Jess replied.

"How do you figure that?"

"Because you'll be dead."

"You sound awfully sure of yourself for such a young punk."

"You're about to find out if you plan on pulling that pistol."

"You planning on using that double-barrel you got there?" asked the man who had stood up first.

Jess glanced at the shotgun. He knew that Andy had cocked his double-barrel. He had heard him cock it while he was talking with the other two men who were still standing at the bar. "No, I only use that when I'm dealing with four assholes. For two assholes I only need this," Jess replied as he motioned his head down towards his pistol. "So, which one of you want to be first?"

Jess hardly had gotten the words out of his mouth when both men went for their guns almost simultaneously. The one on Jess's right, the second man to stand up, was faster and Jess hit him with the first shot, square in the middle of the chest. He dropped to the floor. Jess fanned the second shot, which found the other mans stomach not more than a fraction of a second later. He stumbled backward and sat himself down in a chair, his gun dropping to the floor.

"You son of a bitch!" he yelled, "you gut shot me! I swear I'm gonna kill you for that!" Jess cocked his head slightly and smiled at the man. Then he stepped forward and picked up the man's gun. "You're going to need this, aren't you?"

Jess handed the gun back to him. The man was literally dumb founded by this. Jess walked a few steps backward from the man and slowly put his pistol back in its holster. Andy and the two men at the bar were watching this but they couldn't believe what Jess was doing. Andy raised the shotgun up above the bar just in case.

"Well," Jess said, "I guess all you have to do is cock that hammer back and shoot me. That's what you wanted, wasn't it?" The man's eyes went wild.

"You son of a bitch!" The man yelled as he pulled the hammer back to shoot Jess. He never got to pull the trigger. He never even heard the gunshot that killed him. Jess fanned the shot and hit the man right between the eyes. The man's brains sprayed over onto the next table behind him and then he fell backwards in the chair, dead as the floor he landed on.

"Holy shit!" One of the two men at the bar said. "It's time to get the hell out of this town." The two men hurried out of the bar and headed for the livery. They got their horses and rode out but not before they told a few men about what they had just witnessed. Jess walked back to the bar and Andy got him a fresh beer.

"Well, that ought to slow them down a bit, now that they know you won't hesitate. Those two were pretty good gunslingers. It won't be more than an hour and everyone in town will know what happened."

"That's the plan, Andy," replied Jess as he took a long sip of beer. "That's the plan."

# Chapter Three

**T**HE TWO MEN WHO HAD BEEN watching Jess from across the street had seen some of what had taken place in the saloon. They had been thinking about trying to collect the blood money on Jess, but now they had some serious reservations about it. The other two men, who had left the saloon after witnessing the gunfight between Jess and the two men at the table, stopped and talked to them on the way out of town. The two men who had been watching from across the street headed for the livery and mounted their horses. When they rode up to the saloon, they stopped for a moment. Jess was still standing at the bar, watching them through the door. One of the two men stared at Jess, and for a moment, Jess swore that the man was going to dismount and challenge him right then and there. Then Jess saw a change in the man's eyes and knew that there would be no challenge. The man looked at his partner. They both had the same look; the look of fear. They both rode out of town.

Jess' plan was working so far. Two men down and at least four men run out of town. That in itself didn't even the odds, but it certainly made them better. Hopefully, before the night was over a few more men would value their lives more than money or their reputation and leave town while they could still ride a horse sitting upright. At least he hoped so.

"Well," said Andy, "seems like you scared off a few of 'em."

"Looks like it."

"Don't get your britches all bunched up in the crack of your ass. There's sure to be more of them coming into town tonight. You'll have more trouble than an elephant tryin' to use one of them typewritin' machines in a few hours. Tomorrow will be worse for sure, I'm telling ya."

"Boy, you sure do know how to light up a man's life, Andy."

"Just telling ya, that's all."

"Well, thanks for being ready with that scattergun back there. I appreciate the help."

"Hell, you didn't need my help. I reckon you could've taken all four of em by yourself."

"Yeah, but it was the thought that counted," Jess said with a slight grin. Jess finished his beer and headed to the livery, which also served as the blacksmith shop. He asked Tony if he could sleep in the top of the livery tonight and Tony told him he could have anything he needed. Jess had not wanted to stay with Jim and Sara since that might possibly put them in danger. He fully expected some of Carter's men to come for him in the middle of the night and he didn't want to risk their lives. He set himself up above where Gray was stabled. Then, he visited with Jim over at the store. "How's business been?" asked Jess, as he found Jim stocking some ammo behind the counter.

"Business still ain't what it used to be, but for sure a damn sight better. Some of my old customers are trickling in, one by one. The sheriff came by right after I saw him ride back into town, probably from visiting Carter and informing him that you were in town, but he didn't come in like he used to. He just stood around outside and watched."

"I warned him not to bother you or your store ever again. He obviously didn't take me seriously or he has a hearing problem," said Jess. "I suppose he needs a little reminder."

Jess started for the door but Jim wouldn't keep silent. "Jess, don't go messing around with him," Jim pleaded. "It's not worth it. He didn't say anything or bother the customers; he just stood outside and watched."

Jess stopped outside the doorway and turned back to Jim. "It doesn't matter, when I say something, I mean it and he understood exactly what I warned him about. He's obviously decided to test me to see how far he can push me and he's about to find out right now."

Jess walked straight from the store to the sheriff's office. He walked in and found the sheriff sitting at his desk with his feet propped up on the desk. There was another man sitting in the office with the sheriff. Jess figured him to be one of Carter's men. "Sheriff, are you a patient of Doc Johnson?" asked Jess.

"Well, he is the only pill-roller in town so I guess so. Why?"

"Because you obviously have a hearing problem and since it's going to start affecting your health, maybe the Doc can help you out with it?"

"Whatever do you mean, Mr. Williams? Is there some kind of problem?" asked the sheriff in a nervous but sarcastic tone of voice. He seemed a little braver since he had another man in the room with him. "And how would bad hearing, if I had bad hearing, affect my health anyway?"

The other man in the room began to stand up but before he got his rump off the chair, which was to the left of the sheriff's desk, Jess glared at him with eyes that could bore a hole through a chunk of granite. "You sit your ass back down in that chair unless you're ready to be fitted for a pine box and I won't say it again."

That riled the man who was probably in his early forties and not used to being talked to by a young man who didn't even look like he was past twenty yet, but he did, however, sit back down in the chair.

"Now see here," protested Newcomb, "this is my office and I'm the Sheriff of this town unless you've forgotten that already."

Jess walked up and shoved Newcomb's feet off the desk, his boot heels slamming on the wood floor. "You're no sheriff. You're just another hired gun with a tainted badge pinned on you by a mayor who works for a man who thinks he owns the town. If you think for one minute that I'll respect that badge as long as it's pinned on you, you're making a bad assumption and one that could cost you your life. I don't give a shit about you, your badge, the mayor who pinned it on you, or the piece of crap paying you both."

When Jess had walked over to the desk, he had partially turned away from Carter's man in the chair. He could still see him out of the corner of his eye. He heard, more than saw, the man reaching for his gun. Jess pulled his gun, squeezing the trigger as he brought it across his belly and fanned a shot that hit the man in the chest. The barrel of Jess' gun was only a few inches past his left elbow and Jess could feel the heat from the blast. The man fell back onto the chair, breaking one of chair's legs and sending him to the floor. The chair could probably be fixed with a little work but the man, however, could not. He was dead when he hit the floor. Newcomb stood up and Jess took his left hand and slapped Newcomb so hard it put him

# Brother's Keeper 41

against the wall. Not a punch, but open handed, which was much more insulting and exactly why Jess did it. Newcomb never tried to reach for his gun, he knew better after seeing Jess draw. Jess grabbed Newcomb by the neck with his left hand and rammed him into the wall. Jess put his pistol back in its holster and pulled Newcomb's gun out. Newcomb froze in absolute terror. "Oh…God, you're not going to shoot me are you?"

"Not yet. But I will guarantee you this. If you ever go within one hundred feet of Jim and Sara Smythe or their store, you'll need an undertaker instead of something for the pain."

"I won't ever bother them again. You have my word. But, what did you say about pain?"

Jess didn't bother to explain what he meant. He took Newcomb's gun and cracked him hard across the nose with the butt of the pistol. Jess could hear the bone snap in his nose and the blood came gushing out of Newcomb's nose so fast that Jess had to quickly step back so as not to get any blood on his shirt. Newcomb grabbed a white cloth out of his front pocket and held it to his nose with both hands. The cloth quickly turned red from the blood. "Damn it! You broke my nose! You're a crazy man!"

"Maybe I am, but when you need something for the pain, you be sure to go to the new general store to get it, understand? If I so much as see you walk in front of Smythe's General Store you'll be seeing the front end of my pistol instead of the butt end of yours and don't give me a reason to warn you again. If I have to, it'll be your last day on Carter's payroll and your first day in hell."

Jess turned and walked out leaving Newcomb cussing and hollering about his nose and saying something about how Carter was coming to town tomorrow. He had blood all over his face and his shirt. *That sure was messy,* Jess thought to himself. He still had Newcomb's gun in his hand. He unloaded it and threw it in the dirt. It hit the dirt about a second before a bullet hit the dirt not more than two inches from Jess' left foot. Jess reacted with pure instinct. He knew that the bullet came from high up and to his left from the way the dirt sprayed up from the impact. He quickly moved to his right a step and as he did he saw two figures on a roof across the street about ten feet apart. Jess fanned two shots and hit both men dead on. One of the men fell forward off the roof, bounced off the short overhang and fell onto the boardwalk while the other man stumbled backwards and out of sight on the roof. Jess ducked and made a full turn around scanning everything he could to see if there were any more threats. He saw none. One of the townsfolk who had watched the failed ambush walked over to the body that had fallen onto the boardwalk. Jess quickly reloaded his empty chambers before holstering his pistol and walked over to the body.

"That's old Ned Cullen. He won't be missed much," the man said, spitting some tobacco in the dirt.

"Is he one of Carter's men?" asked Jess.

"He was, but I guess he's off the payroll now."

"Do me a favor and go up to the roof and see who the other man is."

"What if he ain't dead yet?"

"Don't worry, he's a goner. I caught him square in the chest. If he's not dead yet, he's not long from a meeting with his maker."

The man walked through an opening between two buildings and walked over to the back of the building where the man had been shot and went up the back steps and onto the roof. Sure enough, the man Jess had shot in the chest was lying face down, dead in a pool of his own blood. The man went back down and told Jess it was another one of Carter's men but that he didn't know his name.

"Thanks for the help, Mister."

"No problem. Most of us here in town understand what's going on. You're fighting for us and we sure appreciate it. We ain't gunfighters but we'll do what we can to help. Carter's had an iron grip on this town since you left and it's high time someone did something about it. Sure can't count on the new sheriff; Carter owns him lock, stock and barrel, just like he owns the mayor."

"I have a hunch the sheriff might back off a little."

Just as the man was giving Jess a look of puzzlement the sheriff came storming out of his office with a rag that was dripping blood all over the boardwalk. Newcomb was heading straight for Doc Johnson's office, and cussing up a storm. The man looked at Jess and said, "What the hell happened to him?"

"I gave him something else to do to occupy his time other than bothering Jim or Sara Smythe."

The man chuckled at that. "I think it's gonna work," the man said.

Jess had noticed through all of this that the blacksmith, Tony, and the Barkeep, Andy, had appeared in front of their doors. Tony had his Winchester rifle in his hands and Andy had his double-barrel. They nodded their heads to him as if to say that they were watching his back and he could count of them when the time came. It gave Jess a comfort level he was not used to. He nodded back and they knew exactly what he meant. Thanks for watching my back. They went back into their respective establishments and back to work. Normally, Jess would apply for any bounty that these two men might have had on their heads, but he knew that he could not rely on Newcomb to assist in that so he figured to hell with it. He did, however, remove a very nice pistol and holster from the very dead Ned Cullen, along with fifty dollars that he found in his front pocket. He figured that he would give the pistol and holster to Jim Smythe to sell. He climbed up the back steps to the roof where the other man lay dead and he picked up a very nice model 1876 Winchester rifle and another thirty dollars. The dead man's pistol and holster wasn't worth taking it off him.

He figured that the ambush was a result of Newcomb's trip out to see Carter earlier. He realized that this was a personal war between himself and Dick Carter but it was also a fight for the townspeople. This town had been part of his life and the townspeople had stood by him and his family when they had needed it the most. His pa had been friends with most of the long time residents. His pa would have wanted Jess to help these people and that's exactly what he was going to do. Even if it cost him his life, which was entirely possible, the way things were going. Two more down, he thought to himself. The odds were still bad, but they were getting better by the hour. He knew that he would have more trouble tonight and he would be prepared for it, as always.

Jess decided to go back to the saloon and get something to eat. Andy's daughter, LeAnn, was an attractive woman, with medium brown hair and brown eyes. She had a nice shape but you could tell she was a sturdy woman and quite a talker. Andy had once commented that she could talk a man right out of his passions. LeAnn did most of the cooking and serving at the saloon. Simple meals like stew, beans, cornbread or steaks and not much else.

Jess took a seat at a corner table and Andy brought him a beer. "Andy, you better bring me some coffee and make it strong. I think I'm going to need to be awake most of the night."

Andy nodded, knowing exactly what he meant and went back and got Jess a hot cup of coffee. "Can I get ya anything else?"

"Well, I am sort of hungry. How about a plate of whatever smells so good back there?" Jess said, nodding in the direction of the kitchen. "Oh—and Andy, thanks for today."

"It was my pleasure, Jess. It weren't nothin' compared to what you're doin' for all of us."

About five minutes later LeAnn came out from the kitchen carrying a huge plate of stew and homemade bread. It smelled like heaven. She put the plate down in front of Jess and poured him another cup of coffee.

"My, my, my, Jess Williams, you sure look as cute as you did when you left here a few years ago. I remember you coming into town and picking up supplies for your pa. Don't you remember me? I used to see you over at Smythe's place picking out candy? Didn't you see me in there? I used to go there every time you came into town. How have you been? I heard you shot a lot of men already and that you're faster than a rattlesnake and do you have a girlfriend or a woman you're partial to and…"

"Damn it, LeAnn, let the man alone to eat his meal. He don't need to listen to you jack your jaws all day long. Get your ass back there in the kitchen where it belongs!" Andy hollered.

Jess never said a word; not that he would get one in anyway. He just looked at LeAnn and smiled while she had talked. Now, he watched her as she threw her head back and stormed back into the kitchen. Just as she got to the door, Jess said, "Yes and no." LeAnn turned around with a look of puzzlement on her face.

"Yes, I do remember you at the general store—and no, I have no woman that I'm partial to."

LeAnn smiled one of those devious smiles. "Well, maybe we need to change that." Jess didn't respond; he just looked at her, now regretting the answer he had given. I sure have to learn when to keep my mouth shut, Jess thought to himself.

"I told ya to get yer ass back in the kitchen, now!" Andy yelled. LeAnn threw her father a kiss and went back to cooking. Jess looked at Andy who had this strange look of frustration and hopefulness all wrapped up in one bewildering look.

"I shouldn't have said that, huh Andy?"

"No you shouldn't have but I'm shore glad ya did." Now Jess had a strange look on his face. He shook his head and went back to eating, as he said, "No way, Andy."

Andy's head just kind of hung a little low, his hopes dashed. "Damn women, you can't live with them and you can't shoot 'em."

Jess chuckled as he began to eat the heaping plate of pork stew. The bread was as good as any biscuit's he had ever eaten—almost. He finished his meal and went back to the livery and asked Tony if he would keep watch while he took a little nap up in the top of the barn. Jess knew he wouldn't get much sleep tonight and he wanted to rest while he had the chance to do so without someone ambushing him and the way he figured it, the next ambush would take place in the late hours of the night.

"You go on up and make yourself comfy, Jess. I'll wake you before I leave, which won't be for another three hours or so," Tony told him.

"Thanks, but make sure you holler up to me, even if you leave for five minutes."

"I will, don't you worry none about it." Jess felt comfortable that he could nod off and finally get some rest. He knew he was going to need it later. He could hear Tony downstairs and he could tell that Tony had took to doing work that caused the least bit of noise and Jess thought that awfully nice of him. Tony was a good man and one that Jess figured he could count on when the going got tough. He finally fell off to sleep with his left hand on his double-barrel lying across his stomach. He woke to gunfire and Tony hollering up to him.

"Jess! Jess! You better come on down here!" Jess scrambled to his feet and climbed down to the bottom level. "There's shooting over at the saloon. Been about three shots so far. I was heading over there with my rifle, but wanted to wake you first."

"Thanks," Jess said, shaking the cobwebs of sleep off as he slung his shotgun into its back sling. "But why don't you let me handle it and you wait here with your rifle. You keep a watch on the tops of the buildings just in case they try that little trick they pulled earlier again. This might be another set-up for me."

"Alright, but I'll come a runnin' if you need me."

Jess headed for the saloon. He kept a close watch on the buildings in case this was another ambush. Tony watched the tops of the buildings but saw nothing going on. Jess walked up to the front door of the saloon and looked inside. He saw LeAnn holding a rag to Andy's shoulder, which was bleeding quite profusely, from what was obviously a bullet wound. Andy was sitting down at one of the tables and he looked like he was in more pain than a dog walking on rocks with a nail in his paw. The two men at the bar both looked like they had been drinking more than their share of whiskey. Neither of them looked like gunslingers to Jess, but one of them still had his pistol on the bar, obviously the one who had shot Andy. The other man was short and paunchy and he looked like he didn't want to be there. Jess knew he would not be the problem. Jess walked in and both men looked at him. The one who had his pistol on the bar placed his hand on the butt of the pistol, but he didn't pick it up. He saw a look in Jess' eyes that prevented him from doing so. The man did, however, keep his hand on the butt of his pistol and his thumb on the hammer. The other man looked at Jess, but said nothing. He simply put both of his hands on the bar as if to say he wasn't going to be a part of this. Both men were looking at Jess who walked to his left a little closer to Andy and LeAnn but not so close as to put them in the line of fire. The man holding the pistol spoke. "And who might you be?"

Jess didn't answer. Without ever taking his eyes off the two men, he asked Andy how he was doing. "How the hell ya think I'm doin'! I've been shot, goddamn it! I'm bleedin' like a stuck pig and that bastard right there shot me," hollered Andy, glaring at the man at the bar.

"Well, I would not a had to if'n you hadn't reached for that damn shotgun back behind the bar."

"I wouldn't a had to if you'd of shut yer yap like I warned ya." Andy said, moaning with pain.

"Well, she does have a nice ass! A little extra meat to it, but that's how I likes my women, strong and meaty," the man said as he spat some of the liquid from his chew onto the floor. Andy went to say something but LeAnn beat him to it.

"You ain't gettin any of this ass or anything else for that matter, Mister."

"You know you want it. You're jest playin' hard to get. I likes that too."

"You are nothing but a filthy pig! You get the hell out of here!"

"And who's gonna make me?" the man said in a leering voice. LeAnn went to answer but Jess cut her off mid-sentence, which in itself, was quite a feat.

"I guess that would be me."

The man, who had been eyeing LeAnn up and down, looked back at Jess. "Let me tell ya somethin', boy. I been eatin' young-uns like you fer breakfast the last twenty years. You ain't makin' me do nothin' unless I want to."

"I hope you're hungry, then, because you'll be eating something in about one minute, which is just about all the time you have to leave."

"I'm real scared. Ain't you scared Barry?" He said nodding back to his partner behind him at the bar, who had not moved or said a word during all of this.

"Cole, I think we otta just leave," Barry said, still not moving his hands from the bar.

"I ain't goin' nowhere, less I want to! This little shit ain't makin' us do nothin'!"

"You've got about another thirty seconds or so left. I advise you use them wisely," Jess warned the man.

"You suck my dirty shorts, boy! Case you missed it, I got my hand on the butt of my pistol and your'n is still stuck in your holster. I think you're the one who otta get whilst ya can!"

"You're down to about fifteen seconds," Jess replied, calm as a cat curled up on a blanket.

"And jest what do you plan on doin' after that, boy?"

"I plan on putting a little lead in your diet."

"You ain't got the gonads for it, boy."

"Five seconds," Jess said; his right hand at the ready. Andy moaned again. Cole's face got red like an apple. Cole Parker wasn't the smartest man you would ever meet, which is probably why he didn't see in Jess what his partner, Barry Jacobs, had seen. If he had, he would have ridden out of town while he had the chance. Jess saw Cole tighten his grip on the butt of his pistol. Cole figured all he had to do was cock and shoot. He figured he had the advantage over this young man standing him down. He figured he'd shoot this kid and then get his hands on LeAnn. He figured dead wrong. He actually got to lift the pistol off the bar but he never got to finish cocking the hammer back before Jess' shot caught him square in the chest. The man looked surprised and tried to speak but nothing came out except a little spittle with some blood and tobacco mixed in with it. He fell forward and landed face down on the wooden floor with a heavy thud. His partner, Barry, never moved a muscle, which is the only thing that saved his life. Jess' pistol was still out and the barrel was smoking and pointed straight at Barry Jacobs, and as usual, his left hand was ready to fan another round.

"I ain't pullin' on ya, Mister," Barry said, keeping his hands on the bar. "I know who ya are and my momma didn't raise no fool. I'll jest be leavin' if'n that's okay?"

"I think that's a wise decision Barry. When you leave, keep on leaving, right out of town and don't come back, ever."

"I'll be gone in five minutes, you can be sure of that." Barry took one look at his pal on the floor on his way out. He never put his hands down by his side until he got outside the saloon. He was taking no chance that Jess would consider him a threat. He wanted to live another day and find a new pal and maybe one with a little more sense. Jess reloaded and holstered his gun and looked back over at Andy who was still bleeding. He started to speak but LeAnn beat him to it.

"Why, Jess Williams. I've never seen anyone draw a pistol that fast before! That man never had a chance. You sure are something and…"

"Would you just shut yer ever lovin' jaws, woman, and go and get the Doc before I bleed to death right here in this damn chair!" LeAnn snorted at her father and headed out the door to go and get Doc Johnson. Before she got to the door Andy hollered out again.

"I swear by God that the next man that comes in here and wants ya, I'll let him take ya!" LeAnn stopped for a moment and looked at her father and said,"well, Jess was the next man in here." She looked at Jess and headed out the door for the Doc. Andy looked up at Jess with a look like a hungry dog begging for some scraps.

"Don't look at me." Jess exclaimed. "Not a chance in hell!" Andy lowered his head and just moaned. Not from the bullet wound in his shoulder though.

# **Chapter Four**

**D**OC JOHNSON AND LEANN both came running into the saloon and the Doc immediately went to look at Andy's wound. "Well, you're lucky, Andy. The bullet went right through the flesh and it doesn't look like it did that much damage. Come on over to the office and I'll fix you right up."

"Lucky? Since when is it lucky a man gets shot?"

"I'd say you're a damn sight luckier than this fellow lying here," the Doc said, nodding at the dead man lying on the floor of the saloon. Andy moaned and let the Doc help him out of his chair. LeAnn helped also and she started walking out of the saloon with Andy and the Doc.

"Where the hell do ya think your goin' woman?" Andy asked LeAnn, groaning with pain.

"I'm going over to the Doc's place with you."

"Like hell you are! You gotta run this damn place till I git back from the Doc's. He don't need any help causing me any more pain than I got right now!"

Doc Johnson had a look of indignation on his face. "On second thought," Doc said, looking at Andy's shoulder, "maybe I should explore around a little just to make sure there are no pieces of bone or lead floating around in there."

Andy just moaned some more knowing that he would pay for his remark. He looked over at Jess and said, "I shouldn't have said that, huh, Jess?"

Jess shook his head in sympathy and simply said, "Nope, you sure shouldn't have."

The Doc took him out and walked him over to his place. That left Jess inside the saloon with a dead man and LeAnn. Suddenly, he wished he hadn't shot the man or at the very most just wounded him.

"Well, Jess Williams, I guess I should give you a great big kiss for saving Daddy and me. What do you think about that?" Jess felt strangely uncomfortable. It was a feeling he hadn't experienced before and he did not like it one bit.

Tony from the Livery came in before Jess could respond. He looked at the dead man on the floor and looked back up at Jess. "You sure are having a busy day, ain't ya?"

"Yeah, and I don't see it slowing down much either. Tony, could you get some men over here and get this body over to the Undertaker? I have to go see Jim and Sara."

"Sure thing, Jess, I'll tend to it right now." Jess nodded at LeAnn and before she could say anything to stop him, he was out the doors of the saloon like a stampeder. The fact that he got out before she spoke was nothing short of a small miracle. Jess hadn't really planned on visiting Jim and Sara; he had used it as an excuse to get out of LeAnn's sight. She looked a little too much like a starving cat eyeing up a big bowl of milk. He decided that he would visit the general store and have a cup of coffee with Jim and Sara anyway. He always enjoyed that. Jess found Jim stocking some shelves since business was picking up. Sara put on a pot of coffee and the three of them sat down.

"Business must be pretty good if you're restocking shelves already," Jess said.

"Sure is, thanks to you. I'm still not sure it was the right decision for you though."

"How's that?"

"Carter's not going to stop until he gets you. He ain't the type. He ain't used to losing. He's already tried to have you killed and I hear tell he's coming into town tomorrow to make sure you don't get out of town alive. He's a mean cuss and he won't stop until one of you are dead."

"I figure you're right about that. This will never be over until one of us is dead and there is no getting around that. That's why there's no sense trying to get out of this. He'll hunt me down even if I leave town. I might as well end it here, right now, one way or another."

Jim lowered his head a little. "Well, I just feel kind of responsible for it. Hell, we could've retired and just let that old cuss get his way," said Jim, not really meaning it.

"You know as well as I do that that would never have satisfied him anyway. Men like Carter are used to pushing people around and making them do what he wants them to do. That's going to end right here and soon. You've got a right to run your business and the only reason you're being punished is because the two of you are my friends. I won't stand for that."

Sara got up and got the coffee and poured three cups. She got out some cornbread and put it on the table. "You know Jess," Sara piped in, "Jim's right. We could survive okay with the way things were. It's not worth you getting killed over. I'd rather burn this place down and leave town with what we could carry in a wagon before seeing anything happen to you."

"That's exactly why I won't leave. You two are good people and my friends. I won't just abandon you and leave town. I could never live with myself. Besides, Carter is the kind of man who needs to learn that he doesn't own the world."

"What are you going to do when he comes to town tomorrow?" Jim asked.

"I'm more concerned with getting through the night, right now. As for tomorrow, I'll deal with it when it gets here. I can tell you this though. If Carter comes to town, I'll kill him for sure. His hired guns may get me in the process but he will be the first one to go down. He's the one who caused all this grief and he's the one who's going to pay for it and not with all his money, he's going to pay for it with his life."

Jim and Sara looked at one another and knew there was no way they could talk Jess out of any of this. And they also knew that he was right. Even though they didn't agree with the direction in life that Jess had chosen, they knew that men like Carter would just push and push the common people until they gave up, and when that finally happened, he would push some more until he had everything they owned. They both knew that Carter would never leave the town alone, even if he did succeed in having Jess killed. He had the town under his thumb now and he would never give it up. That was the way it was with most rich and powerful men. Once they had the taste of power, the only way they would give it up is when you pried it from their cold dead fingers.

Jess picked up a nice slab of warm cornbread and buttered it heavily. He began to eat it but his mind wasn't really on the cornbread even though it tasted wonderful. He was deep in thought about something else. Not about Carter or the fact that there were as many as a dozen men who would shoot him on sight for the money or the reputation. He was thinking about his twin brother, Tim

Sloan. He knew that once he settled things in town, and if he survived it, he would have to turn his attention to his brother. He would have to find him and find out how and why his brother had come to know Blake Taggert, one of the murderers of his family. But he couldn't think about it much right now. He had to keep focused on his immediate problem, trying to keep from getting killed by one of Carter's thugs or even Carter himself. While Jess steadfastly refused to stay overnight at Jim and Sara's, he did agree to take a short nap. He figured he would head to Andy's Saloon shortly after dusk. He had gotten two good hours of sleep before Sara woke him. He grabbed a quick swallow of coffee and headed down to the saloon.

Jess watched carefully while he walked over to Andy's. He noticed Tony sitting slightly inside the door of his livery, with his Winchester across his lap. Jess nodded to him and felt very fortunate to have a friend who would stick by him in a time like this. Men like that, in fact, were not all that common. Most men would have went home, had their supper and resting between some cool sheets, but not Tony. Here he was, watching the rooftops and any other ambush points he could see from his vantage point. Jess stopped outside of Andy's, looking in to see who was in there. He saw Andy behind the bar and Andy gave him that look that said it was okay to enter. Jess walked in and surveyed the room. There were over a dozen men in the saloon and Jess quickly sized them up. There were only two men who might be a problem. The rest were there for the show, if there was one. Andy brought Jess a hot cup of coffee and Jess sipped it slowly.

"Didn't plan on seeing you back here so soon," said Jess.

"I wouldn't want to miss any fireworks."

"You might get shot again."

"They'd just put me out of my misery."

"Misery?" Jess asked, with a grin. "You've got it made. You've got a great saloon to run here and a wonderful daughter by your side."

"Who the hell you think I was talkin' about when I said misery?"

Jess shook his head and smiled. Just then, LeAnn came out of the back room with a few plates of food. "Why Jess Williams, the way you ran out of here today, I didn't think I would ever see you back in here," she said, obviously a little miffed by Jess' quick departure earlier.

"I missed Andy," replied Jess. LeAnn threw her head back and stormed back into the kitchen area.

"I think I understand," Jess said to Andy.

"Huh? 'Bout what?" Andy asked, somewhat confused.

"That thing you said about misery."

Andy nodded, finally catching on. Jess stayed at the saloon for the next several hours expecting something to happen, but surprisingly, nothing did. There were a few men who had given Jess more than a few glances but they were just curious and Jess knew they would not be a problem. About two o'clock in the morning, the place was almost empty. There was one man at the bar who was totally inebriated and Andy kept trying to get him to go home. LeAnn had left already and there were two men who were deadlocked in a poker game, neither one of them wanting to give up. Jess thanked Andy and headed to the livery to get what little rest he could. Tony was gone from his spot when Jess got there. Jess climbed up to the top and he pulled the ladder up with him. He figured there was no sense in making it easy if someone decided to pay him a visit in the middle of the night. Jess checked the floor for squeaks and found a quiet spot in a dark area and he threw down some hay for a little cushion. Then he found a small chunk of wood on the floor and he placed it close to where he was going to sleep. He was thankful for the blanket and pillow that Tony had placed up there. Jess hung the back sling with the double-barrel on a nail within easy reach and lay down with his pistol in his hand, resting on his stomach.

Men like Jess never really slept soundly. They couldn't take the chance. They could, however, sleep through certain natural sounds. Sounds like frogs croaking or crickets chirping. They could sleep while owls hooted and coyotes howled. But certain noises, noises that didn't seem to fit or belong to the natural order of things, would suddenly startle a man like Jess and wake him. It was just that sort of unnatural noise that the ambusher in the bottom of the livery made that sentenced him to a certain death. He had brushed his left elbow against a wall where there were some bits hanging up and the metal on one of the bits bumped the wall ever so slightly. Jess' subconscious woke him. He wasn't sure what he had heard, only that he had heard something out of the ordinary, something that didn't quite fit, and that meant danger.

He slowly rose from his makeshift bed and stood up, backing himself up against the wall where it was pitch black next to his shotgun and waited, watching for any movement. There were two men. One was standing just inside the front door of the livery, a pistol exposed in his right hand. Jess couldn't see the other man but he could tell the man was below him by watching the face of the man in the doorway nodding in the direction of the man below Jess. The man at the door was pointing his pistol up to the top of the livery. Jess knew he had only seconds to act before they would spot him. He picked up the small chunk of wood he had found on the floor earlier. Then he very quietly reholstered his pistol and pulled the shotgun out of its sling.

Jess threw the piece of wood to the right of the man in the doorway. As the exact same instant that the wood hit the floor, Jess cocked both barrels. Just as the man in the doorway shifted his attention to the sound of the wood hitting the floor Jess let him have the first shot and the man's head exploded like a melon. Before the man fell, Jess stepped off the top and jumped straight down to the floor, turning around in the opposite direction towards where he figured the other man was. Before Jess' feet hit the floor he spotted the man and let him have the second barrel just as the man's shot went wild, missing Jess by at least five feet. The shotgun blast hit the man full force in the middle of his chest. The force slammed him against the wall and he hit the ground, never to move again.

Tony lived behind the livery and Jess could hear him running up the short trail and saw him enter the back door. He had his Winchester and an oil lamp in his hands. Tony looked at the two men and looked at Jess who looked no worse for wear. "You okay Jess?" asked Tony, putting his rifle across his left arm and setting the lamp down on a worktable.

"Better than these two boys."

"Can't argue with you on that."

"You know these two? Are they working for Carter?"

"That one by the front door is one of Carter's men. Never seen that one though," Tony said, nodding in the direction of the other dead man lying in a pile of hay. "Must be one of the many fans you've gained since you came to town."

"I do seem to have a lot of people interested in me, don't I?"

"You are becoming right popular, and that's a fact. Hell, you ought to run for Mayor. You would win hands down."

Just then, Andy came running up to the front of the livery, his double-barrel in his left hand. He was breathing heavy and moaning about his shoulder. "Jesus Christ," Andy exclaimed, "don't ya ever take a break?"

"Only when they let me, Andy."

"Well, the odds are gettin' better. Hell, you must've killed damn near a dozen men today alone," said Andy.

"That's how those rumors get started. Actually, it's closer to a half-dozen," Jess replied.

Andy cocked his head and gave Jess that funny look. "Like it really matters."

"Well," Tony said, "I'll take care of the bodies. Jess, why don't you go on back up and get some rest. I'll stand guard again so you can get some sleep. You're going to need all you can get for tomorrow."

"Yeah," Andy agreed, "I'm sure you're gonna have quite a day tomorrow. Probably worse than today, if that's at all possible."

"You know, Andy, you're just a little ball full of good news," replied Jess as he used a rake to pull the ladder back down so he could climb up to the top.

"Don't get me riled up. I'll send LeAnn over to ya."

"God no, I'd rather deal with a few more armed ambushers," Jess replied. Andy and Tony both laughed at that.

Tony took care of the bodies and sat guard until about five in the morning. Andy went back home after having a cup of coffee with Tony. Jess had listened to the two of them chat back and forth before he finally fell off to sleep. Jess remembered shuddering a little just before he fell off to sleep. He thought it might have been from the chill in the night air but he realized it was really from the thought of Andy sending LeAnn over like he had threatened. A few hours later Tony woke Jess and Jess climbed down and had a few cups of strong hot coffee with Tony. They sat there and watched the small town come to life. People were slowly coming out and moving around. Jess smiled when he saw two people walk into Smythe's General Store inside of a half-hour. He smiled mostly because not one person had yet entered Carter's General Store except for the clerk that Jess had met when he had went into Carter's store yesterday. Jess spotted Sheriff Newcomb opening his office, his nose still bandaged from his encounter with Jess.

"Nice piece of work on the sheriff by the way, Jess," said Tony.

Jess nodded. "Why thank you, Tony. I thought so myself."

Tony and Jess watched two men walk out of Andy's Saloon and stretch. It was the same two men who were deadlocked in the poker game last night. Either they played all night or had fallen asleep at the table. The sun was up and the night chill was slowly disappearing. It seemed like such a peaceful day and yet Jess knew that this day would be anything but.

| | |

While Jess and Tony sat there watching the town come alive, Dick Carter was sitting in a chair on the front porch of his huge ranch home, deep in thought about his son, Red. Surely Red had been a pain in the ass most of the time but like any father, he still had loved his only son and Jess had taken him from him. Red had been such a pain in the ass growing up that Carter's wife wouldn't even have

# Brother's Keeper

anything to do with Red so Dick Carter raised the boy the best he could and of course, Red had picked up a few of his father's bad habits. The worst one was Dick Carter's bad temper. Dick had wanted Red to inherit the sprawling ranch that he had built from the ground up and now there would be no one to leave it to except his wife, and he wasn't happy about that. Their marriage had been a sour one from the start and only went downhill from there.

He thought about drawing up an agreement with his friend Cal Hardin who owned the ranch next to him. The agreement would specify how much Hardin would pay for Carter's ranch and everything that went with it in the case of Carter's demise. That would make Hardin the largest ranch owner in the area but that wouldn't matter to Carter since he would be dead anyway. Dick thought of how Cal had reluctantly agreed to hold the ten thousand dollars in bounty money to be paid to a man by the name of Tim Sloan when he could bring the dead body of Jess Williams to Hardin to identify. Cal Hardin thought the idea was wrong but he owed Carter a favor. Carter had helped him get rid of some rustlers when Hardin's men couldn't seem to handle it. Carter's men took care of the problem hastily, eliminating the rustlers within a week's time.

Then Carter's thoughts turned to Jess Williams. He was obsessed with the thought of killing Jess. He was absolutely crazy with revenge. He wasn't thinking straight and he realized that, but there was nothing he could do to stop himself; it was simply his nature. He planned to ride into town today with six of his best hired guns, but not until the late part of the afternoon. He already had a few men in town and a few more riding out today to try to kill Jess, and if they failed, he would see to it himself. As he stood to stretch, he watched as two of his hired guns rode out towards Black Creek. He knew what their mission was.

To find and kill Jess Williams, anyway they choose. They could ambush him, shoot him in the back or shoot him while he slept. Carter had two more men who would leave in a few hours and their mission was the same in case the first two failed. Carter didn't care about the morality or the rightness of it. He just wanted Jess dead, like his son.

| | |

After several hot and strong cups of Tony's coffee, Jess borrowed a razor from Tony and shaved his little bit of youthful stubble and washed up a bit. Then he walked over to Smythe's General Store and sat with Jim and Sara and had some breakfast. Jess could see the worried look on Sara; she was on the verge of tears. She knew what was coming today and she was deathly afraid for Jess. It was about nine in the morning when they finished a meal of eggs, bacon, ham, fresh biscuits and apple pie.

"Sara," said Jess, "you sure can cook. That was surely one of the best meals I've had in a long time."

"I'm glad you enjoyed it. I hope it won't be your last, though."

"Ah…come on now," Jim piped in, "Jess can handle himself. He's pretty damn good with that pistol of his."

"Maybe, but he's facing a dozen hired guns, not just one man in the street," said Sara.

"I have a hunch that Jess will have more help than he thinks before this thing is over," Jim added.

"What do you mean?" asked Sara.

"I've heard some of the other men talking and they say they're thankful that Jess is here and trying to help out the town. I heard that when trouble starts today, there's going to be more guns than Jess' talking. I know that Tony over at the livery will throw in and Andy over at the saloon

# Brother's Keeper

will be ready with his scattergun. I heard a few other men say that they will be keeping their rifles handy for the next few days. Jess, you ain't in this alone. I aim to throw in with my double-barrel too when trouble starts."

"My Lord!" Sara exclaimed. "You wouldn't know which end is the barrel. You'd just shoot your foot off or something. Are you out of your mind?"

"If Jess is willing to risk his life for our problems, the least we can do is back him up and help him fight our battle. If that means losing a foot, then so be it." Jim said it so proudly, as if he was a politician making a speech and running for office. Jess had sat there watching them go back and forth and his smile finally turned to a quiet laugh. Both of them turned to look at Jess, Jim smiling and Sara looking concerned.

"Listen," said Jess, "I appreciate the help, but don't risk your life unless you have to. I can handle Carter and his men with a little help from Tony and maybe even Andy. I didn't ask anyone to throw in with me, but if they want to, I can't stop them and I'm not sure I would want to. There is nothing wrong with people fighting for their own town."

Jess got up and hugged Sara and thanked Jim and walked out into the street. It was a little after nine in the morning and it was indeed a beautiful day. The air was cool and crisp but the sun was shinning bright and the cool of the morning was dissipating quickly now. The sky was a bright blue with no clouds in sight. Jess almost laughed at the irony of it. It was such a beautiful day. A beautiful day that he knew was soon to turn bloody and deadly. Jess wondered how many men would lay dead before the day was over. He knew one thing for certain though. Dick Carter would hit the ground dead before Jess would and he made himself a vow of that right then and there.

# Chapter Five

**T**HE TWO MEN TOOK THEIR TIME to saddle up. They were in no particular hurry even though they had been assigned a very important and deadly task. Blaine Roth was as tough as nails and one look at his face would tell you that. He had a scar on his left cheek and his face was tanned and leathery. He had gotten the scar from a bar fight with another hard case several years ago over a woman. It wasn't the only scar on his body. He had been in more fights than he could remember over his forty-four years, including several gunfights. He wasn't considered fast with a gun but he wasn't the type to get too easily rattled. He had once faced off with two men in a gunfight and stood his ground like an oak tree. He hit the first man square in the chest and even though he knew the other man had already fired his first shot, burning a hole in the soft flesh of his left side just below his ribcage, he took careful aim and hit the other man with his second shot. Both men lay dead in the street and he went back into the saloon, ordered a bottle of fine whiskey and told the barkeep to collect the money for it off the two dead men lying in the street.

Gene Horn was nothing like Blaine Roth. He was always clean-shaven, neatly dressed and he wasn't one to get into saloon fights. Some of his friends had even taken to calling him Pretty Boy for a nickname. He was, however, very quick with a pistol. He had killed several men and had never been hit. Horn seldom drank or frequented saloons. He had just reached the age of twenty-two a few weeks back and he was somewhat of a loner, spending much of his off-time reading or practicing his pistol skills.

Both men did have one thing in common though. They both wanted to collect their share of the three thousand dollars of blood bounty on Jess Williams' head. Carter had ordered them into town first this morning with another two to follow a few hours later. If Jess survived that, Carter would lead a group of six of his best hired guns into town and personally see to Jess' death, one way or another. Both men mounted their horses and headed out to Black Creek. They had rode in silence for about fifteen minutes before either one of them spoke.

"What are you going to do with your half of the money?" Horn asked.

"Ain't you getting a little ahead of yourself?"

"What do you mean?"

"Hell, boy, we ain't even got to town yet, much less killed this Williams kid."

"Well, there's two of us and one of him and I am pretty damn good with a pistol. And you have that double-barrel there. Hell, I'd say he's pretty much finished when we get there."

"Listen up Pretty Boy," Roth replied, "you should never assume that you have the upper hand when facing down another man. That will kill you quicker than a chunk of lead in your chest."

"You're not rattled about going after this kid, are you? I mean, yeah, he's fast and all and he has that fancy pistol of his, but he's too young to be that fast. Hell, I've been practicing with a pistol longer than he's been able to hold one in his hands."

"I ain't rattled. I'm just telling you that you never really know what's going to happen when it comes right down to it. I plan on finding him and killing him. But the truth is either he'll get me, or I'll get him. It's that simple."

"Well, don't you worry, Blain, I'll be there to make sure that it's him that goes down."

Blaine Roth looked back over at Horn. "Just remember. We ain't playing fair, neither. I don't plan on back shootin' him, but I don't plan on giving him any quarter either. We face him together and we shoot first. If I don't get him with my scattergun, you make sure you put some lead in him with that six-shooter of yours, you got that?"

"Don't you worry about me; I'll have two chunks of lead in that kid before you can cock that double-barrel. You can count on that and when it's done, I'm going to take that fancy pistol and holster of his for myself."

"I ain't counting on anything," replied Roth, still trying to make his point. Roth knew that Horn was indeed pretty fast with a pistol and the truth was it did give him a small level of comfort. On the other hand, Roth was twice as old as Horn and that gave him twice the life experience. Enough experience to know the reputation of some of the men that Jess Williams had already killed. And Roth knew that they were all men who were fast with a pistol and probably faster than the young gunslinger riding next to him at this very moment. For a brief moment his common sense told him to ride past Black Creek and head for Texas. The only thing stopping him from doing that was the thought of three thousand dollars. That was an awful lot of money even if he did have to split it with his partner. They rode the rest of the way in silence.

| | |

Jess decided it was a nice day to visit the Mayor of Black Creek. He had already warned Sheriff Newcomb and since the sheriff worked for the mayor, Jess figured it was only fair to give the same warning to the mayor. That way there would be no misunderstanding about Jess' intentions.

Nigel York was not a gunslinger. He didn't even carry a pistol and if he did, he would probably shoot himself with it. He was in his late thirties and a man who liked to dress neatly and chase the women. He had worked for Carter over the years running errands for him in Black Creek. Things like running supplies out to the Carter 'D' ranch or taking messages to other ranch owners. He was a coward but more importantly, a yes man for Carter, which is why Carter ran him for mayor. It wasn't much of a race though. Carter had everybody in town so scared that no one would run against Carter's man. Even the incumbent Mayor decided it was time to retire instead of challenging Carter. Nigel had a small office in town and he was sitting behind a desk reading a newspaper and enjoying some hot coffee when Jess knocked on his open door.

"Yeah, who is it?" asked York, not bothering to look up from his paper.

"I thought I would pay a visit to the Mayor and introduce myself," replied Jess as he walked inside the room. York finally looked up from his paper. His startled look told Jess that York recognized him immediately and York had a look of fear in his eyes. He stood up and backed away from his desk until his back hit the wall.

"No need to introduce yourself, Mr. Williams. I know who you are and I saw what you did to Sheriff Newcomb.

You can't run around assaulting people whenever you feel like it, especially officials of the town."

"Really, why not?"

York looked down at the floor for a moment as if he would somehow find an answer written on the floorboards and not quite sure how to respond. He looked back up at Jess. "Because it's against the law," York replied, a small hint of defiance in his voice.

"Who's law?"

"The town's law."

"Don't you mean Carter's law? The law he bought and paid for?"

"I am the legal and duly elected Mayor of this town. I won the election fair and square. If you don't believe me, go ask Judge Hollingsworth, he'll tell you."

"Of course you won. No one ran against you. What a stroke of luck for you, don't you think?"

"Maybe, but I'm still the Mayor, and Newcomb is still the sheriff of this town and you're going to have to abide by the laws of this town and its officials."

Jess shook his head, amazed at how men could fool themselves into such a false sense of reality. "Listen up York, let's get something straight. I don't have to live with anything. I don't have to respect you or the sheriff. Both of you are bought and paid for by the same man and neither of you are working for the benefit of this town. You're both working for the man who is paying your salary. The same man who is trying to have me killed and the same man who is trying to run my good friends out of business."

"There's nothing against the law about Carter starting up a new store in town," York interjected, before Jess could continue.

"Shut up and let me finish because I'm not going to say it again. You and your pal, Newcomb, are nothing but hired gunmen to me. I have no respect for your authority or Newcomb's since it was bought and paid for with the same money that's trying to have me killed. Which, by the way, is against the law, but I don't suppose you're going to do anything about that, are you? I'm going to give you the same warning I gave to Newcomb and I'm not going to repeat it. If I have to, you won't have to worry about your next reelection. You stay out of this and you leave Jim and Sara Smythe alone, understand? If I find out you have even so much as looked in the direction of their store, I swear to you that I will come back here and blow one of your kneecaps clean off. Now, did you understand exactly what I said, or do you need me to repeat it for you?"

York's eyes went to the floor. He was absolutely terrified and his knees were getting so weak he thought he might collapse at any moment. "I understand. I won't bother the Smythes' again, ever."

"Good. I'm glad to hear it. You can pass on a message for Judge Hollingsworth too. He used to be on good terms with my pa but that was before Dick Carter put the judge on his payroll. Tell him if he stays out of my way, he'll live, but if he gets in the middle of this, I'll treat him the same as any of Carter's hired guns. Have a nice day, Mayor."

Jess turned around and walked out of York's office and back out into the street. He thought about Judge Hollingsworth. Hollingsworth had been a pretty good man in years past. His penchant for women and whiskey, along with his love for money had been his downfall. The fact that Dick Carter could supply him with all three was the reason that Dick Carter now owned Judge Hollingsworth. Jess remembered how his pa had helped Hollingsworth one time when some cowboys were trying to rough him up before he had become the Judge. Hollingsworth had never forgotten that and had always told his pa that if he ever needed anything, all he had to do was ask. Jess didn't want to hurt Hollingsworth but he would if forced to, but he also figured that there would be no need for a judge in this whole situation. It wasn't like Dick Carter was trying to have Jess arrested and put on trial for killing his son. He was trying to have Jess murdered and he was willing to pay well for the deed.

He noticed Tony down the street sitting there like a rock, just inside the large door to his livery with his rifle across his lap. Again, Jess felt good that someone was watching his back but he noticed that Tony was now looking down towards the sheriff's office. Jess saw what Tony was looking at and he knew immediately what it was; more trouble. Blaine Roth and Gene Horn had already tied their horses to a post and were walking into Newcomb's office. Jess walked quickly across the street to where Tony was now standing.

"What do you think those boys are up to, Tony?" asked Jess, already knowing the answer.

"You are joshin' me, right?" Tony answered with a somewhat comical grin.

"I suppose so. Well, look's like things are about to heat up again."

"I'd have to say you are right about that. I know one of those men that went into Newcomb's office. He works for Carter and he is one mean son of a bitch and he ain't gonna come at you fair. He'll shoot you on sight when he sees you and he's carrying a double-barrel with him. My guess is that Newcomb's already told those boys where you are."

"No sense in hiding then, wouldn't you say?"

"Guess not," replied Tony, a grim sound in his voice.

Jess pulled the double-barrel out of the back sling and removed the strap from his pistol. He peeked out around the large open door and he saw both men were still in Newcomb's office as he cocked both barrels. Jess glanced back at Tony and with a nod of his head; he was out the door and walking briskly across the street, his hand on the butt of his pistol. He went behind one building and worked his way between Andy's Saloon and Jackson's Hardware, which was the smallest hardware store Jess had ever seen. He was standing in the middle of the opening looking across at the sheriff's office when both men came out of Newcomb's office. Jess could see Newcomb standing in the doorway pointing at Jess. Tony had guessed it right. The instant that Blaine Roth saw Jess he opened up with both barrels. Jess had barely gotten his back to the wall enough to get some cover when Roth's blast took out one of the windows of the hardware store as well as a few chunks of wood from the corner of both buildings. Jess could hear the pellets hitting the wall opposite him.

Jess knew that the slightest hesitation would cost him his life. A half second after the shotgun blast hit, Jess crouched down and moved to the left just enough to see the two men and then he opened up with both barrels. He saw instantly that the man with the shotgun was hit and as he spun around and hit the dirt, the spent shotgun shells he was trying to remove went flying in the air. Jess didn't know for sure if it was a fatal shot or not but he figured it was good enough for the moment. He saw the other man who had already been running off towards the right of the man with the shotgun but Jess heard Tony's rifle crack and the man went down like a sack, but not before the man got off two shots from his pistol. One of them took another chunk of wood out of the hardware store about four inches above Jess' head and the second one hit the dirt not more that two feet from Jess. Jess quickly reloaded the shotgun and put it back in the sling and walked quickly across the street, his pistol now in his hand, his eyes scanning the street quickly. "Tony, cover me!" he hollered out.

"Got your back, Jess," Tony hollered, as he walked out into the middle of the street.

Jess walked towards the first man who was moaning and wriggling around on the ground. The double-barrel was well out of reach and the man's right hand was missing a few fingers. Jess looked over at the younger man who was lying on his back in the middle of the street not moving, his gun also out of reach. Andy had come out from the saloon with his double-barrel and Jess nodded to him to watch the younger man. Jess walked up to the man who was still moaning loudly. He looked down at the man who was defiantly looking back at Jess. Roth was bleeding from several areas including both of his legs.

"Do I know you?" asked Jess.

"Screw you, kid," replied Roth.

"I suppose you were after the money, right?"

"Yeah, but I guess it don't matter now, does it?"

"Nope, sure don't," replied Jess, with a matter-of-fact tone to his voice. "Looks like you're hit pretty bad. I figure you'll bleed out in a few minutes or so."

"Maybe not, if you get me to a doctor."

"Doctor?" Jess responded with a hint of anger in his voice. "You just opened up on me with that scattergun with no warning and tried to murder me in cold blood for money and now you want a doctor?" Jess shook his head. "Not today, Mister. What you're getting today is a meeting with your maker. I'm not going to let the Doc patch you up so you can come after me again, and you and I know that's exactly what you would do. Sorry, but I don't play it that way. I have to go check on your partner over there." Jess turned and walked towards the other man.

"You bastard. You can't just let me die here in the middle of the street!" Roth hollered.

"I'm afraid you're dead wrong about that, Mister," replied Jess, not even turning his head back to the man as he said it.

"Well, Andy, how's his partner?" Jess asked as he walked over to the younger man lying on his back in the street. The front of the man's shirt was covered in blood and there was a good pool of blood soaking up the dirt.

"He's a goner. He just passed on while you were having that delightful little conversation with his partner over there. You ain't really going to let him lay there and bleed to death, are you?" asked Andy.

"Absolutely," Jess said, looking back at Roth who wasn't moaning as loud now. "That man is a cold-blooded murderer who has killed before and will kill again. I'm not giving him a chance to kill anyone else ever again, especially me."

"All right then, I guess it's your show. Can't argue with ya anyway. He sure would've come back at ya the first chance he got. That's Blaine Roth and he's sure enough a hard case and that's a fact."

A few people were now gathering in the street and that gave Newcomb enough courage to come out of his doorway and onto the porch, but not enough courage to step down into the street. "You can't just let him lay there and die. Someone should go and get the Doctor," Newcomb said, his voice a little shaken.

Jess glared at him and noticed a sign that was hanging above Newcomb's head that said 'Sheriff's Office' on it. It was hanging with a small chain on each end of the sign and two hooks that were fastened to the porch ceiling. Jess never said a word as he snapped off a shot from his pistol cutting one of the chains in half causing Newcomb to first duck and then look up. He looked up just as the sign swung downward striking Newcomb square in the nose. He let out a scream and a few curse words and grabbed his nose and began running over to the Doctor's office. Doc Johnson had been standing in the doorway to his office, watching the entire incident. Jess looked at Andy and Andy just shook his head.

"What?" asked Jess.

"I think you're beginning to get a mean streak in ya."

"Maybe, but he did deserve it. He's the one that pointed me out to these two."

"Like they weren't gonna find ya anyhow?"

"Well, they didn't need any help and besides, I did warn him." Jess reloaded and holstered his pistol.

"Looks like Roth is just about done in. He ain't breathin' regular," said Andy, nodding in Roth's direction. Roth was in his final death throes. Blood was beginning to wet his lips and he was barely breathing. Jess and Andy watched him take his final breath.

"Two more down, and who knows how many more to go," said Jess.

"Too many," said Andy. "It's gonna be a long day."

"I believe it," said Jess. He knew he was in for more trouble today. He didn't know when or where it would come from but he knew for certain that it was coming. Andy went back to the saloon and Jess turned to Tony who had walked up, still holding his rifle and still watching the rooftops.

"Thanks, Tony. I appreciate the help."

"No problem. I ain't the only one who will throw in with you when you need it."

"That's a little comfort. I have a hunch that by the end of the day, I'm going to need the help. I figure Carter's coming to town later today but not until a few more of his men try to take me out."

"I see it that way too."

"Tony, will you do me one more favor?"

"Sure, you name it."

"When Carter does come to town, leave him for me."

Tony smiled an evil smile. "No problem."

Jess decided to take another walk around town. As he started down the street, the Undertaker was walking towards the two dead men who lay in the street. As the Undertaker passed Jess, he smiled and nodded as if to say thanks for the work. Jess nodded back and then smiled at the irony of the thought that while he and the Undertaker were in two completely different occupations, they both profited from the same thing; the death of men. He thought about all that had happened since his return to Black Creek. He had hoped that his visit would have been a pleasant one but instead it had turned deadly with this battle for his life because of Dick Carter. Jess hated men like Carter almost as much as he hated the men who had brutally murdered his family. He hated him for what he represented and what he stood for. Power, money, and the willingness to use it for all the wrong reasons. That was about to change—and Dick Carter wasn't going to like it.

# Chapter Six

**IT HAD BEEN A HARD THREE DAYS** ride to the town of Holten, from Black Creek, Kansas for Terrence Hanley. He only stopped once in a small town along the way. Just long enough for a quick bath, a few shots of whiskey at the saloon and a stop at the general store for a few supplies. He arrived in Holten late in the afternoon. He stabled his horse, got himself a room for the night and headed for the sheriff's office to see what he could find out about Tim Sloan.

Russ Mathers had been the sheriff of Holten for about a year. He wasn't what you called a great sheriff, but he did okay for a man in his late fifties. He let a lot of things slide, only getting involved in the most serious of affairs. If a gunfight happened between two men, he would let it go on as long as it was a fair fight. Mathers was walking out of his office and heading for some supper when Terrence Hanley walked up to him.

"Afternoon, Sheriff. My name is Terrence Hanley and I wonder if I could have a quick word with you?"

Mathers stuck his hand out and smiled. "Nice to meet you, Mr. Hanley, what can I do for you?"

"I'm looking for a man by the name of Tim Sloan. I've been told you know him and could probably point him out to me."

"Oh yeah, you must be the man with the message. I remember getting a wire a few days back from a man by the name of Carter asking me to give Sloan a message to wait for someone who would be bringing him a letter. I only remember it because this man Carter said he would pay Sloan five hundred just to wait for you. That true?"

"Sure is, Sheriff. I have the money on me right now and ready to deliver it to Sloan after he reads the letter."

"Well, all right then. You can find Sloan at the saloon, which is where he spends most of his time. He's a pretty good card player, even though he's a young one. His father and him ran a pretty successful poker game here the last few weeks or so. His father left yesterday and Tim stayed around waiting to see if someone really would show up and pay him the money and of course, to try and squeeze a few more dollars out of the gamblers here in town. I hope you ain't looking for any trouble with him though. He may be young but he's damn fast with a pistol and he ain't real friendly, if'n you know what I mean. He's killed one man so far and pissed off quite a few more since he's been here."

"Not me, Sheriff. I'm no gunslinger. I'm just here to deliver a message. After that, I plan to ride out tomorrow and head straight back to Carter's ranch."

"That's a good plan. Anyway, there's the saloon down the street where he hangs out. I'm sure you'll find him down there, probably locked in another poker game. Food's pretty good too. I'm heading down there if you want to walk with me."

"Thanks Sheriff. To tell you the truth, I am mighty hungry and I would appreciate it if you would introduce me to Sloan."

Both the sheriff and Hanley walked down the street to the saloon. The place was a little on the shabby side but at

# Brother's Keeper

least it was clean. Hanley walked into the saloon behind the sheriff and went straight to the bar and ordered a whiskey. The place was pretty busy with several people at the bar and two or three tables occupied. Six men who were obviously long into a poker game occupied one table. The sheriff walked over by that table and waited. Five of the men were probably in their mid-twenties to mid-thirties, and one looked young enough to be a kid. That man was Tim Sloan. He was dealing the cards and when he was done dealing the sheriff spoke up. "Sloan, I got a fellow who wants to talk to you."

Sloan looked up at the sheriff with a nasty look of disgust on his face. "Can't you see that I'm in a damn card game here, Sheriff? I ain't got time to meet someone right now. Tell him to come back later."

The sheriff smiled. "It's that guy who was supposed to bring you a message, remember? He's got the five hundred dollars with him, so he says."

That peaked Sloan's interest immediately. He had been waiting for the messenger and he had decided recently that the guy wasn't going to show up. Sloan pushed himself away from the table and told the other five men to deal him out for a while. A few of them complained but they started a new deal as Sloan stood up. "So, where is this guy with the money and the message?"

"Right there at the bar, sipping a whiskey," replied the sheriff, pointing directly at Hanley.

Sloan looked him over carefully and then walked over to the bar next to Hanley and ordered a whiskey. "So you're the guy who has a message for me and five hundred dollars just to read it, is that right?"

"Yes I am, and yes I do. My name is Terrence Hanley and I'm bringing a message from Dick Carter." Hanley put his hand out to shake hands with Sloan, but Sloan didn't offer his hand. Hanley felt strangely uncomfortable and he took another sip of his whiskey. This young man he was facing seemed to have an empty look in his eyes. It was a look that said a lot, and yet nothing, all at the same time.

"Where's my money? You have the five hundred?"

"I have it. But you have to read the letter before I give you the money. Those were my instructions."

"Well then give me the damn letter," replied Sloan, another nasty look on his face. Hanley was getting a little perturbed at Sloan's nasty disposition and for a moment he thought about walking out and going back to Black Creek and telling Carter he couldn't find Sloan. But he knew that would cause him problems either from Sloan, or from Carter and right now, he didn't know which was worse. There was something about this young man that scared Hanley. He reached into his back pocket and pulled out the letter, which was still sealed with Carter's stamp on it. Sloan grabbed the letter from Hanley and sat down at a table, leaving Hanley at the bar. That was fine with Hanley, he wanted to get this over with and get away from Sloan. Hanley had met his share of mean and nasty men in his lifetime but this young man, however, was one of the worst that Hanley had met so far.

Sloan sat down and opened the letter. He read the letter as follows:

This letter is to be read only by Tim Sloan.

Mr. Sloan,

My name is Dick Carter. After you read the contents of this letter, the man who delivered it to you will pay you the sum of five hundred dollars whether or not you agree to the terms of my offer. The five hundred is yours simply for waiting and reading my letter. Here is my offer.

You have a twin brother by the name of Jess Williams. I don't know if your father told you about your twin brother or not, but I can assure you that I am telling the truth. Now, here is my offer. I will pay you the sum of ten thousand dollars if you kill your brother, Jess Williams, who killed my only son. I know what I am asking you to do is out of the ordinary, but ten thousand dollars is a lot of money. I will be truthful and tell you that your brother is very quick with a gun and will not be easy to face down. If you agree to my terms, make your way to Black Creek, Kansas as quickly as you can. There are men here who are trying to collect a bounty I have placed on his head as you read this letter. If he is still alive when you get here, that will mean that I am already dead and you must contact a man by the name of Cal Hardin. He has the ten thousand dollars and instructions to pay you the money as soon as you bring the dead body of Jess Williams to him to identify. I hope you will take the job. Nothing would please me more, even in my death, than to know that Jess Williams' own brother would collect the money to kill him. God speed.

—Dick Carter

Sloan folded the letter back up and sat there momentarily thinking about its contents. He knew about his twin brother. His father had told him all about what had happened. Of course, by that time, Tim had as bad a disposition as his father and he really didn't care. Sloan smiled at the evilness of Carter's proposal. It was something that he himself would have thought up. Sloan looked back over at Hanley, who was sipping another whiskey at the bar. "I'll take my five hundred now."

Hanley slugged down his drink and turned around and walked to Sloan's table and placed an envelope on the table. Sloan opened it up and counted out five hundred dollars. He smiled. He liked money and what it could buy him, expensive whiskey, the best whores, and a stake in another poker game.

"Any message you want me to take back to Mr. Carter?" asked Hanley, after Sloan finished counting the money.

Sloan looked up at Hanley with a look that ran a chill up Hanley's spine as well as causing the hair on the back of his neck to stand straight up. "Yeah, tell him I'll be collecting my ten thousand as soon as I can get to Black Creek."

Hanley's curiosity got the best of him when Sloan had mentioned ten thousand dollars. "Ten thousand dollars? What in the hell would Dick Carter want you to do that he would pay you ten thousand dollars for?"

Sloan sneered at Hanley. "Well, I guess if he had wanted you to know that, he would have let you read the letter."

Hanley nodded, not wanting to pry any further. He had done what he had been assigned to do and as far as he was concerned, his part in this matter was over with. He did, however, still wonder what the hell his boss had said in the letter, but it was not his business. Hanley walked over to another table where Sheriff Mathers was sitting, eating what looked like a pretty tasty steak and a large helping of potatoes. "Looks mighty good, Sheriff, mind if I join you?"

"Grab yourself a chair and sit down. The food is real good and I'm sure they have another steak in the back there."

Hanley ate his supper and chatted with the sheriff for about an hour and then the sheriff left to make his rounds for the evening. Hanley thanked the sheriff and told the sheriff that he would pay for his meal. After all, he had just earned five hundred dollars. The sheriff thanked him and walked out of the saloon. It was dark outside now and a little chill was creeping into the saloon. The bartender put some more wood in the stove and it didn't take long for Hanley to feel the warmth. Hanley decided to sit at the table and order a bottle of good whiskey. He had nothing else to do and he wasn't ready to turn in yet. Sloan had gone back to his card game and was winning quite repeatedly, which was evident by the remarks from the other players. Hanley hadn't asked what was in the letter to Sloan and he didn't ask what the ten thousand dollars was for, mostly because it just wasn't his business. He had done his job and was paid very well for doing it. He wondered how everything was going back in Black Creek. He figured that Jess Williams was probably dead by now, already gunned down by Carter and his hired guns.

His thoughts were interrupted by some commotion over at the card game. One of the players was getting louder about his complaints about Sloan's uncanny luck. The man who was getting upset was Cobb White. He was in his mid-thirties and had maybe a little too much to drink, which is what gave him the courage to start complaining about Sloan's gambling skills.

"I'm telling you no one is that lucky! You can't win that many hands without cheating somehow," hollered White.

"Now settle down, Cobb. I can't help that you keep losing your money. Maybe you should just take what you have left and go on home. Maybe your luck will change tomorrow," Sloan replied, staying calm but obviously not feeling too bad about taking Cobb's money.

"I ain't got any damn money left! I started this game with two hundred and now all I have is twenty dollars left."

"Well, that's why they call it gambling," said Sloan, smiling sarcastically.

"I've about had it with your smart-ass remarks too!" hollered White.

"Now, I already told you to take your money and go home. I think that's the best thing you could do right now, before you get yourself into something you can't get out of."

"You kiss my ass, kid, I ain't scared a you!"

"Maybe you should be."

"Maybe you should show us the cards you got stuck up your sleeve," White said, as he stood up, shoving his chair backwards. Sloan remained unusually calm and placed his cards on the table. Then he slowly pushed his chair back and stood up, glaring at White. Hanley noticed that Sloan had already removed his hammer strap from his pistol. You could sense that White had a momentary lapse of courage, which is normal for a man to have just before an impending gunfight. A sober man with common sense usually backed down about this time. However when you've had one too many whiskeys, common sense seems to take a holiday. Pile that onto the fact that most men are more afraid to back out of a gunfight than to continue in it, is the reason that Cobb White stood his ground, even when he knew he shouldn't.

Sloan slowly unbuttoned his sleeves one at a time and rolled each one of them up for everyone to see. There were no cards. The truth was that Sloan was cheating but he didn't need to hide cards in his sleeves to do it. He would just palm whatever cards he needed from the deck. Sometimes it didn't work, but more often than not it did and he won the majority of hands. His father had always told him that you never want to win every hand and you never want to be caught with cards up your sleeves or in your pockets. Walking away with a smaller profit after a night's work is better than lying dead under a large pile of money. It was good advice and he had heeded it; most of the time.

Tim Sloan's father, Eddie Sloan, had only taught him to do a few things in life very well. How to gamble, lie and cheat were some of those things. More importantly though, he had taught Tim how to draw a pistol, and he had taught him very well. Sloan was an accomplished poker player by the age of eight and an expert gunslinger by the time he was twelve years old. Both professions went together perfectly, and it was times like this that proved it. Sloan's father had bought Tim a beautiful pistol and holster for his tenth birthday. The pistol was a beautifully engraved, silver plated Colt .45 Peacemaker and a black left-handed holster that was made in Mexico by a man who was an artist with leather. The holster was cut lower in the front and the barrel of the .45 was slightly shorter than most, with the front site removed, which allowed it to clear the holster quicker.

"Well now, Cobb. Did you see any cards up my sleeves?"

Cobb looked at the other four men at the table, looking for any help or encouragement. He found none. "I didn't see any, but you were cheating just the same. Maybe I can't figure out how you did it, but I know that you did."

"So, what do you want to do now?" asked Sloan, the sarcastic tone turning more serious now.

"I want my damn money back. I'll go play it in a fair game."

"Listen, Cobb. I ain't giving you your money back. Like I told you, take what you have left and go on home. If you don't, you might be making a bad mistake."

"Just give me my money back and I'll leave."

"You don't seem to be listening and I'm getting tired of talking. Now what's it going to be?"

Cobb White had a few beads of sweat on his forehead now. He had looked at the other four men, who were still sitting at the table, chairs pushed back. He knew that he wasn't going to get any help from any of them. None of them had uttered a word since the argument had begun between the two. Cobb knew that he should take what he had left and go home but he just couldn't make himself do what he knew he should do. He couldn't bring himself to back down now. Then, he made a fatal error. He drew on Sloan.

Cobb went for his gun but he never had the slightest chance. He had only gotten a grip on the butt of his pistol when Sloan's gun seemingly flashed out of its holster and blew a hole in Cobb's heart. Cobb stumbled backwards tripping over his chair and collapsed on the floor, never to complain about a card game again. Sloan whirled his gun around with his left hand and slipped it back in its holster as slick as silk. Then, he simply sat back down in his chair and picked his cards back up as if nothing had happened. The other four men looked stunned but slid their chairs back in and continued the game. They didn't care if they went home broke; they simply wanted to make it home alive. Hanley watched all of this from his table. He had watched many gunfights before and none of them were what you could call nice. Men would kill each other over the smallest of things, things certainly not worth dying for, at least, in Hanley's mind. He was, however, surprised by three things. The incredible hand speed of this young man by the name of Tim Sloan was the first. The second thing was the calm that he had displayed during a gunfight. Those two things were uncommon in most men and probably the reason that Carter had sent a message to Sloan. The third thing, and probably the most important, was the pistol and holster that Sloan was wearing. The holster was a lot nicer than most men had and the pistol was a silver engraved Colt .45 Peacemaker. He still didn't know what the letter to Sloan had said, but he pretty much figured out now what Carter wanted from Tim Sloan. Carter wanted Sloan for his pistol skills. Hanley downed another shot of whiskey, paid the bartender, and walked out of the saloon without saying a word or even looking over at Tim Sloan. All Hanley wanted to do now was get away from Tim Sloan.

As Hanley walked down the street towards his hotel, he met the sheriff who was heading down towards the saloon. "Turning in, Mr. Hanley?"

"Yeah, I'm tired and need a good nights sleep. Besides, I'm getting itchy to get out of town, if you know what I mean."

The sheriff grinned. "I know exactly what you mean. I suppose that ain't Sloan lying on the floor over at the saloon, is it?"

The sheriff had a wishful look on his face. Hanley knew what he was hoping for. "No, it ain't Sloan, but I kind of figured that you knew that already, Sheriff."

"Yeah, suppose I did. Can't blame a man for hoping though," grinned the sheriff.

"Guess not. Well, if it's any consolation Sheriff, I believe you'll be rid of Sloan first thing in the morning."

The sheriff smiled. "I guess good things do come to those who wait."

"I suppose so, Sheriff." The sheriff headed down for the saloon and Hanley went to his room and turned in.

It was early sunrise and Hanley was splashing some cold water on his face in his room when he heard a horse galloping below his window. He looked out and saw Tim Sloan riding out of town seemingly in a hurry. Hanley wasn't surprised. Even though he didn't know what the money was for, he knew that ten thousand dollars would make men do things they wouldn't usually do. Hanley decided that maybe he would stay in town another day. He would rather ride behind Sloan than to catch up to him or even worse, to have Sloan following him out on the trail.

Dick Carter watched the second team of men ride out from the Carter "D" ranch. He didn't know whether the first two men out this morning, Gene Horn and Blaine Roth, had been successful in killing Jess or not, but that didn't matter. If they had, they would meet the second team on their way back and then notify Carter that the job was done. If not, Carter would ride out with his best six hired guns and finish the job himself, one way or another. He didn't care if he got himself killed in the process. All that mattered to him now was that Jess Williams died in the process.

The two men on the second team were Woody Hampton and Flynn Dugan. Both men were hard cases and pretty good with a gun. Woody was especially good with a rifle and used it whenever possible. Flynn fancied himself as an expert with a pistol. Neither of them had any problem with ambushing a man and killing him, even if it meant shooting a man in the back. They were simply well paid man-killers and they didn't play by any set of rules.

It was early afternoon back in Black Creek, Kansas. Jess was sitting with Andy at the saloon making small talk. As they sat there, two men rode into town and hitched their horses across the street at the sheriff's office. It was Woody Hampton and Flynn Dugan. Jess and Andy watched them and they knew they were watching trouble.

"Well," Andy said, "seems like ya got more problems, Jess."

"You're always so quick to spread the good news, Andy. Anybody ever tell you that?"

"Yeah, seems like I heard that once before from a young smart-ass."

"Wonder who that might be."

Andy cocked his head again in that 'you know what I'm talking about' look. Andy got up and walked behind the bar and got his double-barrel while Jess sat at the table, waiting for the inevitable. After about ten minutes, Jess got up and walked to the bar. "Do you think maybe they're not involved in this?" asked Jess.

"Not a chance. I recognized both of those two. That's Woody Hampton and Flynn Dugan. My guess is they plan to ambush you the second they spot you."

Jess carefully walked over to the window and peeked out and looked around as best he could so as not to make himself a target. He saw nothing, but they had to have gone somewhere. He wondered if the men knew where he was yet. He couldn't see from his position whether or not Tony was watching what was going on, but he had to hope that he was. He looked back at Andy who was standing at the bar and keeping an eye on the back door. "Well, Andy, it seems like I got more work to do."

"I'm beginnin' to think you're one of them real smart fellers."

# Chapter Seven

JESS WAS STILL PEEKING OUT THE front window from time to time and Andy was standing guard behind the bar, keeping an eye on the back door just in case the two men knew that Jess was in the saloon. Andy's nerves were getting frayed. He didn't like waiting for something to happen.

"What the hell are they waitin' for?" asked Andy, not really looking for an answer.

Jess was standing to the right of the front window and he looked over at Andy. "Maybe they're waiting for you to show your pretty face."

"I don't think it's me they're waitin' for. Besides, this face ain't been pretty in a hell of a long time now."

"You'll get no argument from me on that one." Andy glared at Jess and mumbled something that Jess couldn't quite understand.

"You in a hurry to get shot again?" asked Jess.

"It ain't gettin' shot that's bothering me so much. It's the waitin' fer it."

"I'm getting tired of waiting too. I might as well try to get this over with. Those two boys have had too much time to think about what they're planning. I'm going out the back door and take a look around and see if I can spot them."

"Okay, but be careful."

"I'm always careful. You watch your back."

Jess slowly walked to the back door. The screen door had a spring on it and Jess grabbed a broom and pushed it out a little and let it spring back. It made some noise but didn't attract any fire, which is what he wanted to know. He walked over by the screen door and peeked out and looked around to see if he could spot any ambush. What he did see was a lot of junk and debris in the back of the saloon. "Hey, Andy," he quietly called down the hallway.

Andy poked his head around the corner. "What?"

"When this is over, how about cleaning up the mess back you've got back here."

"Give me a break for Christ's sake. We got more important things to worry about right now like gettin' shot," said Andy, a look of frustration on his face.

Jess stepped out the screen door and down the two steps. He pulled his double-barrel out of the sling and checked it to make sure it was loaded. He knew it was, but it was just an automatic thing he did. He worked his way along the back wall until he got to the opening between Andy's Saloon and Jackson's Hardware. He decided that was too close to Andy's Saloon. If they knew he had been in Andy's, they would spot him too easily in that opening. He made his was along the back of the hardware store to the next opening and he began to work his way along the walls while looking up at the rooftops and the windows of the two buildings looking for the two men he knew were looking for him. He had just about made it to the opening when he heard the words—"Hey, Mister." Jess spun around with the double-barrel and just as he lined up with the voice he had heard, he spotted a head darting back into a window of the one building. "Don't shoot, I'm not armed," a voice came out from behind the window.

# Brother's Keeper

"Okay, but you come out of that window with a gun and I'll blow you and half of that window apart."

"I'm just trying to help. I know where those two men are that are after you."

"Where are they?"

"One of them is up on the roof of the Sheriff's office with a rifle, and the other one is on the roof of the building next to mine. I saw him climb the back steps of the hardware right after they came to town. I think he's still up there because I heard some noise up there just a minute ago."

"Thanks, Mister. I appreciate it."

"No problem. I know what you're trying to do to help the town out. I don't like that damn Carter one bit either."

"Keep your head down when the shooting starts."

"You ain't talking to no fool."

Jess worked his way to the back again. He found the steps that led to the roof of the hardware next to the tailor's shop. He waited for a moment to decide how he was going to proceed. He looked at the steps which looked pretty old and dried out. He decided what his plan would be. The only problem with the plan was that half of the plan relied on Tony being at the ready from his vantage point at the livery. Jess had to only hope that Tony had already spotted the other man who was across the street or that he would spot him when he came out of hiding, which is exactly what the man would do when he heard the gunshots that were about to happen. Jess slowly climbed the back steps and he kept his feet to the outer edges of the steps. There were a few creaks and noises as he climbed the steps but they were so slight that Jess was sure that the man wouldn't hear them.

As he got to the top, Jess removed his hat and slowly raised his head and peeked over the top. He found what he was looking for. There was a man standing behind the fake front of the building holding a rifle and peeking around the edge looking around the street. With the other man on the other side and down several buildings, they would have Jess in a good crossfire if he went out into the street or even walked out of just about any building along the street. It was a good plan but one that was about to go bad for the two men who had planned it, although they didn't know it yet. Jess put his hat back on and stepped onto the roof staying low and very deliberately walked towards one side of the rooftop so that he could keep himself out of sight of the man across the street on the roof of the sheriff's office. He couldn't go much further forward for fear that he would expose himself to the other man. There was a ledge that was about a foot or so high all around the roof so Jess figured that he could hit the ground for cover if the man across the street opened up on Jess. So far, so good, Jess thought to himself. Jess figured it was time to have a little conversation with the man. The man looked to be in his thirties and fairly well dressed. Jess didn't know who this man was but it was Flynn Dugan. Dugan was watching the street and the buildings across from his ambush point and obviously never figured he would have to watch his back. That was about to be a fatal mistake that the man would never make again.

Jess had him in his sights with the double-barrel and decided to at least warn the man first. He didn't know why he should have to; the man standing there was surely going to shoot him on sight with no warning or hesitation. But Jess wasn't quite able to do that although he internally fought himself over it. *Why not just pull the trigger on this man? He would do it to me. Why play fair with a man who doesn't? Why not treat this man exactly the same way he was about to treat me?* This was a running argument that

Jess was having more and more often with himself, but there was still something in him, some sense of fairness that was still embedded in his mind that just wouldn't allow him to shoot a man without the man at least having a warning. He decided to call him out.

"Hey," Jess called out to the man, "have you seen him yet?"

The man made the slightest movement as if he was going to turn and then he froze in place and Jess could see that for a moment the man was trying to process what was happening. It only took Dugan about three seconds to figure out what had happened and then it took him another two seconds to decide what he would do about it. Jess saw the move coming. Dugan had both hands on his rifle but he slowly shifted the rifle to his left hand, still with his back to Jess. He knew there was no chance that he could get off a shot with the rifle while spinning around. That left Dugan's right gun hand free and it was slowly moving towards his pistol. Jess knew exactly what he was going to do and simply watched and waited for him to do it.

Flynn Dugan thought he was fast and the truth was; he was pretty fast. But not fast enough for a man, who was holding a double-barrel, cocked and pointed at you and just waiting to pull the trigger. Flynn dropped the rifle with his left hand and spun to his right pulling his pistol out. The pistol had just cleared the holster when Jess opened up with both barrels. The blast hit Dugan so hard that he flew back and went right over the edge and bounced off the short roof over the wooden walk below the building. Before Flynn hit the walk a rifle cracked and a bullet whizzed by Jess, missing his head by inches. Jess dropped down flat on the rooftop, his pistol now in his right hand. Then he heard another rifle crack but it didn't seem to be coming from the roof across the street.

Jess slowly crawled to the front of the rooftop he was on and peaked over the edge. He looked across the street in the direction that the rifle fire had come from and saw nothing. Then, he noticed Tony walking out into the middle of the street, his rifle still trained on the roof where the other man, Woody Hampton was.

"Jess, I'm sure I hit him!" hollered out Tony. "I'll keep the rooftop covered while you go check him out. Jess holstered his pistol, reloaded the double-barrel and put it back in its sling, and quickly climbed down the steps and ran between the buildings and across the street. He ran behind the sheriff's office and climbed the steps slowly. He peeked over the top of the roof half expecting another rifle shot but what he saw was Woody Hampton, leaning up against the front ledge of the building, holding his chest, his rifle lying about six feet from him. Jess walked up to him, his pistol now in his hand. He picked up Hampton's rifle and threw it off the roof.

"I found him Tony," Jess called down, "you hit him for sure, but he's not dead yet."

"Me and Andy are keeping an eye on everything down here. You be careful up there. Don't give that snake a chance, Jess."

"I won't, and thanks to both of you for the help again."

Jess looked at the man who was bleeding profusely. The man hadn't said a word; he was more occupied with trying to stop the blood from flowing from the hole in his chest. "You don't look too good, Mister. I don't think you've got long to go."

The man looked up at Jess. "Just be thankful you threw my rifle off the roof, else I'd plug you for sure."

"Mister, about the only thing you're going to do is plug a hole in the ground when they bury you."

"Yeah, well...Carter will be putting you in the ground before this day is over. He's coming for you and there is nothing you can do to stop him." The man coughed and let out his last breath. Jess simply watched him die. If Hampton had lived another few seconds, he would have heard Jess' response. Jess knew he was speaking to a dead man but it didn't really matter. What he said was more for himself than anyone else. His voice was low, firm, and deliberate. "I wouldn't have it any other way."

Jess made his way back to Andy's Saloon. He passed the Undertaker again and the Undertaker still had that strange smile on his face as he passed by Jess and nodded to him. Jess, Andy and Tony sat down at a table and Andy brought out a good bottle of whiskey.

"I didn't know you had any good stuff here," said Tony.

Andy had a hurt look on his face. "I do if you got the money to pay for it."

"I can't afford that stuff," replied Tony.

"It's on me," Jess replied. "Actually, it's probably on Carter. I found fifty dollars in the front pocket of the guy you plugged earlier. Besides, it's the least I can do after you just saved my life."

"Well, I don't know about that, but I will drink this fine whiskey. Thanks." They sat there for what seemed an eternity but in reality it was only about fifteen minutes. It was a strange thing about time. It seemed to slow down after an event such as men shooting it out with one another and some living, and some dying. Maybe it was because the one's who survived savored the following few minutes after their brush with death. It wasn't something they thought about, it was something they felt and yet couldn't put a finger on. They slowly sipped the fine whiskey and savored the good flavor.

"Well," Andy broke the silence, "since I'm the one who always points out the good news, I think things are about to get a whole lot worse in a few hours."

Tony didn't say anything and Jess looked at Andy, shaking his head. "You just can't let a man have a good moment, can you?"

"Well, someone had to say it! What do ya think Carter's gonna do? Let us sit here all day and drink this fine whiskey? I'll tell ya what he's doing. He probably on his way into town right now with a bunch of professional killers and they ain't coming to town to thank ya for killin' all their friends. They're coming to kill you, me, Tony, and anyone else who will help you."

"Well then, I guess we better have a plan. Taking on two men is one thing. Taking on six or eight is quite another. Tony, if you still want in, I'll need you up on a rooftop with your Winchester where you can see them coming and warn us," Jess said.

"No problem. I'm with you, all the way," Tony replied.

"Andy, I'll need you with that double-barrel. As a matter of fact, go down and see Jim Smythe and borrow two of his so you have three of them loaded and ready. You can do a hell of a lot of damage with three scatterguns. Don't fire off both barrels at once though. Make sure you get six separate shots out of them before you have to reload."

"Okay," replied Andy.

"All right, then. In the meantime, if you know anyone else who wants to help, tell them to stay in their houses or their stores and cover us with rifle fire or whatever they have. If they keep Carter's men ducking, it will give us the edge to take them out as quickly as we can."

"Sounds like a good plan," Tony said, trying to smile.

"It's the only one we've got right now," replied Jess, as he got up and started walking out of the saloon.

"Where are you going?" asked Andy.

"I got something I need to tend to right now. Oh, and by the way. Don't let Carter or his men get off their horses, understand? I figure they'll ride right into town as if they own it. If they get a chance to dismount and run for cover, that's bad for us. If they try to do that, just open fire on them and don't stop until every last man is down."

"So, we don't give them any warning? We just plug them even if they haven't fired a shot?" asked Tony, not really caring much about it but just wanting to know for sure.

"Don't worry, they'll have a warning. But only one and it won't last long. I'll see to that." Andy and Tony nodded and Jess walked out and headed for the mayor's office. He found Nigel York at his desk writing a letter.

"Afternoon, Mayor. How's your day going? Better than mine, I hope."

"Well…uh…I suppose my day is going okay so far. What do you want?"

"I'm here to inform you that your day just got worse."

York was terrified of Jess. Of course, he was a coward and was terrified of most other men. "What do you mean? What do you want with me? I'm not the one shooting at you."

"No, but you have played a part in the overall plan to have me killed and I'm not going to give you any opportunity to help again in any way."

"What are you going to do? You're not going to shoot me, are you?" York asked, afraid to hear the answer.

"I should plug your sorry ass right now or maybe save the cost of a bullet and just beat you to death with a big stick, but for now, I'm at least going to make sure you can't do anything to help your boss. Get up."

"Where are we going?"

"Down to visit your friend, the sheriff."

"What for?"

"You'll see. Now get up and don't make me say it again or I swear I'll just plug you right there in your seat and that would save me a whole lot of aggravation."

York got up and walked out of his office and Jess headed him down towards Sheriff Newcomb's office. York walked into Newcomb's office first with Jess right behind him. Newcomb was getting himself a cup of coffee when he heard them come in and turned around. His smile quickly turned to a frown when he saw Jess. "I didn't have anything to do with those men who tried to kill you today," said Newcomb, trying to defend himself.

"You sure were quick to point me out though, weren't you?"

"They already knew who you were, honest," Newcomb replied, nervously.

"It doesn't matter now anyway. Get your keys and pick a cell for the mayor here."

"You're going to lock up the Mayor? You can't do that."

"I'm getting awfully tired of you telling me what I can or can't do. The way I see it, I can do anything I want to do as long as I'm willing to die for it. Now get the keys and pick a cell before I start to work on that nose of yours again."

Newcomb put his hand over his still bandaged nose and knowing there was no point in arguing with Jess, he got his keys and picked out a clean cell and opened the door. Jess pushed York into it and York sat down on a chair in the cell.

"You're next," said Jess, as he removed Newcomb's pistol from his holster.

"Huh, what...you're locking me up too?"

"You catch on real quick. Get in there with your partner. I don't have any time to fool around with the two of you and I'm not going to give you the chance to help Carter when he gets here."

Newcomb got into the cell with the Mayor and closed the cell door. Jess made sure it was locked. Then he took Newcomb's gun and broke the key off in the lock. He looked at both men who were now seated. "The next time I lay eyes on either one of you, one of two things will happen. One, you'll both be on a horse riding out of town, or two, and don't ever doubt this for a second, the undertaker will be fitting you both for a pine box, understand?" Both Newcomb and York nodded in the affirmative, Newcomb still with his hand over his nose as if somehow shielding it.

Jess walked out and stood out in the middle of the street. He looked up and the sky was a beautiful blue color with just a hint of hazy clouds up high. He spotted Tony up on the roof of the livery and Andy in the window of the saloon. He looked over at Smythe's General Store and saw Jim Smythe sitting on the porch with a double-barrel. I sure hope he doesn't shoot his foot off," Jess thought to himself, after remembering what Sara had said.

"Well," Jess said to himself, "it's a good day to die—for Dick Carter."

# Chapter Eight

IT WAS ONE OF THOSE PEACEFUL serene days that made people feel good to be alive. The sky was beautiful with a rich blue color to it and just a hint of faint clouds high enough to dress it up without blocking any of the sunlight. It was all lost on Dick Carter, though. He didn't see any of the sunlight. He didn't see any of the rich blue sky. All he saw was dark looming clouds and all he could feel was hatred down deep in his dark and brooding soul. A seething hatred that caused his head to slump slightly lower than normal and made his eyes look into some strange beyond that no one else could see because it wasn't really there. He now realized that the four men he had sent into town today had failed and were most likely dead.

Dick Carter was sitting on the front porch of his sprawling ranch home. Deke Moore was sitting on a chair opposite the front screen door, carefully watching his boss slink into that strange beyond that Deke could not see and yet he knew it was there; at least it was for Dick Carter. Deke was waiting for what he knew was inevitable, and he knew he wouldn't have to wait much longer. He tried not to stare at Carter but instead he would just glance over to his left every few minutes and try to read the look on Carter's face. Carter was so deep into his dark thoughts that he never noticed Deke glancing at him even though he knew he was there on the porch with him. Deke was never too far from Carter. Deke was the best man Carter had with a gun. He was twice as fast as any of the other five men Carter had picked to go into town with him this afternoon. Deke's job was to keep Carter alive first and foremost. Beyond that, he would kill anyone Carter told him to kill. It didn't matter to Deke if it was an unarmed man, woman or even a child. Deke was simply a hired killer with no conscience at all. The consequences of his actions had long ago been lost on him. He just didn't care anymore.

The other five men who would ride into town with Carter today were all good with a gun and all quite experienced at killing. They were men who would not hesitate to shoot and would give no quarter to any man. Homer Densley and Butch Ramsey had come to work for Carter recently. They had heard that Carter was hiring gunslingers and paying well. They had been working together as bounty hunters for a few years before coming to Carter about two months ago. They were both looking forward to their share of the three thousand dollars.

Vic Nalley had been with Carter the longest. He had been a field hand for about five years with Carter and had honed his skills with a pistol to the point that Carter decided to pay him as a hired gun. The pay was much better and there wasn't much labor involved. Most of the time was spent sitting around waiting to run off the next rancher or possibly killing some poor soul who was either brave enough or dumb enough to defy Dick Carter's wishes. Nalley had welcomed the move.

Nick Priestly was the oldest of the bunch. He wasn't the fastest with a pistol, but he was probably the most dangerous of the lot. Some said he was so mean that he already had a reserved seat in hell. He had killed his share of men and raped his share of women. One of the most talked about stories around the ranch about Nick was the one about the whore he had pleasures with one night. At the end of the night, he beat her to death with the butt of his rifle just for charging him a little more than what he thought he should pay.

Warren Malarky was a young Irish lad who had worked as a gunman for the last two years. He had a good sense of humor and was always telling jokes around the campfire. He had come from the East to escape murder charges after killing a man in his brother's pub. All five of them were waiting in the bunkhouse for the order they knew was coming. They had all cleaned and oiled their weapons and made sure they were loaded and had extra ammo for all of them. It was a ritual that they performed often. A hired gunman relied on his tools of the trade and if they failed to keep them in proper working order and at the ready all the time, it could cost them their life. All that was left was to mount up and ride.

Dick Carter slowly rose his head up from where it had been hanging. He looked straight out in the direction of Black Creek. He stared out in that direction for a whole two minutes. Then, he slowly turned and looked straight into Deke Moore's eyes with a cold hard stare. "Deke, tell the boys to saddle up and get my horse ready."

Deke didn't have to respond. He knew it wasn't necessary. He simply got up from his chair and slowly walked over to the bunkhouse where the other five men were waiting. He walked in to find the five men sitting around and just chatting small talk. Deke stood just inside the door looking the five men over. He felt comfortable with them. Warren Malarky was the first to speak. "Is the boss man ready for his little ride into town?" Warren asked.

"As a matter of fact, he is. Mount up boys and get the big man's horse for him. It's time to earn our pay and maybe a big bonus."

"I like the sound of that," replied Warren.

"Especially that bonus thing," said Homer.

"Just remember, this Williams kid is one tough hombre. He might be young but he has put down some mighty fast gunmen already. You boys don't give him any quarter at all. Just plug him when you get him in your sights," Deke said, as he walked back out towards the house. He saw Dick Carter, who was standing now, checking his pistol out. Deke couldn't shake the ominous feeling that would not leave him alone today. He wanted to try to talk Carter out of this whole business, but he knew there wasn't the slightest chance of that. There was something that just didn't feel right and yet he couldn't quite put his finger on what it was. The one thing he did know for sure is that whenever he had that feeling, things usually went bad. But he was loyal to the bone to Carter and he would take a bullet for him. Carter had been very good to Deke over the years and Deke wasn't the kind of man who would walk away from someone just because the going got tough. He walked up to the front of the house and looked at Carter. Carter holstered his pistol and walked down the two steps and over to Deke. He stared deep into Deke's eyes as if trying to read what Deke was thinking. He could sense Deke's uneasiness about the whole matter and the truth was he felt it too. Yet, all he saw in Deke's eyes was loyalty. "Deke, let's go kill that bastard who killed my boy."

"You're the boss," Deke replied, "the boys are ready and so is your horse." Without turning away from Carter,

Deke waved his hand and the other five men mounted their horses and walked them over to where Deke and Carter were standing. Carter and Deke mounted their horses and Carter led the way into town. Carter had a strange look about him. It wasn't so much a look of someone who was going to avenge a death, but more like someone who was going to their death. The other five men could feel it and they too wondered about it but the thought of three thousand dollars pushed it from their minds.

Jess made one final check around the town. Tony was up on the rooftop of the livery with his rifle. Andy was sitting just inside the doorway of the saloon and he had placed a heavy wooden table against the wall next to a window. He figured that would give him a little extra protection. Jim Smythe was standing behind his counter and had his double-barrel leaning up against the wall next to the open door. On a table next to it lay at least a dozen shotgun shells in a bowl. Jess also noticed another man up on the rooftop of Smythe's General Store. He had a rifle and he waved at Jess. It was the man who had identified Ned Cullen. That made two rifles and two shotguns on his side and even though he wasn't sure about how much help Jim Smythe or the man on his roof would be, but the extra fire would distract Carter's men nonetheless. He felt more comfortable. At least as comfortable as any man who was facing down a bunch of murderous hired guns could be.

The ride to Black Creek started out as a slow and somber one. As they neared Black Creek though, Dick Carter's ears got redder and redder and then his face began to take on a slight tinge of red color. There was a slow crescendo of hatred building up inside Dick Carter, driving him forward. Deke, who was riding next to him, noticed the change as well as the change in Carter's pace. He was slowly pushing his horse faster until the horse was in a slow gallop. Then, as the buildings in Black Creek became visible around the last bend, Carter pushed his horse a little faster. The seven horses stirred up quite a dust cloud. Tony had just stood up to stretch a little when he noticed the dust. "Rider's coming in!" hollered Tony, so as everyone could hear. "I count seven riders."

Jess was on the opposite end of the main street from where Carter and his men were riding in. He was heading towards the spot he had picked out between Andy's Saloon and Jackson's Hardware. He heard Tony's call and saw the dust at the other end of town. There was no time to get to the spot he was heading for and he quickly looked for any other cover. For a split second he began to head for the first building on his left and then he looked back down the main street and saw seven men riding abreast down the street as if they owned it. He could see that Dick Carter was in the middle of these men and he knew that they were all there for only one reason—to kill him. For some reason, and he never quite knew why, a sudden change came over him and he stopped in his tracks and turned to face the seven riders slowly coming towards him. He realized that he was putting himself in an extremely dangerous position and yet he just didn't care. Rage began to surge in him as he thought about the unfairness of life. Here he was, guilty of nothing but killing Carter's son for the cold-blooded murder of the previous sheriff of the town, and now seven men, six of whom he had never met, were getting ready to kill him for money. So, there he stood, right in the middle of the street, staring down at the seven men, not moving one inch. If you had been standing next to Jess you would have heard him say to no one but himself and in a strong and most deliberate voice, "I wouldn't have it any other way." His strap was off his pistol and he had already picked out his first target—Dick Carter.

Tony had quickly ducked down out of sight but he had watched Jess turn to face down Carter's men and he wondered if Jess hadn't all of a sudden gone plumb loco. He remembered what Jess had said earlier about Carter so Tony trained his rifle on one of the other six men. Andy had moved to his spot next to the window and had his double-barrel trained on the men who had just ridden slightly past him. Jim Smythe was shaking in his boots, but he had his double-barrel sticking out the front window. He had never killed a man before, but he would if it meant saving Jess. The man up on Smythe's roof had his rifle trained on the men also.

All of a sudden, Carter and his men stopped dead about one hundred feet from where Jess now stood like a statue. Everybody tensed and Tony put a slight bit of pressure on the trigger of his rifle and had it aimed right at the side of Homer Densley, although he had no idea who the man was and didn't really care either. No one moved. It was as if for a moment or two, time stood still.

Dick Carter was staring straight down at Jess, his face the color of a red apple. Deke was looking around a little but since they had ridden slightly past them he didn't spot any of the other men who were helping Jess. Homer Densley leaned over to his pal Butch. "Kid's kind of stupid to just stand there and make it easy for us."

"Ain't no kid that stands down seven men in the middle of the street," replied Butch.

"I ain't ever seen anything like this before," said Warren, "that boy must have gonads bigger than a bull."

"What do you think he plans on doing, Butch?" asked Homer.

"Making us all rich," replied Butch.

"I think you boys are right about that," Malarky chimed in.

Deke was listening to the chatter and watching Carter's face. He didn't like the feeling he was getting and he leaned over to Carter and whispered to him. "Mr. Carter, are you sure you still want to go through with this? We could turn around and go on back to the ranch. There have been enough men killed already over this kid. He just ain't worth it," said Deke, sure that none of the other men heard him. Dick Carter never heard a word. He was in his own little reality where all he saw was Jess Williams' body lying in the street riddled with bullet holes. All he could hear was Jess Williams screaming out in pain as he lay dying. A chill ran up Deke's spine as Dick Carter began to move his horse forward at a slow walk. Carter had pulled a few feet ahead of the other men and they followed along still abreast and covering most of the street. "Look alive, boys," Deke said, "I don't like the feeling I got about this."

"Let's just shoot this little bastard and go have a drink," grunted Nick Priestly.

"We follow the boss man's lead and you know that Nick," said Deke in a somewhat scolding voice.

Carter walked his horse straight at Jess and stopped within ten feet of where Jess was still standing, his feet seemingly planted to the ground like an oak tree. Everyone tensed again, waiting for the fireworks to happen. Deke and the other five men moved up to where Carter was. Jess kept his stare straight into Carter's eyes but he still kept the other six men in his view. He had already spotted Deke Moore to Carter's immediate left and he figured him for a quick draw by the looks of him. Jess had already figured by the discussion that this man was the leader of the other men. Jess decided that this man was his second target, with Carter being his first. For the second time in a few

# Brother's Keeper

minutes, time seemed to stand still again. Carter leaned a little forward in the saddle and looked at Jess with as much pure hatred as any one man could muster. "You killed my boy, Jess Williams," said Carter, his voice actually shaking from the seething hatred he felt in his heart for Jess.

Jess didn't respond right away. Instead he shifted his glance to the three men on the right, and then to the three men on the left making sure his eyes locked on each and every one of them for just a second. Then, he turned his eyes back directly at Carter and Carter saw something that surprised even him. He saw more hatred in Jess' eyes than he himself had ever felt, even at this moment. It was then that Carter realized that this young man before him was no kid, but a hardened killer of men. Yet, Carter could not turn back now; he had to finish this, no matter the outcome.

"Mr. Carter," said Jess, "you have exactly one minute to turn around with your men and head back to the ranch and end this thing once and for all and I mean everything. That includes trying to have me killed, the bounty on my head and your grip on this town. If you don't, I will surely kill you right there on your horse."

Carter glared back at Jess. "Like you killed my boy? Well, I ain't going to be so easy. I'm not going anywhere until your sorry ass is lying in a pool of your own blood right here in the middle of this god damned street."

Jess cocked his head ever so slightly and you could see what looked like a hint of a slight smile beginning to form on his lips. "You know what, Mr. Carter? I wouldn't have it any other way," replied Jess, in a firm voice. Dick Carter began the movement of getting off his horse and what stopped him was what Jess had to say next. "By the way, Mr. Carter—your time is up."

Then, Jess did something that was out of the ordinary even for him. Maybe he was just plumb tired of playing by someone else's unwritten rules, or tired of playing fair with men who didn't know the meaning of the word. Maybe it was the fact that he was facing off with six professional killers hired and paid for by Dick Carter of whom he had no beef with and maybe it was a combination of all of these things, but whatever it was, he had simply had enough.

Carter had no sooner righted himself in the saddle and was getting ready to make one more comment to Jess and then go for his pistol when Jess—moving at lightning speed—drew and plugged Carter square in the middle of the chest. Jess fanned his second shot at Deke Moore but Deke's horse had been startled by the gunshot and jerked ever so slightly and the slug hit Deke in the left shoulder, knocking him out of the saddle. As soon as Jess had fanned his second shot he began running to his right to avoid being hit and to keep from getting hit from the fire that was beginning to rain down on the group of men still on their horses. The shots were coming from both directions as well as from above and from ground level. Deke hit the ground about the same time that Carter's dead body landed. Shots were ricocheting everywhere. Tony had hit Homer Densley in the neck with a rifle slug. Butch Ramsey had taken a shot at Jess, barely missing him, when Andy's double-barrel barked and blew him clean off his horse. Vic Nalley threw a shot at Andy and took a chunk out of the wood wall as the slug went through it and stuck solidly in the wooden table Andy had placed in front of him. Jess fanned a third shot and hit Nalley in the chest and he hit the dirt, dead. Nick Priestly had taken a few pellets from both Andy and Jim Smythe's scatterguns but not enough to put him down, but enough though, to thoroughly piss him off. He threw himself off his horse just as a rifle slug from the man on Jim Smythe's roof zinged past his head. As he hit the dirt he looked through the legs of the horses looking for Jess' legs. He took a wild shot and the slug poked a hole in Jess' left pant leg. The horses were scattering now and there was dust flying everywhere. As soon as Jess found an opening, he fanned two shots at Priestley. The first one hit him in the shoulder and the other one hit him in the top of his head, blowing half of his brains out of the back of his head.

Warren Malarky took a few pieces of buckshot but had not gotten off one shot yet. Slugs were whizzing past him in rapid succession and he quickly realized there was no hope. He figured that he might have a chance if he made a run for it and he spurred his horse and headed out at a full gallop away from the bloody carnage that was going on in the street. With his left hand, Jess grabbed at a rifle in the sling on Nick Priestley's horse as it began to move away from the commotion. He put his pistol in his holster and then he levered a slug into the barrel of the rifle. He glanced at the other six men lying in the street to make sure they weren't able to take a shot at him. Andy was running out of the saloon now and Jess hollered at Andy to watch the six men and then he lifted the rifle up and sighted it on the back of Warren Malarky who was now heading past Jim Smythe's store blasting away with his pistol. Jim was trying to get behind the front wall when one of Malarky's shots hit him in the leg. Jess fired and the .45-70 slug from the Winchester hit Malarky in the middle of his back, exiting out the middle of his chest and then hitting his horse in the back of the head. The horse's front legs buckled and the forward momentum caused the horse to roll forward and flip onto his back, pinning the now dead rider underneath. Neither of them moved again. Jess threw the rifle down, pulled his pistol back out of his holster, and hollered out to Tony who was now standing on the roof watching everything.

"Tony, go and see if Jim's okay!"

Tony didn't respond, he just took off and headed down off the roof and over to see about Jim Smythe. Jess began reloading his pistol as he turned back towards the bloody mess in the street. He looked at Andy who was watching the only one left alive. Deke Moore had been dazed by his fall off his horse and the slug in his shoulder, but he was still very much alive. Jess looked over at Carter who now lay motionless in a pool of dark blood, which was already seeping into the dry dirt of the street. He looked at the other four men who lay dead in various grotesque positions scattered around the street, each in his own pool of blood. Then he looked back down the street at the dead man still pinned under a very dead horse.

"One hell of a shot there," remarked Andy, as he too, looked down the street. Jess said nothing but simply nodded at Andy. It was then that Andy noticed something different in Jess' eyes. There was a dark and foreboding look to them that Andy had not seen before. It actually made Andy a little uncomfortable. Jess holstered his pistol and Andy noticed that he didn't put the hammer strap in place, which was unusual and out of the ordinary for Jess, which is why Andy noticed it. Jess turned his attention to Deke, who was now sitting up holding his shoulder. The fog in Deke Moore's brain was beginning to clear now and he was beginning to feel the pain in his shoulder a little more. Jess stared deep into Deke Moore's eyes as if trying to read something in the man. He found what he was looking for.

"What's your name, Mister?" asked Jess.

"Deke Moore, not that it matters."

"It matters."

"To you maybe, not to me."

I usually like to know the names of the men who try to kill me."

"So now you know it and now you can kiss my ass."

"I'll pass on that." Jess looked around at the dead bodies again. So did Deke.

"Those were all good friends of mine you killed," Deke remarked.

"Maybe I killed them, but I'm not the one responsible for their deaths. Your boss there Carter is the one responsible for every bit of this. I didn't ask for none of this," replied Jess, anger rising in his voice now.

"Well, I guess that don't matter now," said Deke, "there are six men dead, just the same."

"Actually, I count seven," countered Jess, his face hardening even more.

"Kid," Deke replied sarcastically, "you sure are good with that pistol, but your mama obviously never taught you how to count."

"Actually, she taught me how to count to ten before I was five years old. Could you count to ten when you were five?" It took a full five seconds before Deke finally figured out what Jess was getting at. He looked over at his pistol lying in the street where Andy had thrown it. "I'll tell you what kid, you give me my pistol and then we can face each other in the street like men, fair and square. My right arm still works fine. What do you say?"

"Well, Mr. Moore, It seems like the bad news is that you chased fair clear out of town when you seven men rode into town today to kill me. I got a hunch that fair won't be back until sometime tomorrow."

"Well, you ain't gonna' just shoot me, are you?" asked Deke.

Jess looked at Deke square in the eyes and that's when Deke Moore saw it. "What do you think?" replied Jess. Deke lurched for his gun but it was too far away. Jess drew his pistol and put two slugs solidly into Deke Moore's chest. Deke fell back into the dirt on his side.

"Jesus God Damn Christ!" hollered Andy. "You can't just plug a wounded and unarmed man like that!" Jess holstered his pistol, but not before reloading the two spent cartridges.

"It seems as though I can—because I just did."

"And you don't feel even a little bit bad about it?" asked Andy, a confused look on his face. Jess looked down at the street where Warren Malarky lay dead pinned underneath his dead horse.

"Well," replied Jess, "I do feel bad about the horse." Andy cocked his head and gave Jess one of those strange looks.

"Well, I do. I like horses," said Jess, defending his comment.

"You remember that thing I said before about thinkin' you're gettin' a mean streak in ya?" asked Andy.

"Yeah?"

"Well, just so ya know, I ain't wonderin' about it anymore."

Tony had been walking up to Andy and Jess when he watched Jess plug Deke Moore in the street. Tony stopped for a moment and hung his head and said "damn" in a whisper that only he could hear. He continued towards the bloody carnage in the street until he was standing in front of Jess and Andy. "Damn shame this had to happen like this but then again, we didn't ask for it either," said Tony.

"How's Jim?" asked Jess.

"He's fine. He took one in the leg but it went clean through. The Doc is with him now."

"That's good and don't either of you two feel sorry for any of this. These men all came in here to kill me along with anyone else who got in their way. They got exactly what they deserved. You can be sure of one thing; I wouldn't have been the last person these men would've killed. You probably saved a dozen innocent lives that would've been taken by these murderers over the years if they had rode back out of here. And Carter there would've owned this town, lock, stock and barrel and would have run it the way he wanted. That's what you need to think of."

Both Tony and Andy looked at the seven dead men and as they did, they realized that what Jess said made sense, even though it didn't seem to fit the normal way a man would think. They knew that these were hardened professional killers who had killed before and surely would have killed again. You could see the expression of both men change.

"Andy," said Tony, "I think maybe we did a good thing today, even though it might not feel like it right now."

"I'm beginnin' to think so, too," Andy replied, still shaking his head. "But I do think our boy here is gettin' just a little loco."

Jess looked down at the dead bodies and looked at Andy. "Well, I might be a little loco, but I'm alive and they aren't. Now, I'm going over to check on Jim. Tony, strip these men of all their guns and money and give it all to Jim. It will make up for most of the money he lost due to Carter's new store. You can keep all of the horses."

"Hey, what the hell do I get?" retorted Andy, "I coulda got shot again, ya know."

"Well Andy, you can have that poor horse I shot over there," answered Jess, as he looked down at the horse still lying on Warren Malarky's dead body.

"What the hell am I goin' to do with a damn dead horse?"

"You serve steaks in your saloon, don't you?" asked Jess as he turned and headed for Smythe's. Andy gave Jess another one of his looks and then he glanced down at the dead horse. "Well, I guess they probably won't know the difference anyway. What do ya think, Tony?"

Now it was Tony's turn to give Andy a comical look. "Have you eaten one of your steaks lately?" Andy had a hurt look on his face. Then they both turned to watch Jess as he walked over to check on Jim Smythe.

"Did you see what he did to that last fella?" asked Andy, never taking his eyes off Jess.

"Yeah, I sure did. I guess I can't blame him, but it ain't something I could've done."

"I don't think I could've either," said Andy. "That boy's gettin' hard as nails. One thing is for sure, ain't no one in this town gonna mess with that boy now, after what he did today. Well, I guess we might as well start cleanin' up the mess." Tony nodded and they both started to strip the men of their valuables. The Undertaker showed up with his usual smile and loaded the bodies on a wagon, never saying a word.

As Jess walked over to check on Jim and Sara, he wasn't thinking about the dead men lying in the street. That was over with and there was no reason in his mind to waste any more time thinking about it. Besides, his thoughts were somewhere else. His thoughts were on his brother—and how he was going to find him.

# Chapter Nine

JESS FINALLY GOT A FULL NIGHT of sleep. With a little prodding, he had agreed to stay at Jim and Sara's. He slept in the same room he had stayed in the night his family was murdered. When he awoke, he dressed and washed his face out of the same bowl of water he had used on that fateful night when his family was murdered. When he looked at himself in the mirror, which was something he didn't care to do very often, he noticed how much older he looked. It was then that he realized how much older he actually felt. He wondered about his brother and whether or not he looked a lot like him. He wondered what his brother was doing right now. Where did he live and what kind of life did he have. Too many questions and not enough answers, he thought to himself.

He strapped on his gun belt, checked his pistol, and made it down the stairs. He could smell the food all the way down. Jim was sitting at the table feeding his face and Sara was busy at the stove as usual. "Well," Jess said as he pulled out a chair and sat down, "I see that bullet in the leg didn't slow down your appetite any."

"Hell no, a man's got to eat, especially when he's trying to heal up. Dig in, Jess, you got to be hungry after yesterday."

"As a matter-of-fact I am starved for sure. It sure smells good, Sara."

"It's always good. Now dig in because I'm making more eggs and bacon right now and I have more fresh biscuits in the oven."

"You don't have to tell me twice," replied Jess, as he filled his plate. Jim and Jess ate without saying a word for about five minutes and Sara swore they sounded like two men eating their last meal before being hanged. Sara put some more food on the table and finally sat down to join them. She fixed herself a plate and after she took a bite or two, she turned to Jess. "Jess, maybe I shouldn't ask but…doesn't it bother you at all after killing those men yesterday; especially that last man? The man you shot while he was sitting in the street, unarmed and helpless?"

Jess put down his fork and picked up his coffee cup and took a long swallow before answering. "Sara, I don't expect you to understand some of the things I do. I suppose I look at things in a different way than most folks. Maybe I never had enough upbringing to teach me what is supposed to be right from wrong and maybe that's a good thing. Actually, if I had learned what most people think is right and wrong, I wouldn't be here today. I'd be dead already. Think about it. It's not like I came to town yesterday and shot a few of the townspeople for no reason. With the exception of Carter, the men I killed yesterday were all hired professional killers who kill innocent people for money and if someone won't pay them to do it, they would do it just for the fun of it. I didn't know any of those six men and yet they came into town yesterday to murder me, and I'm sure they wouldn't have stopped there, men like that don't. Once they start killing, they usually keep killing until they satisfy their twisted desire to see other people suffer. Men like that deserve to die. Those are the kind of men who murdered my family. There are a lot of them out there causing innocent people a lot of grief, and I plan to kill every damn one of them I can. I live by a few simple rules. If a man tries to kill me, I will brace him and I won't stop until he is dead. I certainly won't let a man who has tried to kill me for no good reason, get patched up and come at me again. That's why I shot the man sitting in the street yesterday. He would have been hunting for me as soon as he was well enough to ride a horse. What sense would that make when it was him that tried to kill me for the money and simply because Carter told him to?"

"What if they had killed me?" continued Jess. "What if Carter decided to tell those men to come here and murder Jim and then rape, torture and kill you just for helping me? Picture that in your mind for a minute. And don't tell me that it can't happen because that is exactly what happened to my ma and little Samantha, and there was absolutely no reason for it. Think about the terror and the horror and the helplessness you would feel until they finally put a bullet in your head. Try to imagine the terror and horror my ma and little Samantha went through. That's how you have to look at it. That's how I look at it and when I do, I can justify my actions. That's what I'm trying to prevent. Do you think they would have told Dick Carter no? They would simply do it, collect their blood money for a job well done and go over to the saloon and have a nice bottle of whiskey on the money they collected for killing and raping you. And they wouldn't feel one bit of sorrow for it either. They'd laugh and joke about it until they were too drunk to stand up. Ask yourself, Sara, do you really want men like that walking the streets armed? The law can't do anything about those type of men until they do something bad and even then, most of the time, nothing happens to them. Most of the time there is no law to turn to."

"I had no beef with Deke Moore or any of those men. Hell, I had never seen him or any of them before yesterday. As for Carter, he deserved to die. I killed his son in a fair fight and for a good reason. Ray Diggs was a good man and a good sheriff. Red killed him for no reason. Carter would have kept trying to have me killed as long as he lived and I figured the only smart thing to do was to end that, right or wrong. So, to answer your question, I suppose I could feel bad about it if I thought about it long enough, or thought about it like most people. Actually, I probably did every one a favor by killing those men yesterday. I'm sure I saved some innocent lives that would have been taken by those men. They weren't done killing and you can be sure of that. Those are the kind of men that I will kill, and I won't stop killing them until I can't find another one to put down. I won't feel sorry for it either, even if you can't bring yourself to understand it all."

There was a long and awkward moment of silence at the table while Sara and Jim thought about everything that Jess had said. Jim understood it plainly and the truth was Jim agreed with what Jess had done, even though it somehow seemed wrong at the time it was happening. Sara was having a much harder time understanding how men could kill one another at all. She did, however, have to agree that it was better that Carter and his men died than to have Jess shot down dead in the middle of the street, and having Dick Carter running the town under his iron rule. She also took a moment to try to picture in her mind about what Jess said could have happened to her and Jim and it made her shudder to her inner core with fear. Sara put her hand out and touched Jess's face and smiled at him. She gave him a look that told Jess that she was trying to understand it all.

"Well, no matter what, we love you and I'm glad you're here with us today. I'll just have to try to understand the rest of it. It may take some time, but I'll try."

"That's all I ask for," replied Jess.

Jim interjected with a big smile. "Okay, now let's all dig in before this great food gets cold." Jess agreed and dug in for seconds.

Andy was wiping down the bar when Tony walked in. Andy grabbed the pot of coffee from the iron stove and two cups and they sat down at a table. "You don't make a half-bad cup of coffee, Andy."

"It's always good when it's free."

Tony took another sip. "You know, it does taste better now that you mentioned that. Andy, have you seen Newcomb or York anywhere yet today?"

"Nope, but I sure saw 'em last night. It wasn't long after Jess let them out of jail that I saw the two of 'em high tailin' it outta here. I guess they figured they was both plumb out of a job."

"Lucky for them they left. I heard some of the men talk about getting a rope and giving them what they deserved."

"I don't think we'll be seeing their sorry asses here in this town again," said Andy.

Tony smiled. "I think you might be right about that. Of course, we don't have a sheriff anymore. I was thinking about asking Jess if he wanted the job. I already talked to some of the other men in town and they said it was fine with them. What do you think, Andy?"

"Hell, I'd love to have him as our sheriff but I don't think there's a damn chance in hell that he'd take the job."

"Why not? We could pay him good and maybe it'll settle him down some. It might be good for him."

Andy gave Tony one of his comical grins. "Hell, in case you haven't picked up on it yet, that boy's on a mission in life and the last thing he's planning on doing is settlin' down."

"Well, I'm gonna to ask him anyway, just in case."

"Good luck. If you're successful with that, maybe you could talk to him about my LeAnn."

Now it was Tony's turn to grin. "I may be good, but I ain't a miracle worker." Andy groaned. Tony got up and walked to the door and turned back around to Andy. "What's the special for tonight?"

Andy cocked his head. "What do ya think?"

Tony just shook his head and walked out and headed to Smythe's General Store where he knew Jess was. Sara welcomed him in and escorted him to the kitchen. Jim and Jess had finished with breakfast and were chatting and sipping hot coffee. They both greeted Tony and Sara fixed Tony a plate over his objections.

"Tony thanks for throwing in with me yesterday. I appreciate it."

"Couldn't do no less. It wouldn't be right to let you take on all our problems by yourself. Jess, how would you like to be our new sheriff?"

Jess almost choked on his coffee. "Well, don't you just get right to the point?"

Tony smiled. "I've already talked to several of the men and they agree. I know that you could have the job just for the asking. We can pay you well and it might be a good move for you." Jess didn't have to think long about it. "Tony, I appreciate the fact that you would offer me the job of sheriff and thankful that the town would have me, but my interests are elsewhere. I'm a bounty hunter now and there are a lot of bad men out there to hunt down."

"I understand that, Jess," replied Tony, "but some of them are bound to turn up here from time to time and when they do, I'd sure like to know that you were here to protect the town."

"I understand that Tony, but I think after yesterday, this town can protect itself pretty good. And if anything did happen, you get in touch with me and I'll be here as fast as a horse can carry me. You have my word on that. Besides, I have to find my brother now. I found out that he knows one of the men who murdered my family. I need to know why; and I need to know if my brother knew about any of it. I'll be leaving soon to look for him."

"Jess, you never told us anything about your brother knowing any of the men who murdered your family?" Sara interjected.

"Actually, we haven't had much time to talk since I got to town."

"Ain't that the truth," said Jim, shaking his head.

"When I was in Red Rock, Texas, Sheriff Clancy told me that when Taggert had left town before I got there, he left with a man by the name of Jim or Tim Sloan. I'm not positive that it was my brother but I'm guessing it probably was," Jess said.

"So, where are you headed for?" asked Tony.

"I figure I'll start out by heading back down to Red Rock. That's where he was spotted last as far as I know. Maybe I'll pick up some information or a lead on him from there."

"Well, good luck, and if you change your mind, the job's still open," replied Tony, as he dug into the plate of food Sara had put in front of him.

"I see you changed your mind about eating," Sara said with a smile.

"Well, I figured it was a good idea since I might miss supper tonight."

"Why is that?" asked Sara. Tony looked over at Jim and Jim looked at Jess and they all laughed, which left Sara wondering what was so funny.

"I don't think you'd want to know," Tony said as he dug in again.

Sara now realized that this was one of those man discussions of which she would not get to share in and she simply gave up trying. "Jess," said Sara, "are you sure you won't stay for another day or so?"

"I'd love to, but I can't. I have to find my brother and find out what he knows. Hopefully, from there, I can find out about my father. I need to know who they are and what kind of men they are, especially after hearing about my brother riding with Blake Taggert back in Red Rock."

"If he's anything like your real father, you might not like what you find," Sara replied.

"I realize that but I need to find out, especially now that I found out that he might have had something to do with one of the men who murdered my family. I have to find out how he knew Blake Taggert and more importantly, if he knew about Taggert and what he had done."

"I still wish you would stay, at least for a day."

"I can't, Sara. But I promise to visit with you and Jim as soon as I can, I promise."

"Well, I guess that's all I can hope for," Sara said with a frown.

"I rounded up those supplies you asked for, Jess," said Jim, changing the conversation.

"I'll stop by and pack my saddlebags on my way out. What do I owe you?"

"Not a damn penny and don't you argue with me on this one. You've already done enough for me and Sara, as well as the whole town. I threw in some extra ammo for you too."

Jess could tell by the tone in Jim's voice that there was no point in arguing with him. "All right, I'll let you get away with it this time." Jim let out a grunt and nodded.

Jess went over to the livery and saddled up Gray. He thanked Tony for everything and then he stopped by the saloon to say goodbye to Andy. Andy was busy wiping down some tables. "So, ya didn't take the sheriff's job, huh?" asked Andy.

"No, I appreciated the offer, but I have to find my brother."

"You know, it's gets mighty lonely out on the trail. You just might want some company."

Jess knew exactly what Andy meant as he looked over at the swinging door to the kitchen. "Not a chance, Andy, not a chance."

"Well ya can't blame a man for tryin'."

"Thanks for everything, Andy, and I'll be back around before you know it."

Jess was almost out the door when LeAnn came running out of the back. "Why, Jess Williams! Are you trying to run out without even saying goodbye to me or letting me thank you proper for everything you done for us?"

"I'm kind of in a hurry, LeAnn. You're welcome and goodbye." Jess said it as fast as he could and then he nearly ran down the steps and grabbed the reins of his horse. He could hear Andy laughing in the background and what sounded like LeAnn throwing another one of her tantrums. He walked Gray over to Jim's and loaded everything he needed and hugged Sara and thanked Jim again and rode out, heading for Red Rock. He hoped he would find a lead on his brother there.

He had gotten a late start leaving Black Creek and he was in no real hurry so he didn't make it that far south the first day. He stopped a little early and cooked up a rabbit he had shot along the trail. He fried up some pan bread and cooked some beans to go with it and it was quite good. He had several cups of coffee and turned in for the night.

He made better time on the second day. He found a nice spot to make camp on top of a small hill that had a rock ledge on one side. There was a small creek running at the bottom of the hill less than two hundred yards from where he made camp. The wind was blowing pretty strong and the ledge would protect him from the chill somewhat and contain a little more heat from the fire. The nights were getting quite cold this time of year. He had packed an extra blanket that Sara had given him and he sure was thankful for it. He wondered about maybe picking up a packhorse to carry more supplies since he would probably spend more of his time on the trail than in towns.

He had already eaten his meal and was finishing up the coffee that was left when, off in the distance; he could see the glow from another campfire. He stood up and tried to estimate the distance but that was hard to do at night. It was far enough away though that he didn't figure for any trouble. Even though it was quite a distance to the other fire, it was a small one and Jess figured it was just another lone man on the trail. Jess was not one to take chances though so he looked around his area. He noticed that the ground was quite rocky and gravely coming up the small hill where he was camped. There was a lot of scrubbrush around the area.

He took out the ball of string that he had gotten from Jim at the store and he tied a piece of the string to the end of one bush and then he attached a can to the other end and placed the can gently into another bush. That left the string dangling about six inches above the ground so that if someone tried walking up the hill, he would hit the string and pull the can out of the bush and that would make enough noise to wake Jess. He only had the one empty can but he decided that he would save more cans and have enough of them to cover a larger area. Of course, he could always count on Gray to give him a heads-up, but this would give him an extra level of comfort. He leaned back on his saddle and laid the shotgun next to his left leg, just in case he would have the need for it.

He woke a few times in the night but not from someone tripping the string. He always woke several times during any night. It was just something he did. He rose at dawn and made some breakfast and coffee. He rolled the string around the can and packed it in his saddlebags. He decided that he would make more and use them anytime he camped out on the trail. He saddled up Gray and headed out south again.

He wondered who the man across the way was last night. He decided that he would get himself one of those telescopes he had seen in Jim's hardware store. Maybe it was a traveling salesman with a wagon full of products to sell. Maybe it was a lawman on the trail of someone or maybe it was that someone the lawman was trailing. It didn't matter though; he had something more important on his mind. Find his brother Tim Sloan and confront him. That was his mission now and he would not be diverted from that.

# Chapter Ten

**I**T WAS A THREE-DAY RIDE TO Black Creek, Kansas from Holten for Tim Sloan. He didn't mind the ride though. He liked to be out on the trail and the truth was, he liked to be alone most of the time. Sure, he liked playing poker and stealing other men's money and he liked the company of whores and dance hall girls, but he was a loner for sure. He had packed enough supplies for the ride before he had left Holten because he didn't want to stop in any towns along the way. He couldn't afford to get distracted now. He had a mission and his mind was on the big prize. Ten thousand dollars was a hell of a lot of money for killing one man. Hell, Sloan had killed men for as little as a twenty-dollar bet in a poker hand so for ten thousand dollars, he would kill a dozen men. But he only had to kill one man and even though that one man was his only brother, as far as he knew, it didn't bother him in the slightest.

His father, Eddie Sloan, had told him about his twin brother and how he had separated them at birth. His father hadn't told Tim the whole truth, however. He hadn't told Tim about the whore by the name of Sally that took care of Tim until he was about four years old. He hadn't told Tim that he beat Sally to near death and left her in a little town without a penny when he decided that he didn't need her help anymore. Tim vaguely remembered someone holding him and taking care of him and he could remember that it was a woman with soft skin and a hint of lilac, but that was about all he could remember from his early childhood.

His father had told him about his real mother, a worthless woman by the name of Becky. He had told him how she was a filthy whore and didn't want anything to do with Tim or his brother Jess after giving birth to them. He told Tim about how Becky had run off three days after their births and threatened to throw the two babies into the creek to drown rather than have to raise them. He told Tim about how he had found someone to raise his brother and that he had taken Tim to raise by himself along with the help of a woman by the name of Sally. He told Tim that his real mom, Becky, had died from a beating a man had given her while she was working in a whore-house in a small town somewhere in Texas. Tim hated his real mother for what she had done to him and he grew up hating pretty much everything else in life.

Of course, what Tim didn't know was that his father lied about all of it except for the fact that his real mother's name was Becky, but that didn't matter. He believed what his father had told him mostly because no one had told him otherwise and also because he grew up with his father going from one whorehouse to another and from one gambling house to another. He grew up among thieves, murderers and whores, and before he had a chance to form any of his own opinions about life, he was already tainted. Tim simply ended up being a product of his environment. It was not the life he had chosen; it was simply the life he had been handed.

Tim Sloan had killed his first man when he was only twelve years old. Sloan hadn't started the fight, the other man had spotted Tim sitting outside a gambling establishment where Tim's father was deadlocked in a high stakes poker game and he decided that the pistol and holster was too nice for a twelve-year-old kid to have and he wanted it for himself. He demanded that Tim take the gun off and give it to him and when Tim told him to kiss his ass, the man challenged him. Tim obliged and shot the man straight through the heart before the man got his gun out of his holster. From that day on, no one considered him a twelve-year-old kid anymore; they considered him a killer who had a lightning fast left hand.

And now, he was a young man just a few months shy of seventeen. A young man who had already killed several men and now on the trail of his twin brother and when he found him, he would kill him for the ten thousand dollars of blood money that Dick Carter had promised him. He would not hesitate or feel bad about it; he would just do it for the money. He didn't think about the morality or the fairness of it. He hadn't learned those lessons from his father. He had only learned to cheat, lie, steal and how to kill men. Yes, he was a product of his environment and quite a bad one at that.

Tim made camp the first night by a small creek. He ate a simple meal consisting of bread and coffee. He was just about to turn in after putting a few more pieces of wood on the fire when he caught a slight glare from a distant fire. The fire looked like a campfire but it was up higher like it was on the top of a hill. For a moment he thought about checking it out. Maybe it was someone he could rob; but then again, it might be a lawman on the trail and that might put a dent in Tim's plan. He decided not to tempt fate. He had more important things to do and one that would pay him a lot more money than whoever was at the other campfire had, and all he had to do was find and kill one man.

In the morning, he made coffee, ate some cornbread with some fried bacon and broke camp. He always traveled light and he never really ate much, only what he needed to sustain himself. As he rode north, his thoughts turned to the campfire he had spotted last night. He wondered about who it was but not because he cared. He was simply occupying his time. The trail was always lonely and you had a lot of time to think of all sorts of things. But then his mind turned to the idea of ten thousand dollars. He began to think of all the things that ten thousand dollars would buy him. He thought about the fine whiskey. He thought about the best whores, the really good-looking ones that weren't scarred up or ugly as an old mule's ass. He thought about a new set of clothes and a new hat and even a new stake in a high dollar poker game. Then he thought about how he was going to get all these things and that led him to think about his brother again. If anyone could have been there to see it, you could see an evil grin begin to form on Tim's face.

| | |

Jess hadn't been riding very long since breaking camp. He was following a creek, which ran almost straight south. He stopped and filled both of his canteens with water. It was starting to warm up a little with the sun out and it felt good on his face. He loved the open range. It was lonely but at the same time, so peaceful. It always helped him to gather his thoughts. He thought about what he had done back in Black Creek. He thought about the man sitting in the street that he had simply shot and sent on to meet his maker, wherever that was. He wondered if he should have given him his gun and gave him a chance to face off with him but he couldn't think of a good reason to have done so. The man was a murderer and hired gun. He had come to town to kill Jess and who knows how many others. Jess was not afraid of a fair fight but seven against one simply wasn't fair. Sure, Jess had help from some of the townspeople but the seven men riding up to him while he stood his ground in the middle of the street didn't know that. They intended to shoot him down like a dog and that would have been the end of it. Of course, he did have to wonder to himself about the sanity of standing down seven men in the middle of the street. That might have been just slightly on the edge of crazy. And, of course, he really did feel bad about killing the horse. He thought about how lucky he was to have survived the showdown with Carter and his men. Then again, he wondered if it was fate playing a role in his life again. He mounted Gray and continued along the creek.

The creek suddenly made a sharp turn to the west and Jess decided to cross at a shallow part. He allowed Gray a moment to get a drink. He could hear Gray drinking the water and he took his hat off, stroked his hair back, and looked around. He looked down the creek and way off in the distance; he could barely make out what looked like a man stooped down at the creek next to a horse. He wondered who it might be. For a moment, he wondered if it could be his brother but after he entertained the thought, he figured the odds of that were almost nonexistent. Gray finished his drink and Jess crossed the creek and continued south.

Terrence Hanley finished filling his canteen and started northward again back to Black Creek. He wondered if he still had a job when he got back to Carter's ranch. Not because he thought Carter might fire him, but because he wondered if Carter was still alive. He kept a slow pace, not wanting to run into Sloan on the trail. He wondered more than once on his trip back to Black Creek if he shouldn't just take the five hundred he had in his pocket and head out farther west and find himself another ranch to work at, but he couldn't bring himself to do it. He had started a job and he needed to finish it. That was his way. He wondered who the man was he had seen on in a distance at the creek. He knew it wasn't Sloan since the man was heading south and Hanley had been following Sloan's trail all the way back to Black Creek. *Probably just another drifter*, Hanley thought to himself.

| | |

Tim Sloan could see the town of Black Creek, Kansas from the road. It was still a mile or so away but he could see most of the buildings from the road. He had passed a few farms along the way and now he was coming up to a house on the outskirts of town. He saw a man who was working on replacing some old weather-beaten fence posts. He decided to stop and talk to the man. The man working on the posts noticed Sloan and he stopped his work and stood up. He took a rag from his back pocket and wiped his hands off and looked up at Sloan as Sloan reined up by the man.

"Howdy, Mister," the man said, putting the rag back in his pocket. "Can I help you with something?"

Sloan looked the man over for a moment. "Actually, you might be able to. Do you know where I can find a man by the name of Cal Hardin?" Sloan asked.

"Well, I sure can. The Hardin ranch is down the road the same way you're heading. It's about four miles past the town and on your right side as you go. You can hardly miss it. The Hardin ranch is one of the largest in the area. He's got a big gate area and a big sign atop the gate rails that says 'HARDIN' on it. He's not a bad fellow for a rich man. I do some work for him now and again and he always pays well and he's never treated me bad either. You tell him Charlie says howdy."

"Thanks, Mister. I appreciate it," Sloan replied, trying to be friendly, which wasn't easy for him.

Sloan continued down the road and passed the turn into the town. He wanted to get to the Hardin ranch and speak to Cal Hardin and get as much information as he could about the job he was being paid to do. He finally came up to the gate to the Hardin ranch and he turned down the road. He could see the house, which was about five hundred feet back from the road. He noticed several men sitting on horseback in front of the house. They seemed to be in some discussion about something, probably about who was going to do what for the next day or something like that. Sloan thought about the everyday drudgery of being a ranch hand and the thought repulsed him. They spotted Sloan and two of them broke from the group and rode over to meet Sloan. They reined their horses up in front of Sloan, putting themselves between Sloan and the Hardin house. Sloan did not excite easily. He simply stopped and waited for the men to do exactly what he figured they would do. Art Wheye and Newton Cash were the two men who had rode over to Sloan.

Art was the first to speak. "Can we help you with something, Mister?"

Tim, always cold and deliberate with his actions, took a moment to look the two men over. They both wore pistols and they looked tough enough but they were not gunslingers and Tim knew it with one look. Sloan looked over at the other men who were now all facing in his direction and watching to see what would happen next. Sloan figured he could take these two in front of him but that was not what he was here for, at least, not at the moment. "I'm looking to speak with a man by the name of Cal Hardin. I was told to look him up by a man named Dick Carter." Wheye and Cash both knew that Carter was dead, which is why they both looked at one another with a look of we know something that you don't.

Cal Hardin had just finished his supper and he was looking out the window to see what was going on. His wife, Ruth was peeking over his shoulder. "Is that Jess Williams? What do you suppose he wants with you? I thought this whole damn mess was over with," she said with more than a hint of worry in her voice.

"It damn sure looks like him, but it ain't," Cal replied, after taking another look at the young man who had been stopped on the ranch road.

Cal went to step back and go to the front door and when he did, he stepped on his wife's left foot. She let out a howl that sounded somewhat unnatural and Cal, stumbling to get his footing back, yelled at her. "God damn it woman! How many times have I told you not to stand behind me like that! Finish up cleaning the dishes instead of worrying about things that don't concern you!" Ruth let out a breath of disgust and went back to cleaning up. Cal walked outside onto the porch and waved at the two men in front of Sloan.

"Let him come on in," Cal said. The two men backed up their horses just enough to allow Sloan to pass. Sloan, not one to be friendly, didn't even nod at the men as he moved past them. He acted as if they no longer existed. He kept his gaze on the man on the porch waiting for him.

"Sure enough not the friendliest guy I've met," said Cash.

"You ain't wrong 'bout that," replied Wheye.

"You know what else I noticed?" added Cash.

"What?"

"He looks a lot like that Jess Williams kid."

"Damn if you ain't right about that too, Cash," replied Wheye, "but I wouldn't call Jess Williams a kid anymore."

"Why not? Hell, I'm more than twice his age."

"Yeah, but he's already killed more men than any other one man I know. And after what he did to Deke Moore the other day, well…he ain't no kid anymore."

"Yeah, that was pretty hard, even though Deke most likely had it comin'. He sure enough killed his share of men up to then." They both started their horses over to the house. They knew that their boss would want some company close.

"You know what?" asked Wheye. Cash looked at him but didn't answer.

"I'm thinking maybe you might be more like three times his age," laughed Wheye.

"Damn that's cold, Wheye. I thought we were friends and all."

"Hell, I never did like your sorry ass." They both laughed as they dismounted their horses and wrapped the reins around the rail on the front porch. Sloan had already tied his horse. He walked up the steps and stood in front of Cal Hardin and took a moment to size him up.

Cal spoke first. "I'm Cal Hardin and my guess is you're Tim Sloan."

"You guessed right. I would like a minute to speak with you, in private, Sloan said, as he looked over at Cash and Wheye, who were not about to let Sloan out of their sight just yet.

Hardin nodded at the two men. "You boys wait out here on the porch. Mr. Sloan and I have something to discuss inside." Both Cash and Wheye nodded and took a seat on the porch. Hardin went inside and Sloan followed. Hardin offered Sloan a seat at the table.

"Can I offer you some coffee or a drink?"

"Coffee would be just fine," Sloan answered.

"Ruth, pour the man a cup and I'll have one too."

Ruth did as she was told. She thought about limping on her foot a little just to get a dig in at her husband. She always liked to get in a dig whenever and however she could. Sometimes it was simply a breath exhaled too loudly and sometimes it was stomping her feet and slamming doors. Her favorite was when she would slam his plate or coffee cup down hard on the table. Cal Hardin ruled the roost and he ran roughshod over his wife most of the time. Ruth wasn't thinking about any of those things right now though. She was a little too distracted by the striking resemblance that Sloan had to Jess Williams. When she finished serving the coffee, one look from Cal was all she needed to know that she was to leave the room. When she did, that left Cal Hardin and Tim Sloan in the room alone. Hardin knew that his men were right outside on the porch and yet, he still felt uncomfortable. He knew that Jess Williams had killed a lot of men already including Dick Carter and most of his hired guns and yet, if Jess Williams were here sitting where his brother Tim Sloan was, he would not feel uncomfortable. The truth was that Hardin still liked Jess and felt sorry for what had happened to him and especially for what had happened to his family. But he did not like this young man sitting here before him but mostly, he did not like what he was here for. They both looked each other over. Tim took a sip of his coffee and sat his cup down ever so slowly as he kept his stare on Cal.

"Well, Mr. Hardin, I understand that you are holding the sum of ten thousand dollars for me, is that right?"

Cal shifted in his seat and leaned forward slightly. "Do you have a letter that you would like to show me?" asked Cal. Tim dug into the front pocket of his shirt and pulled out the letter. He handed it to Cal. Cal read it and looked at Dick Carter's signature. It was his handwriting and Cal was sure of that.

"Goddamn you Carter," Cal Hardin growled. He wasn't speaking to anyone. He was speaking to an unseen entity that may or may not have been able to hear him. "The dirt on your grave hasn't even begun to settle yet and you're still causing people grief." Cal hung his head for a moment before he looked back up at Sloan. He did not like what he was doing but he would do it because he had said he would. A man's word was one of the most important things in life and once it was given, it was given. "That's Carter's signature on the letter but you don't get the ten thousand until you…" Cal's voice broke off for a second "…finish the job."

"Oh, I'll finish it, you can count on that."

"You'd really kill your own flesh and blood, your own brother, for money?"

"Mr. Hardin, I've killed men over a poker bet for a twenty dollar gold piece and I've killed men just for calling me a cheat. I ain't got no brother as far as I'm concerned and the only flesh and blood I have is my father, and I'd even kill him for that kind of money.

"Jess Williams is your brother, I can assure you of that."

"I don't need your assurance, Mr. Hardin. All I need right now is for you to tell me that if I bring his dead body strapped over his horse to you for identification that you will pay me the ten thousand that Carter promised."

"Just so we understand one another, I don't like you or what you are here to do. But I did agree to do what Carter asked, so yes, I'll pay you the money if you are able to do what Carter is paying you to do." Sloan took another swallow of his coffee and slowly stood up. Hardin looked at Sloan's pistol and holster.

"You know, your brother has a pretty fancy pistol and holster himself. He's damn fast with it too. You might want to think this thing over."

An evil grin formed on Sloan's lips. "I've already thought about it. Just be ready to hand me my money when I deliver his corpse to you."

Sloan turned around and walked back outside. Cash and Wheye were still sitting on the porch. Tim walked past them as if they still didn't exist and walked down the steps of the porch. He grabbed the reins of his horse and mounted himself into the saddle with an easy fluid movement. Cal came out onto the porch and both men stood up. All three of them were facing Sloan.

"I don't suppose you know where I could start looking for this Jess Williams?" Sloan asked.

Hardin lowered his head for a second. He was thinking about what he had promised Dick Carter and one of them wasn't helping this Tim Sloan find Jess Williams. He slowly looked back up at Sloan. "Matter-of-fact, no, I wouldn't have any idea."

Sloan smiled that evil grin again. "That's what I thought," replied Sloan, as he slowly turned his horse toward the main road heading into town.

"Not a very friendly feller, huh boss?" Wheye asked.

"Nope. That young man is a lot of things, but friendly sure ain't one of 'em."

"I know one thing he is," Cash piped in. Hardin and Wheye both looked at him with interest.

"He's a damn sight better looking than Wheye here," Cash snickered, getting his dig back at Wheye.

"Guess I had that one coming for sure," laughed Wheye.

"That and a damn sight more, too," replied Cash.

"Now who's being cold," replied Wheye as he and Cash headed back to the other men who were now standing around together over to the side of the house.

Cal Hardin watched Tim Sloan until he was out of sight. The feeling in his gut that started out with an uneasy feeling had now turned to something more like someone slamming you in the gut with a ten-pound hammer. He didn't like what he was being a part of. He wondered about his loyalty to a dead man but then again, loyalty was loyalty, even in death. He had made a promise and no matter how much he disliked the matter, he would keep it. He hung his head again as he recalled his conversation that day that Carter had come to visit him with the envelope with ten thousand dollars in it. Then, he remembered another thing that he hadn't promised Carter as he slowly raised his head back up. As he looked out at the road where he had finally lost sight of Tim Sloan, you could see a slight smile come to his lips.

# Chapter Eleven

TIM SLOAN KNEW THAT CAL Hardin had lied about the whereabouts of Jess Williams. It mattered little to him though. He knew that he would find him sooner or later. Sooner would be better, but later would be just fine with him. He figured that the town of Black Creek was the best place to start. The sun was just about to go down when he finally rode into Black Creek.

Tony, the blacksmith, was just finishing up filing the left front hoof of a beautiful palomino mare when he looked up and saw Jess riding back into town. He stopped what he was doing and grabbed a rag to wipe his hands as he walked outside of the livery. He said, in a very low voice that no one but himself could hear, "well, well, well, I guess maybe that job offer sounded better than he first thought." He kept looking at Jess who was walking his horse slowly towards the livery. The horse was the first thing he noticed. It wasn't Jess's horse, Gray. Tony knew that horse. He had sold it to Jess' father, John Williams. Then, Tony realized that the young man on top of the horse wasn't Jess. It was someone who looked an awful lot like Jess, but the body language was all wrong.

Tim Sloan rode right up to the large man who was standing outside the livery wiping his hands. Actually, the man looked more like a huge bear standing in the street. Sloan dismounted and handed the reins of his horse to the man. Sloan stared into Tony's eyes, which was something he did often. He could read a lot from a mans eyes. It was something that he had learned from working the poker tables. He could usually tell if a man was lying or cheating just by staring into the man's eyes for a moment. He saw something but he wasn't sure what it was. He logged it in the back of his mind. Tony took the reins but said nothing, still staring at the close resemblance this young man had to Jess Williams.

"I'm looking for a room and I assume you can take care of my horse?" Sloan asked.

"Uh…sure thing, Mister, you can find a room at the hotel right there," said Tony, pointing in the direction of the Creek Hotel. "I'll take care of your horse for you." Tim noticed the odd behavior of the blacksmith but he simply nodded and headed down to the hotel to get a room. He figured he would settle in and then start asking some questions about the man he was looking for. Tony went about stabling the man's horse and as soon as he was finished, he headed straight over to Jim and Sara Smythe's place. He had heard that Jess was looking for the brother he never knew he had, and while Tony wasn't the smartest guy in town, he knew that there might be something to what he had just seen.

When he arrived at Smythe's General Store, Jim was on a step stool stocking the top shelf and Sara was holding a box. She was handing Jim small bottles of some unknown elixir that probably delivered an unknown reaction to whoever was dumb enough to drink the stuff.

"Well, hello Tony, what do you need?" asked Sara.

"I need to talk to the both of you about what I just saw," Tony replied with enough anxiousness in his voice to cause both Jim and Sara to stop what they were doing. Jim came off the step stool wincing in pain every time he put pressure on the leg he had been shot in. Sara put the box on the counter.

"What did you see that has you so rattled, Tony?" asked Jim.

"You know that brother that Jess is looking for?" asked Tony.

"Yeah," replied Jim.

"Well, I think I just stabled his horse. I thought it was Jess come back to town at first until he got right up close to me. Then I realized it wasn't Jess but someone who looked a lot like him. I think it might be his brother."

Sara had a worried look in her eyes. "Oh lord Jim, what if it is his brother? What are we going to do?" Sara asked nervously.

"We ain't going to do anything until we find out who this man is. Hell, maybe it's just someone who looks a lot like Jess. I mean, what are the odds that he would show up here in Black Creek? Let's not get too excited until we know for sure. Besides, Jess ain't here anyway," Jim replied.

"What do you want me to do?" Tony asked.

"Just keep an eye on him but don't talk to him or tell him anything, especially anything about Jess, and make sure you warn Andy too."

"I'll go see Andy right now." Tony headed out for Andy's.

Sara put both her hands on her face. "My lord, Jim, I'm worried. I don't want any more trouble. I don't know that I can take it. I want it all to go away."

"Now Sara, stay calm and don't you worry. Things will all work out the way they are going to work out no matter how much you worry about it. Jess ain't here and all we have to do is keep quiet and not let on about Jess. Maybe this guy just looks like Jess."

Andy was busy wiping down the bar when Tony came in. Andy could see that Tony was excited about something. "What's up, Tony?" asked Andy.

"Well, we ain't sure yet, but a young man came into town a few minutes ago and I have a hunch that he might be that brother that Jess is looking for."

"You gotta be kiddin' me?" said Andy, with one of those strange looks he gives when he tilts his head slightly.

"I ain't kidding. I thought it was Jess coming back to town when I first saw him ride into town. If it ain't his brother, he sure could pass for him."

Just then, the swinging doors to the saloon opened and a young man stepped inside and stopped, the doors swinging a few times behind him. The young man's eyes swept the room completely and when he was seemingly satisfied that he was aware of his surroundings, his eyes fixed on Andy. Andy looked him over for a minute. The young man wore a very nice black left-handed holster with a silver engraved Colt .45 in it. The holster was tied down and you could tell by the look of this young man that he knew how to use it. There was a dark and foreboding look about the young man. His eyes were cold and his expression one of contempt for anyone but himself. Andy couldn't believe the resemblance. Tony turned away from Sloan and said in a low voice that only Andy could hear—
"I told ya."

Sloan slowly walked up to the bar and Tony turned around again. Sloan could tell that Tony was concerned by something but he felt no threat from him. He sauntered up to the bar and looked into Andy's eyes.

"Well, barkeep, do you sell whiskey in here or not?" Andy didn't move for a second. He was staring back at Sloan.

"Uh…yeah, we got whiskey. You want the good stuff or the rot-gut."

"I'll take the good stuff." Andy got a bottle from the back shelf and poured Sloan a shot. Sloan downed it and Andy refilled the glass. Sloan looked over at a table where two men were engaged in a poker game. He looked back over at Andy. "You mind if I get a table started later on?"

Andy looked at Tony and then back at Sloan. "I don't suppose so, as long as it's a clean game."

Sloan smiled at that. "What makes you think it would be anything other than a clean game?" replied Sloan, a hint of agitation in his voice now. Andy paused for a moment.

"I'm just lettin' ya know, that's all," Andy replied, a little attitude beginning to show.

"Also," Sloan said, as he turned to look back over at the men at the poker table, "I'm looking for someone. I was told he was here in town lately. His name is Jess Williams. Either of you two men know anything about him or where he might be?"

Well, there it was. It was the one question that neither Tony nor Andy wanted to be asked and the fact that Sloan asked the question told them the whole story. This young man was surely Jess' brother and he was looking for Jess. Both Andy and Tony looked slightly uncomfortable and delayed in their answer. Andy replied first.

"We don't know any Jess Williams, Mister," replied Andy. Tony nodded as if to say the same thing when Sloan's eyes turned to look at him. Sloan looked at them both and he knew that they were both acting strangely.

"Really?" Sloan asked, not sure they were being honest.

"That's right, Mister," replied Andy, "but if we was to run into a man by that name, who should we say is lookin' for him?"

Sloan smiled and downed his drink. "You can tell him that his brother is looking for him."

Tony turned back towards the bar and looked at Andy. Both had a look of dread on their faces. Sloan threw a few dollars on the bar and walked over to the two men playing poker and asked if he could join the game. They nodded and Sloan sat down and pulled out a few hundred dollars and placed it on the table. Both men looked at the pile of money and began figuring how they were going to spend it once they won it. About an hour later both of them left the bar with empty pockets.

| | |

Cal Hardin walked out to the front porch with a cup of hot coffee in his hand. He called over to Newton Cash. Cash walked over to the porch.

"Morning boss, what do you need?"

"Newton, do you know Terrence Hanley? He was one of the men who worked for Dick Carter."

"Not personally, but I'd know him If I saw him. I saw him a few times at Andy's Saloon. Seemed to be a nice enough fellow, not like those other men that worked for Carter. They were mighty mean. I mean, those rustlers were breaking the law sure enough but what those men did to them—well, I would have done it a little differently."

"So would I, but that's over now and we can't do anything about it. I know I owed Dick Carter and I am a man of my word, but maybe we can do one good thing about this whole damn mess." Cash didn't know about everything or about Hardin's role in identifying Jess and holding the ten thousand dollars for Sloan, so he looked a little confused.

"Cash, I want you to go and find Terrence Hanley for me. I would think that he is still at Carter's ranch. I figure Carter's widow would have kept a few of the hands that survived to help out on the ranch and Hanley was one of the best ranch hands they had. I want to hire him to do something for me. Tell him that I will pay him very well."

"I'll be on my way in five minutes boss."

Hardin nodded and walked back into the kitchen of the house. His wife was busy making some breakfast and she had overheard his discussion with Newton Cash. She was one of those women who tried very hard not to say something or to interject with her husband's affairs, but sometimes she just couldn't help herself. She knew all about the money Cal was holding and she didn't like the whole affair. She liked the young Jess Williams even though she was fearful of him, although if you asked her, she didn't really know why.

"So, what do you want to talk to Terrence Hanley about?" she asked, somewhat sheepishly.

Cal didn't even look up from his coffee cup. "Ain't any of your business, woman, Cal replied, firmly.

"I know about the money you're holding and I know why you're holding it too and I don't like it," she replied, gaining a little bit of courage. Cal looked up at her and handed her his coffee cup.

"You just get me another cup of coffee and let me handle the affairs around here. Do you understand me, woman!" Cal hollered.

Ruth had a look of indignation on her face and it was one that Cal had seen many times before. She grabbed his cup, refilled it, and slammed it down in front of him and stormed out of the kitchen. Cal sat there and said in a low voice that no one else could hear. "What a pain in the ass." He looked up to see Newton Cash heading out towards the Carter ranch. He smiled a little knowing that he was about to try to do something to right things a little.

| | |

Jess was making pretty good time in his journey to Red Rock, Texas. He was looking for a spot to make camp along a creek he had been following for the last few hours when he thought he heard voices. He reined up and listened. He heard them again and though the voices were far off, he could tell that they were loud and angry. He figured there were at least two men. He dismounted and tied Gray to a branch and worked his way towards the voices, his hammer-strap already off his pistol. He worked his way through some trees until he could see the men. There were two men and they were sitting on boulders across from each other. They were obviously engaged in a loud argument with each other. Jess didn't see any horses, and the men had nothing but one canteen and a sidearm each. Neither of them noticed Jess and Jess decided to wait and listen for a minute before announcing himself.

"Goddamn it Carl, I can't believe you did this to us."

"Oh, it's always my fault. It's never your fault, is it Murry, no, never your fault."

"I'm not the one who forgot to check him over to see if he had a knife on him."

"Oh, so I don't check the man's boots and that's my fault?"

"If I would have checked him over I would have looked at his boots."

"You say that now but you didn't say it when I was checking him over. What…you forgot then, but you remember now? Oh, that's good—that's real good, Murry."

"Well, what do we do now?"

"Now you want me to figure things out? You trust me to figure it out?"

"Quit your bellyaching, Carl. I can't help it if you screwed up—again."

"Again! What do you mean again?"

"Just like last time, Carl. You let the last man get the drop on us and he robbed us just like this man did. How are we going to make any money at this business if we keep letting our prisoners get the drop on us? We're supposed to making money at this, not losing money."

"So now it's my fault we're losing money? Sure, let's blame everything on Carl. That's the easy thing to do. Just blame me. You're really starting to piss me off, Murry. It isn't all my fault. You had a hand in this too."

"I didn't let the man keep a knife in his boot, Carl. You did that; remember?"

"Yeah, yeah, yeah, it's all my fault. I'll take the blame so you can feel better, okay."

"Okay."

"Oh, just like that? It's okay? Boy, you're something else, Murry, I'll give you that."

"Well, what are we going to do?"

Carl put his hands up in the air with a look of exasperation on his face. "I told you. You figure it out. You're such a Goddamn genius—go on, you figure it out. It's your turn to screw up. I'm all done screwing up for the day. You're not going to blame me again today, that's for sure."

Murry stood up and started waving his hands in the air. "For Christ's sake, quit complaining about everything and start thinking about what we are going to do next."

"I already told you," hollered Carl, "I ain't doing anything!"

It was then that Jess decided that he would announce himself. He put his hand down by his gun and stepped around the big pine tree he had been standing next to.

"Afternoon, gentlemen." Carl jumped to his feet and Murry's hands shot up straight in the air, followed by Carl's a half of a-second later.

"Easy, men. I don't mean any harm. Put your hands down and relax but don't be going for those pistols, okay?" Jess said, in a calm and re-assuring voice. "My name is Jess Williams. Who might you two be; and how did you get way out here without any horses?" Murry and Carl both looked down at the ground for a moment. Then Murry looked over at Carl.

"Well, we had horses until Carl here gave them away along with our money and everything else we had except one canteen and our six-shooters." Carl shook his head with a look of disgust.

"We got robbed, Mister. I didn't give anything away. And yeah, it's all my Goddamn fault, according to Murry here."

"I'm just telling him the truth, that's all," exclaimed Murry.

Jess didn't want to hear the whole argument again so he suggested that they have a cup of coffee with him. Jess retrieved Gray and got out the coffee and the pan while Carl and Murry collected some dry firewood and got a small fire going. Soon they were all sitting on some big boulders and enjoying a good cup of coffee. Jess decided to find out a little more about the two men who seemed to have been robbed and left stranded miles from any town.

"So, what are you two men doing out here? I got the drift from your argument that you got robbed, but who robbed you?" Carl and Murry looked at one another and quickly looked away as if disgusted with each other.

"We got robbed by our prisoner. We took him into custody in a small town about fifteen miles east of here and we were taking him to Abilene for the reward," answered Carl.

"So, you two men are bounty hunters?"

"Yeah, that's what we are, but we don't seem to be very good at it yet," replied Murry. "We've arrested two wanted men so far and we've been robbed by both of them. Not too good, hey?"

"Don't sound like it."

"Well, we have to get better at it if we want to make enough money to start up our business back East," said Carl, throwing a look at Murry.

Murry started to wave his hands in the air again. "Don't look at me like that, Carl. This whole thing about coming out West and making a fortune as bounty hunters was all your idea, not mine."

"Don't give me that. You thought it was a great idea and you even said so," Carl replied indignantly. Murry was about to reply when Jess figured he would have to either cut in or listen to another protracted debate between the two.

"Where back East?" asked Jess. Both Murry and Carl looked at Jess and forgot about their argument for the moment.

"We're from the City of New York," answered Carl. "We were partners in the supply business."

"What kind of supplies?" asked Jess. Carl started to answer but Murry cut in first.

"Anything you needed. We would supply almost anything any place of business would need. If you needed dishes for an eatery, we would get them and resell them to you. If you needed lumber, we would get it and resell it. Pots, pans, clothing, whatever any business needed, we would go out and get it and then resell it for a profit. Hell, there's about a million people who live in New York and that's a lot of customers." Murry said it as if he was proud of being able to make a profit running a business.

"So, let me get this straight," asked Jess, "you two men left a profitable business back East to come out West and make a fortune at bounty hunting?" Jess asked the question with a hint of humor in his voice. Murry looked over at Carl when he answered.

"Well, Carl thought we could make a fortune. I wasn't so sure, but hey, he's my partner and I thought I should come out here with him and make a go of it." Carl was going to respond but he gave up and just waved his hand at Murry as if to shoo him away.

"So, how much money have you lost so far?" asked Jess.

"As far as we can figure, about five hundred dollars," answered Murry. "That's counting the four horses and saddles, four rifles, miscellaneous supplies and about a hundred in cash." Jess shook his head and tried to contain his amazement.

"What? You think that's funny?" Murry asked.

"I'm sorry," replied Jess, trying to be polite, "but yes, it is kind of funny. You two left a perfectly good business back East to come out here and make a fortune at something neither of you knew anything about. In the process, you've been robbed twice by the very same men that you were trying to collect a bounty on and lost about five hundred dollars worth of stuff in the process and you don't think maybe that's a little bit funny?" Carl and Murry looked at one another and both conjured up a smile as they thought about it for a moment.

"You are lucky in one respect though," said Jess. Both Murry and Carl lost their smile.

"Lucky?" replied Murry, a surprised look on his face.

"Yeah, what do you mean lucky. How the hell can this be lucky?" added Carl, the same look of surprise on his face. Jess shook his head, wondering about the sanity of these two men who obviously had no idea of what they had gotten themselves involved in.

"Yes. You two are lucky to be alive. I'm a bounty hunter myself of sorts and it is a very dangerous business. Most of the men out West that have a bounty on their heads are very dangerous men…killers most of them. You men are lucky you haven't been shot dead and left as feed for the vultures. You might want to think about giving this line of work up and going back East and make your fortune in the supply business."

"We can't do that," Carl said.

"Why not?"

"We did a lot of bragging when we left. Some of our friends said we was crazy and that we would come back broke and riding a mule together. They laughed at us and…well…we just can't go back broke. It would be too humiliating." Carl hung his head as Murry chimed in.

"I told you not to go bragging now, didn't I? You just couldn't keep your mouth shut, could you?" Carl just waved his hand at Murry, too disgusted to reply.

"He is right, though," Murry said to Jess, "we can't go back as failures. We have to make enough to go back and start up our new place of business. If we go back broke, we would never live it down."

Jess felt bad for the two men. They were obviously trapped in a bad situation even though it was by their own stupidity and actions. "What kind of business are you going to start if you do go back?" Both Carl and Murry sat up straight and a look of excitement replaced their look of failure. They both seemed like they wanted to talk at the same time. Murry was first.

"We are going to open up 'Murry and Carl's'. It will be a place where men with money can come and drink only the finest liquors and smoke only the finest cigars available from around the world." Murry said it so proudly as if he had said it a hundred times before, which wasn't far from the truth.

"I say we call it 'Carl and Murry's' but we can talk about that later," added Carl, shooting a look at Murry as he continued. "It will be a small but beautifully decorated place with dark wood and large mirrors on the walls. It will have nice paintings on the walls and the finest carpet on the floor. We will have wine, too, and waiters to serve the customers while they remain seated in plush leather chairs. It will be a place that any man of money will want to go and have their favorite fine liquor. We can make a fortune with it. There are a lot of rich men in New York, and they will spend it at our place."

"It seems like you two finally agree on one thing, except for that name thing," said Jess.

"We'll work that out by the time we get back home to open it," replied Carl.

"Well," Jess said, as he looked up at the sun, which was slowly going down, "it's too late to do anything tonight so I suggest we make camp, have something to eat and tomorrow we can figure out how to get you two some new horses."

"That's mighty nice of you," said Murry. "We can wire for more money if we can get to that town back that way where we captured that man."

Jess unloaded some supplies and made enough beans and pan bread for the three of them. Usually he made the pan bread with just flour and water but this time he made the pan bread by mixing some cornmeal, flour and water together and frying it in some bacon grease. They made some more coffee and sat around and talked for hours. They asked Jess about his strange looking pistol. Jess explained how he had found it hanging on the peg under his pa's hat. It was probably the most conversation he had with strangers in a long time and Jess was actually enjoying it. They finished up and Carl and Murry cleaned up and gathered some firewood for the night. Murry was dropping off a few pieces of wood and he saw Jess with a can and a string wrapped around it. He watched as Jess unrolled the string from the can and placed the can in a bush about twenty yards from the campfire. He watched as Jess tied the string to another bush about six feet away. Jess put a few small pieces of rock in the can. Then, Jess got out three more cans with string wrapped around them and started placing them around the area.

"What the heck you doing with those cans?" Murry asked.

"I put them around my camp every night. I figure that if anyone tries to ambush me at night, it might give me enough warning to prevent that from happening. I've been trying to think up more ways to guard my camp at night and I thought about another one while we were eating. I'm going to place a few medium sized rocks along the area where I would walk if I were trying to sneak up on this camp. That way, if it's dark enough, someone might not see them and step on it and that would make noise or make them stumble enough to give me a warning."

Murry smiled. "You're mighty smart for a young fellow. You want to be partners?"

Now it was Jess' turn to smile.

"Thanks, but no, I work alone. I figure a partner could get me killed. If I had a partner, I might start relying on him and that might cause me to let my guard down just enough to get myself killed. I like the fact that the only one I have to rely on is myself. That's what keeps me on guard all the time. Besides, you already have a partner."

"Yeah, but he's not as smart as you, and he's getting dumber by the day." Jess smiled as he looked over as Carl was walking up to the camp area. Carl didn't see the string and as he pulled the can out of the bush he was startled by the noise and he tripped over a rock spilling the firewood and landing on his hands and knees, cursing up a storm. Murry just shook his head.

"Well, he's all yours, Murry," replied Jess, as he continued to place the cans and rocks around the camp.

"I think the can and rock thing will work just fine," said Murry as he walked over to help his partner up and shaking his head in frustration.

"Goddamn it! Where the hell did that can come from? It wasn't there a minute ago," exclaimed Carl as he began to pick a sliver out of his hand.

"I'll tell you all about it later. Now, go and get some more firewood and watch where you're walking. Jess has these cans all around the area." Jess finished up with his work and they settled in for one last cup of coffee and then they lay down for the night. Jess gave them his extra blanket for some warmth and they thanked him again and again. Jess didn't get much sleep though. He spent most of the night watching Carl and Murry wrestle the blanket back and forth all night.

# Chapter Twelve

NEWTON CASH RODE UP TO THE Carter ranch house. It was the biggest house in the entire area, probably twice the size of Hardin's place. One of the ranch hands took the reins from Newton's horse as he dismounted.

"What can I do for you, Mister?" asked the ranch hand.

"I'm looking for Terrence Hanley. Is he still working for the Carter spread?"

"Yep, he's one of the few hands that Mrs. Carter kept after…well…you know." Newton nodded.

"Yeah, I know all about what happened. Quite a thing don't you think?" asked Newton.

"I was there and saw it. I never seen anything like it afore in my life. I was in the hotel sleeping off a hangover and by the time I got up and saw what was happening; it was over; except for when that kid shot Deke Moore right there in the middle of the street. He didn't even give Deke a chance. That boy's meaner than a basket of rattlers and twice as fast, I'll say that."

"Yeah, but he did have reason. You've got to give him that," said Cash.

"I guess I have to agree with you on that. Anyway, Hanley is over in the barn working. I'll tie up your horse for ya." Newton thanked the hand and walked over to the barn. He found Terrence Hanley working on one of the stalls that had some loose boards. He was pounding away and didn't hear Cash enter the barn. Cash waited for Hanley to stop and when he did, Cash spoke.

"Mr. Hanley?" Hanley turned around and looked at Cash.

"That's me. What can I do for you, Mister?"

"I'm delivering a message from Cal Hardin. He would like to see you."

Hanley narrowed his eyes as if to be able to look into Cash and find out why. "What in the hell does Cal Hardin want with me?"

"He wants to ask you to do a job for him."

"Hell, I'm trying to keep the job I still got here. At least, I hope I still got it. Don't know whether or not I'll have a job tomorrow. Carter's widow ain't happy with most of us and she's fired most of what's left of Carter's old crew, at least the ones who are still alive. What kind of job?" Hanley asked, his curiosity getting the better of him.

"He wants you to go and look for a man and take a message to him."

Hanley put his hammer down and looked Cash over real good. "I've seen you before, in Andy's Saloon, haven't I?"

"Yeah, I've seen you in there a few times. We've never had any words, but I know who you are," replied Cash.

"Cal Hardin seems to be a pretty nice fellow. I've never heard a bad word about him at least. Who does he want me to find?"

"He wants you to find that young man Jess who killed Carter and his men. He wants you to take a message to him."

Hanley took off his hat and looked at Cash with amazement. "Do I look stupid? Do I look like a crazy man? I only ask because only a stupid man who is crazy in the head would go looking for that kid who took down Carter and that bunch that went into town looking for him. I knew those men and they were all damn fast with a pistol and that kid, if you can call him a kid, took out four of them and Dick Carter all by himself. And now, Cal Hardin wants me to go and have a chat with him? No way will that happen. You go find him. Go back and tell your boss I ain't interested in getting dead just yet."

"He said he will pay you well."

Hanley look frustrated. "Why me? Why would he ask me to do it?"

"He said you would know how to find the kid."

"I don't know the kid. Don't think I ever saw him."

"You were the man Carter sent to find Sloan, weren't you?"

"Yeah, but what does that have to do with the Jess Williams kid?"

"From what I gather, they look an awful lot alike. I guess they're brothers."

Hanley looked at the ground and shook his head. "Carter, you mean old son of a bitch you," Hanley said softly, finally realizing why Carter had sent Hanley to find Tim Sloan. He thought for a moment and then he looked up at Cash with a grin.

"Tell Mr. Hardin I'll be there to see him first thing in the morning."

"I'll tell him."

"Good. And when you do, make sure you remind him about the part about paying me really well."

Cash laughed. "Does this mean you're stupid and crazy?"

"I'm sure beginning to see it that way lately," replied Hanley.

Cash retrieved his horse and headed out back to the Hardin ranch. Hanley went back to working on the stall and wondering about the crazy notion that he was going out to find the very same man who Dick Carter had tried to kill. And now Hanley realized that he had found Jess Williams' brother and gave him a message from Dick Carter and Hanley figured out what the message had probably said. And now, he was seriously considering going back out and finding Jess Williams? *I must be crazy*, Hanley thought to himself.

| | |

Whump!

"Jesus Christ!"

Murry jumped up from the ground throwing the blanket down and trying to catch his hat, which had been covering his face. His hat hit the ground and he reached for his pistol and found his holster empty. He spun around to where he thought he had heard the cursing. He was trying to get his head out from the fog of sleep. He looked back to the campfire and saw Jess lying comfortably still.

"Don't worry," said Jess, without even opening his eyes, "it's only Carl. He must've tripped over one of the rocks I placed around the camp." It all suddenly came back to Murry as the fog of sleep began to lift.

"Goddamn it, Carl. I told you to watch out for the rocks and cans," exclaimed Murry.

"Well I can't see 'em in the dark!" hollered back Carl, finally getting up and brushing himself off.

"That's the whole idea, you idiot!" Murry hollered back. Carl let out a string of cuss words that neither Murry nor Jess could hear. Carl came back into the light of the fire. He looked down at the ground at Murry's pistol.

"Well, at least I know how to keep my gun in my holster," said Carl, only too happy to point out a flaw in Murry.

Murry picked up his pistol and dusted it off before placing it back in his holster. "I might need it now since you have alerted anyone within five miles of us as to where we are."

"Well a man has to piss sometime!" grunted Carl as he lay back down.

Jess leaned up on one elbow and looked at the two. "Why don't the two of you go back to sleep and finish your argument in the morning. It's only a few hours to daylight." Murry lay back down and tried to pry some of the blanket out of Carl's grip. Jess closed his eyes and nodded back to sleep.

"Rise and shine, men." Both Murry and Carl woke up to the aroma of fresh coffee, bacon and potatoes frying in a pan.

"That smells damn good," Carl said, as he filled his cup with hot coffee. Murry poured himself a cup also and the three of them devoured the breakfast that Jess had made. Jess poured himself another cup of coffee and sat down on a boulder. Carl stood up and filled his cup again and looked back and forth at Jess and Murry. When neither of them spoke, Carl did. "Well…what's the plan?"

Murry looked at Jess and then back at Carl. Jess could sense that another argument was about to begin and he didn't want to hear it. He cut in before either of them could get a word out.

"I passed a small ranch back that way about three miles before I ran into you two yesterday. I plan to ride back there and see if I can buy me a packhorse from him.

I've been thinking about it for some time now and I've decided I need a packhorse. Then, you two can ride the packhorse into that town you told me about and we can all get supplied up. How does that sound?"

"That's sounds great," Murry said.

"Yeah, that would be mighty nice of you," added Carl. "We'd even be glad to pay you back for everything."

"That's not necessary. Just the pleasure of your charming company has been rewarding enough," replied Jess, as he emptied his coffee cup. "You two stay here and I should be back in a few hours or so."

Carl and Murry both nodded in agreement and began making another pot of coffee while Jess saddled up Gray and rode out back the way he had come yesterday. He found the ranch and the man who owned it was only too happy to sell one of his horses. Jess picked out what he thought was the strongest of the lot. Luckily, the rancher had a used saddle and saddlebags and Jess bought those also. He paid the rancher and headed back to the camp to pick up Murry and Carl. On the way, he thought about what supplies he would need for the packhorse. The more he thought about it, the more he liked the idea. The packhorse would allow him to carry a lot more supplies as well as a back up in case something happened to Gray. He would be able to carry more ammunition, more weapons, water, and even a dead body now and then. He got to camp and picked up Carl and Murry and they headed for the town where Carl and Murry had captured the man who had robbed them.

| | |

Terrence Hanley reined his horse up in front of the Hardin ranch. Newton Cash was sitting on the front porch having a cup of coffee with Cal Hardin. Hanley wrapped the reins around the post and walked up on the porch. Both Hardin and Cash stood up and Hanley shook hands with both men. Hardin called into the house and had Ruth bring out a cup of coffee for Hanley, which he gladly accepted. The mornings were getting a little colder now.

"I understand you want me to go and find this Jess Williams kid?" asked Hanley.

"Yes. I asked for you because I knew that Dick Carter had sent you to find Tim Sloan."

"I took a letter to Sloan from Carter. I never read the letter but I think I have a hunch about what it said."

"I'll tell you what it said," Hardin replied. "It was an offer to pay Tim Sloan ten thousand dollars to kill his own brother, Jess Williams. The letter told Sloan to contact me because I am holding the money for Sloan and I am the one who is to identify the body of Jess Williams if Sloan does, in fact, kill him. Carter asked me to do this for him because I owed him, which I did. I didn't like the whole matter but when you owe a man for helping you out when you need it, then you have to repay the favor, no matter what the favor is."

Hanley had figured as much. "Has Sloan showed up here yet to see you?" asked Hanley.

"He was here yesterday. He showed me the letter and asked me if I would pay him the money I was holding. I told him that I would. I don't like it, but I will do what I promised."

"And yet, you want me to find Jess Williams and what, warn him?"

"That's exactly what I want you to do."

"Doesn't that go against the promise you made to Dick Carter?"

Hardin smiled. "I promised Dick Carter that I would identify the body and that I would pay the money to Sloan. I didn't promise anything else."

"How will I know who this Jess Williams is when I see him?"

"Just look for a young man who looks an awful lot like Tim Sloan. They aren't identical twins but they look enough alike that you should be able to pick him out. He rode out south of here heading for a town called Red Rock, in Texas. That's where he last heard his brother was. He has no idea that his brother was in Holten, Texas, and he also had no idea that his brother is here in Black Creek right now, looking for him. That's what I want you to tell Jess Williams, if you can find him."

"It won't be easy. He's already got a good head start on me and how do we know he didn't make a change in plans by now?"

"We don't. But he is dead set on finding his brother and I don't think he would let anything deter him. Just keep after him and try your best to find him and tell him what is going on. If you fail, I'll understand. If you succeed, I'll pay you a bonus along with your pay."

"Exactly what is the pay?" asked Hanley; wondering whether or not the job was worth it. After all, Hardin was talking about more than just a few days. Finding Jess Williams could take weeks or even months and he might never find him at all.

"I said I would pay you well and I meant it. I will pay you five hundred up front, another ten dollars a day plus all your expenses."

"What is the bonus if I am able to find him?"

"Another five hundred dollars, paid upon your return."

Hanley took a moment to think about it. "That's mighty tempting. I might lose my job, however. Mrs.

Carter ain't going to like me taking off for who knows how long to do this job for you. Hell, she'll probably fire me right off the minute I tell her about this. She ain't exactly a forgivin' woman, if you know what I mean."

Hardin smiled. "I know exactly what you mean. Old man Carter wasn't the easiest man to live with and she sure wasn't the happiest woman I've ever met even on her best days. Don't worry about a job though. If she fires you, you come here to work for me as soon as you get back if you want. Does that take care of all of your concerns?"

"I guess you know how to make it easy for a man to say yes, Mr. Hardin."

Hardin shook hands with Hanley to seal the deal. "I have two of my best long horses picked out for you. That will give you the edge and help you to catch up with him. I expect you to ride long and hard each day. I have all your supplies ready and they will be packed up and ready for you at first light."

Hanley nodded. "I'll ride back to Carter's and pick up a few things and be back here tonight. I might as well bunk here tonight."

"Cash will see to your needs. Thank you, Mr. Hanley, for doing this for me. I will owe you a favor if you are successful."

Terrence Hanley rode out at first light heading south. Jess had quite a head start on him but Hanley figured Jess would be riding at a fairly normal pace. Hanley, however, would be pushing the trail hard to close the gap. The two horses that Hardin had provided were two of the most magnificent long horses that Hanley had ever laid eyes on. They were fast and they had endurance to spare. Hanley would switch from one horse to the other every few hours. He figured that he would ride from dawn to dusk every day until he either got to Red Rock, Texas, or found a lead on the trail. He wasn't sure that he would meet up with Jess on the trail but if he headed as straight as he could to Red Rock, he might get lucky. If not, he would try to find out whatever he could once he arrived in Red Rock. Hanley figured that as hard as he was riding, he might get there about the same time as Jess. He began watching the trail for any signs of a camp. He found one by a creek and he hoped it might have been Jess' camp but there was no way to know for sure. He made a mental note of the hoofprints at the camp and he at least knew that it was a single rider. He pushed on hard until he couldn't see anymore and made camp.

# Chapter Thirteen

**B**AXTER WAS A SMALL TOWN and somewhat off the beaten path. And, like many of the small towns like it, it had only one hotel, one saloon and a few various run down buildings on the single main street. Jess, Murry and Carl arrived in town in late afternoon and Jess stabled Gray and his newly acquired packhorse. They all got rooms at the hotel after making a quick stop at the bank to wire for money. They agreed to meet at the saloon for something to eat in a few hours. Murry and Carl headed for the general for supplies and Jess went to pay a visit to the sheriff. Jess found the sheriff's office, which was no bigger than a closet. It had a small desk, one cell that could hold maybe five people, if they could sleep standing up.

Ollie Bannick was a drunk. He started drinking whiskey after his first cup of coffee in the morning and didn't stop until he passed out each night. He couldn't handle a six-shooter anymore and had even quit wearing one a few years back; most likely because he had shot himself in the foot the last time he tried to use one. He was, however, the only person who would take the job of sheriff in Baxter. Jess found him sweeping up the small jail cell in the sheriff's office. It looked like he was doing more leaning on the broom handle than sweeping but then again; he was on no schedule. He looked up at Jess standing in the doorway. He just stared at Jess for a moment and then he let out a belch that must've lasted a whole five seconds. When he was done he worked his tongue around his mouth as if he was trying to dislodge a ball of cotton and couldn't quite get it out.

"What…what can I do for you, Mister?" Bannick asked.

"I'm looking for the sheriff," replied Jess.

"You found 'em."

"You're the sheriff? I don't see any badge?"

"Damn town don't pay me enough to wear it and I don't even know where it is. I don't like advertising it anyway."

"Why'd you take the job, then?"

"I get free whiskey over at the saloon. Other than that, I get to sleep in the cell here and they pay me ten dollars a month to boot. Ain't much, but it's better than sleeping on the ground."

Jess remembered about what Sheriff Diggs had told him about the lawmen in some of the small towns and how they didn't amount to much. This was yet another example of it. He shook his head. "I came in to see if you had any wanted posters here in your office."

Bannick put his broom against a wall and took a good look at Jess. He focused on the shotgun behind Jess and then his eyes went down to Jess' pistol and Jess could see Bannick's stare linger on it. "Where the hell did ya get that?" Jess had tired of answering that question and he figured it would be lost on Bannick anyway.

"Sheriff, do you have any wanted posters?" Jess asked, acting as if he never heard Bannick's question. Bannick grunted and went to his desk. He fiddled with some papers and found what he was looking for.

"Here," said Bannick, as he handed Jess a piece of paper. On it was a sketch of a man who looked to be in his thirties and with a full head of hair and a bushy beard and mustache. Written on it was Wanted for Robbery and Murder, Lloyd Aker, Reward $5,000, Dead or Alive.

Jess paid extra attention to the words at the bottom of the wanted poster. Preferably Dead! That was a little unusual and he asked the sheriff about it.

"Way I heard it was that he shot a woman while robin' a train," explained Bannick. "Only problem was the woman he killed was the wife of one of the owners of the train. That's why the bounty is so high and that's why they put Preferably Dead on there."

Jess smiled. "Well, that's the way I usually bring them in anyway. Do you have any idea where he might be?"

"Rumor has it he was possibly in a little town less than a day's ride from here called Holten. Don't know if that's true, but that's all I know." Jess borrowed a scrap of paper from the sheriff's desk to write down the name from the poster.

"Hell, take the poster if'n you want," said Bannick.

"This the only one you have?"

"Yeah, but that don't matter none. I ain't gonna bother him if he comes around here. I don't even want to know where he is. Ten dollars and some whiskey don't buy a good sheriff; just one who keeps the cell cleaned out and locks up a few drunks once in a while including myself."

Jess wondered about such people but he simply put the poster in his pocket and thanked Bannick for the poster. Bannick went back to sweeping the floor and Jess headed over to the general store to get some supplies and packed them in the oversized saddlebags he had purchased for his new packhorse. He wondered why he hadn't done this whole packhorse thing earlier. He bought extra pans, canteens, beans, flour, cornmeal, rice and other such things a man needed to survive on the trail. Then, he went to the saloon to get a bite to eat. The saloon wasn't much. He found Murry and Carl sitting at a table and they were sharing a bottle of whiskey. Jess sat down with them.

"How are you two men doing?"

"This stuff taste's like crap," Carl exclaimed, after taking another swallow of the whiskey.

"Yeah," added Murry, "and they said this was their good stuff. I wonder what the bad stuff tastes like."

Jess smiled. "In these little towns out here, they don't get much call for any good whiskey. People out this way don't have the money to pay for it and the ones that do don't come here to drink anyway."

"I don't blame them," Carl replied. "By the way, we hope you don't mind but we told the barkeep that you would be paying for the drinks since we can't get any money till tomorrow," Carl said sheepishly.

"We will pay you back tomorrow, you have our word on that," added Murry.

"I figure you two are good for it. I'll even buy you both a good meal, providing we can get a good meal here."

"They got food. We seen some of the plates coming out of the back and it don't look too bad," said Carl. "You want some of this…stuff?"

"No thanks. I could use a beer though." Jess called over to the barkeep and asked for a beer. The barkeep poured him one and brought it over to the table. They ordered three meals and the barkeep went back into the kitchen area and ordered it. A few minutes later he went back into the kitchen and brought out three heaping plates of food. It was beef stew with two big biscuits lying on top of the stew. They all dug in and devoured the stew. They sat back and let the food settle in. Carl and Murry poured themselves another shot. They winced as they swallowed the cheap whiskey.

"I want to take a bottle of this back home with us," said Carl.

Murry looked at him with a confused look. "What the hell you want to do that for? This stuff tastes like someone wrung out a dirty sock in it. Why the hell would you take any of this stuff back home with us?"

Carl smiled. "I just want to make sure we place it on our shelves with a sign that says: 'We don't serve cheap whiskey like this here.'"

Murry's frown turned to a smile. "You bet your ass we won't. Only the finest whiskey will be poured at our establishment. We won't serve any of this rotgut."

"I think you two have a real good idea with the place you want to open up," said Jess. "That is, if you actually make it back to New York. I just hope you two stay alive long enough to make it back." Murry and Carl both had a hurt look on their faces.

"What do you mean, if?" asked Carl.

"It's like I tried to tell you the other day. This isn't the city of New York or back East. This is the West and the men out here, especially the bad ones who are wanted by the law; don't have any sense of fair play or reason. They would simply put a bullet in you and they usually don't care if it's the front or the back or if you are awake or sleeping soundly. They simply will kill you unless you kill them first and I don't think you boys are good enough with a gun to make sure it's them first."

"We know how to shoot a pistol," Murry replied, almost indignantly. Jess looked at him with one of the looks Andy usually gives Jess.

"Yeah, when you can keep it in your holster so you can find it, that is," said Jess, grinning.

"That was an accident," Murry replied, "and it was only because of Carl here tripping around like an old woman."

"Hey, I told you it was a mistake! I forgot about the rocks and the cans. Don't blame that one on me, Murry," exclaimed Carl. Murry was about to reply again when Jess cut him off.

"That's what I'm trying to tell you two. That one mistake would have cost you your lives." Jess took out the wanted poster from his pocket and unfolded it. He placed it on the table and put his finger on the face of the man on the wanted poster. "See this man? He shot and killed a woman while robbing a train. What do you think he would have done if it had been him sneaking up on our camp the other night? I'll tell you. He would have shot the both of you before you had a chance to pick up your pistol and then he would have drank your coffee, took everything you had and left your bodies for the scavengers to eat. And, he wouldn't feel bad about it either." Jess looked back and forth at Carl and Murry who didn't seem to be listening now. They were both looking at each other and back at the poster again.

"Five thousand dollars!" Carl exclaimed. "That's enough to start our business when we get back."

"Yeah," added Murry quickly. "Five thousand would be enough to get started. Maybe we lighten the inventory a little in the beginning and we don't put the carpet down right away and…"

"Haven't you two been listening to what I'm trying to tell you?" asked Jess, a look of frustration beginning to form on his face. Murry and Carl looked up at him as if they didn't know what he was talking about. All they could think of now was the five thousand dollars and how that could start their establishment back East.

"This is enough money to go back East with," replied Carl.

"Yeah," added Murry.

"You don't plan on going after this man, do you?" asked Jess, afraid he already knew the answer.

"Well…yeah. Ain't that what bounty hunters do?" asked Carl.

Jess shook his head in amazement. "I'm sorry I even showed you this poster. I was just trying to make you understand how dangerous this business is. This man is a born killer and if you two go after him the both of you will wind up with dirt for a blanket."

Jess called over for another beer. Carl and Murry looked at the poster some more and they began talking to each other, planning on how they would sneak up on him and capture him and then turn him in for the reward money and go back East and operate their drinking establishment. Jess was amazed at how naïve some men could be about certain things in life. He had thought about taking a few days and looking for this Lloyd Aker and collecting the bounty. Five thousand dollars was, in fact, a very large reward. He was certain though, that these two men were going to end up dead trying to collect the bounty. He was frustrated with these two but yet, for some reason unknown to him, he liked Murry and Carl. Maybe he liked the fact that they were naïve. Maybe he liked the fact that these two men came from a different place where men weren't as ruthless and cold-blooded as some of the men out here in the West. Maybe it was the fact that Murry and Carl had hopes and dreams of what they wanted to do with their lives and it was a far better picture of what Jess had in store for him. He was destined for a life of killing. Maybe he was jealous of that, but he wasn't really sure that he would change it even if he could. Then, an idea came to him. He took the wanted poster and folded it back up and placed it back in his pocket. Murry looked at him with an almost pleading look.

"Can we have that poster?" asked Murry.

"No," replied Jess, staring at the both of them. Carl placed both his hands on the table.

"So, are you going after that man?" Carl asked, hoping the answer was no.

"Yes."

"Damn it! I knew it!" exclaimed Carl. "I knew it was too good to be true. The one time we could've gotten enough money to go back East and we ain't going to get a chance to collect it."

"Carl, he did find the poster first," replied Murry. "It's only fair that he gets the first chance at the man. After all, he has treated us with kindness and respect," he added. Jess took another long sip of his beer and put his glass down on the table ever so slowly, looking at the glass as if he was reading something that wasn't there.

"I'll make you two a deal," said Jess, looking up at the both of them.

"What deal?" Carl asked impatiently.

"We will go after this man together. If we find him, we collect the bounty. If I let you keep most of the reward, will you promise me you will get on a train and go back to New York?" Murry and Carl looked at each other and they nodded in agreement.

"Okay, it's a deal," replied Murry. "It will mean we have to start smaller but we can make it work."

"Yeah," added Carl, we can even wait on the padded leather chairs and maybe the wood work won't be so nice but it will still be Carl and Murry's, a place where gentlemen will want to come and drink the finest whiskey in all of New York."

# Brother's Keeper

"You said it, partner," as Murry patted Carl on the shoulder, "Murry and Carl's will be the place for gentlemen to go, even if we have to cut back a little bit on the opening expenses." Carl was about to argue the point of the name of their establishment again and Jess was slowly lowering his head in anticipation of another drawn out debate. What stopped him was what, or rather who, walked into the saloon.

The man was tall and slender and dressed quite nicely. What stood out to Jess was the fact that he was dressed too nice for his demeanor. Jess could size men up in an instant and this man was nothing but trouble and his clothing didn't fit in with what this man represented. The man had a fairly nice six-shooter worn low and tied down. He walked to the bar and ordered a drink. When the barkeep tried to take the bottle back the man grabbed the bottle and slammed it back down in front of him.

"I'll be keeping this."

The barkeep, a little man, thought better about making it a big deal, so he left the bottle and waited on a few of the other men standing at the bar. Carl and Murry had been exchanging glances while this was going on and Jess was amazed at how little these two paid attention to their surroundings. Jess scanned the saloon looking for any other men who might be with this one or might be a problem.

"So, you two still want to be bounty hunters, huh?" asked Jess.

"Of course," replied Murry.

"Yeah," Carl added.

"So when are you going to start acting like bounty hunters?"

"What are you talking about?" Carl asked. Just then, Murry took a good look at the man at the bar. He focused on the man for a minute while Jess talked to Carl.

"How are you planning to stay alive when you don't even know what's going on around you, especially now?" Carl looked frustrated and Murry kept staring at the man at the bar.

"I still don't get what you mean," Carl replied.

"I'll tell you exactly what I mean. The man, who a moment ago, walked past the both of you? The man who is standing over at the bar right now? I noticed him the second he walked through the door and I noticed a few odd things about him. One, he is dressed too nice for the way he acts. Two, I'm figuring that he is wanted by the law. Three, he is going to be involved in some kind of trouble before he leaves this bar. Now, I don't know these things absolutely. But I sure have a good gut hunch that I'm right on all three counts."

"Now how could you figure all that out when you don't even know who the man is?" Carl asked, in a sarcastic tone.

Jess glared at Carl "Because if you plan to hunt men, you need to learn real fast how to spot trouble or things that don't seem to add up."

"Actually," chimed in Murry, who had been watching the man at the bar all the while Jess and Carl were talking, "we do know that man."

Carl looked over at the man at the bar. He noticed the clothing. "Son of a bitch," said Carl, "that mans wearing my shirt."

Murry shot Carl a glaring look." "No shit, Carl. He's wearing your shirt; and those are my pants. I can tell you why too. That's the man who robbed us the other day. That's the man we captured at the hotel right here in town.

You know, the one you let get away the other day by letting him keep a knife in his boot."

"When are you going to quit blaming me about him getting loose? I thought we were supposed to share in everything? That means it's half your fault he got the drop on us," Carl complained, a little too loudly. Before Murry was able to respond, the man at the bar, who was obviously disturbed by the loud outburst, turned around and glared at Carl.

"Why don't you shut yer yap and let a man drink in peace!"

Carl and Murry looked at each other trying to decipher from each other's look as to what to say. The man sat his glass down and poured himself another drink without taking his glare off both of them. He put the bottle down next to the glass. Carl and Murry were both standing now and shuffling back and forth. They hardly noticed that Jess had slowly risen and walked up to the bar about ten feet from the man at the bar. The man had noticed it but seemed too focused on Carl and Murry to be distracted. Carl and Murry had both noticed it, however, and they looked over at Jess with confusion on their faces. The man, Curley Simms, noticed them looking at Jess. It was then that Curley Simms recognized the two men.

"Hey, I remember you two eye-ballers," said Simms, "I thought I left you two for the buzzards to pick your bones."

Carl looked at Jess again and Jess simply smiled back as if to say—what are you bounty hunters going to do now? Carl looked at Murry and Murry looked at Jess and saw the same grin and then Carl and Murry looked at each other seemingly trying to figure out what the other one was thinking. They both looked at Curley who had downed his whiskey and refilled his glass again. He took off his hat and slowly set it down on the bar as if that was a sign that he was about to get serious. Then Carl said what Jess thought was about the dumbest thing he had ever heard. When Carl said it, Jess shook his head slowly.

"Curley Simms, we are taking you into custody…again. Give us your gun so we can tie you up and then we are taking you in for the reward money and we ain't letting you us again either." Carl tried to say it with all the conviction he could muster but he would not have even convinced the most cowardly man in the saloon. Curley paused for a moment and then he burst out laughing. Murry shot Carl a glare that would have stopped a train. Carl glared back at him.

"Well…you weren't saying nothing!" Carl defended.

"I sure would have come up with something better than give us your gun so we can tie you up! Where in the hell did that come from?" Murry looked back at Jess and then he looked at Curley Simms who had now finished laughing and was now glaring at Carl.

"I'll tell you what," said Simms. "Why don't you boys just come on over here and see if you can tie me up again?" Carl looked at Jess again.

"Why do you keep looking over at him?" asked Simms. "Ain't anybody in this bar going to mess with Curley Simms. Besides, it would take a man to try me on, not some kid. Besides, I owe you one. I got rope burns on my wrists from you tying me up. Lucky for me I always keeps me a knife in my boot. I can't believe you was dumb enough not to look for it," Curley said as he looked at his right wrist. "I don't think its bad enough to slow me down any on the draw though. Why don't we find out for sure? Why don't you see if you can outdraw Curley Simms? Then, after that, I can try on your partner there; if he's a mind to," said Curley in a sneering voice.

Jess figured this little confrontation had gone on long enough to hopefully teach Carl and Murry a lesson—maybe. It was one thing to talk about taking down a man in a gunfight but it was quite a different thing to actually experience it. "That won't be necessary, Curley. My two partners have asked that you give up your gun and I think you should listen to them," said Jess as he stood away from the bar and looked straight down at Curley. "What did you say the bounty on Mr. Simms was, Murry?" asked Jess, not taking his eyes off Curley who seemed to be agitated by this interruption.

"The bounty was supposed to be five hundred dollars for cattle rustling and horse thievery. We tried to collect it from the sheriff in town here, but he wouldn't even take Mr. Simms into custody," Murry said.

"I understand. I met the sheriff earlier. I don't think he will be of much help in this matter."

"Well, we could still take him to Abilene like we were trying to do before."

"Yeah, but I bet he won't get the drop on you again," replied Jess with a hint in his voice that he knew something that Murry and Carl didn't. Curley had been listening to this conversation between this young man and Murry and he was getting more agitated by the moment.

"Ain't nobody taking me anywhere for anything! You two tenderfoots couldn't keep me before and this young pup ain't gonna help you none. I'm Curly Simms and I'm meaner than all three of you put together." Curley was now paying more attention to Jess than Carl or Murry. Jess kept his stare straight at Curley.

"Murry, did the poster say dead or alive?" asked Jess.

"I think so. Let me look. I kept the poster in my back pocket." Murry took out the piece of paper and unfolded it. He read it aloud. "Yep, it says right here: Wanted, dead or alive, Curley Simms, cattle-rustler and horse thief, Five hundred dollars. Jess smiled.

"Mr. Simms, I usually don't shoot horse thieves or cattle rustlers so I will ask you to give up your gun willingly and allow my two partners to take you into custody to be taken to Abilene for the bounty on your head. I will warn you though, I won't ask you twice."

Curley's anger heightened instantly. "You think you and that fancy lookin' pistol is enough to take on Curley Simms? I'll send you hoppin' over hot coals in hell if'n you try me!"

"I'm going to give you about ten seconds to drop that gun belt," replied Jess. Murry and Carl were really sweating now and neither one of them knew what they should do. They just stood there, Carl looking back and forth between Curley and Jess. Murry still held the piece of paper in his hand. Jess scanned the room again and saw no other threat except for Curley.

"You're down to five seconds," said Jess, in a voice that was calm and nonchalant and yet firm.

"I'm gonna' fill you so full o' holes you won't float in brine," Curley replied, with a snicker on his lips. "Then, I'm gonna take care of your two partners."

"Times up," Jess said.

Curley went for his gun. Curley Simms was indeed pretty fast with a pistol. He actually got to pull his pistol halfway out of its holster. He was thinking how good he was going to feel when he stood over the dead body of this young man who had the nerve to challenge him. What he felt though, was a burning sensation in his chest as Jess' bullet hit its mark. The force made Curley stagger back and lean against the bar, his gun in his hand, which was now down at his side, but not yet cocked. Curley placed his left hand over the oozing wound in his chest trying to stop the flow of blood. He looked at his chest as if he couldn't believe what had happened. His look changed from one of surprise to one of contempt as he glared at Jess.

"You son of a…" He never got to finish his words. He cocked his pistol and began to raise it but he never got it high enough to shoot anything but the floor. Jess fanned two more shots into Curley and Curley hit the floor with a loud thud. No one in the saloon moved, not even Murry or Carl. They both kept looking at Curley's body and the growing pool of crimson red blood on the floor. After a moment or two Murry looked over at Jess.

"I…I don't think I even saw you draw. How can anyone be that fast on the draw?"

"Practice, Murry, lots and lots of practice, replied Jess."

"Hell," Carl said, "we wouldn't have been any help to you, that's for sure."

Jess grinned at them both. "I don't suppose so. Especially since neither one of you removed your hammer straps from your pistols," replied Jess, almost sarcastically. Carl and Murry both checked their pistols at the same time and then simultaneously hung their heads in shame. "You two sure are something else and that's a fact. Well, the least you two can do is haul him down to the undertaker until we can leave town. His dead carcass is worth five hundred dollars."

"Yeah," replied Carl, "and we will be glad to split it with you." Murry shook his head and Jess simply smiled.

"That's mighty nice of you, Carl, since I did all the work. I'll meet you two back here in the morning for some breakfast."

"Sorry," Carl replied, realizing what he had said.

"I swear by Jesus, Carl, I'm going to have your mouth stitched shut," Murry complained.

"What? I said I was sorry. Why is it always me?"

"Because it is always you, you sorry ass!" Carl put his hands up in the air in frustration. Then they carried Curley Simms' body down to the undertaker. Jess finished up his beer and headed over to the hotel for the night.

# Chapter Fourteen

JESS AWOKE BEFORE DAYLIGHT and headed to the livery and checked on Gray and his packhorse. He tried to think of a name for the new packhorse but couldn't think of one yet. He began to think about all the extra things he could carry now and that gave him another idea. He went to meet his two new partners for breakfast at the saloon. Both Carl and Murry had already ordered meals and were about halfway finished when Jess entered the saloon. There weren't many people in the saloon. Jess ordered and sat down to a hot cup of strong coffee.

"You two sleep good last night?"

"Pretty good," replied Carl. Murry simply nodded, not able to answer because of the wad of biscuit he had stuffed in his jaws.

"Good. Listen up, here is the plan," explained Jess. "As soon as you can get the money from the bank, go to the livery. I spotted a good mule there this morning and we can use him to carry Mr. Simms' carcass with us since it's worth five hundred dollars. Then, we will head over to this town of Holten and look for this Lloyd Aker. If we can find him, I'll put him down and then we can collect the reward on him. Then, I can send you two on the train back home, alive I hope. That sound okay with you two?"

Murry finally swallowed his mouthful of biscuits. "When you say, put him down, do you mean like what you did last night?"

"Yes."

"Don't you ever take one in alive?" Carl asked.

"No."

"Well, we ain't going to question your methods. They seem to work quite well," added Carl.

"You can be sure of one thing," said Jess, "Curley Simms won't be robbing you or anyone again."

"I don't suppose so," added Murry, "we found most of our money still on Mr. Simms last night. That should pay for the mule and more supplies we might need. I found my horse and saddle in the livery last night also but he must have sold Carl's horse or let him go."

"My guess is he let him go," replied Jess. "Men like that travel light and keep only what they need. Anything else they need, they usually steal. Anyway, I have to go and get a few more supplies at the general store and I will meet you two at the livery. Make sure you strap Simms down good enough. Once that body starts to stink, you won't want to pick it back up and tie it down on the mule again." Jess headed over to the general store. He walked in and there was a pencil thin man with spectacles behind the counter.

"Morning, young man. What can I get for you today?"

"I need another skillet and five pounds of coffee and I'll take a few dozen 12-gauge shells." The old man went to getting what Jess wanted and Jess was looking behind the counter when he spotted a heavy looking, long barreled rifle. The man came back to the counter with the things Jess ordered.

"Could I take a look at that rifle you have back there?" The man looked over his shoulder.

"Oh, I bet you're talking 'bout the Sharps. That's one damn good rifle. I don't sell very many of them though, in this godforsaken town. I get buffalo hunters now and then who buy 'em. They swear by 'em though. They call it the 'Big Fifty' and some say it's the straightest shooting rifle ever made." The old man gave the rifle to Jess. Jess looked it over for a few minutes. The rifle was much heavier than his Winchester and the barrel was quite long and octagonal instead of round. The rifle had long-range sites on it.

"What kind of ammunition does this thing use?" The man reached down below the counter and brought up a box of cartridges and placed it on the counter.

"This one shoots the .50 caliber cartridge. Some of the hunters I've talked to claim it can kill a buffalo at a thousand yards, although that would be a small miracle if you ask me. It does shoot pretty far though. I took it out back once just to see for myself. I shot it straight out and the dust it kicked up when it finally hit the ground was a pretty good distance. The buffalo hunters I talked to say that for long distance shots, you have to learn to use those sights on it, and you have to cut a tree branch with a fork in it to rest the rifle on. One of 'em showed me how he tied up three sticks with leather to make a rest for the rifle."

"How many cartridges do you have for it?" The clerk looked under the counter and brought up three boxes of ammo for the rifle.

"This is all I have right now. I don't get that much call for them. I can order you more but it would take about a week to get here."

"Don't order them on my account. I'm leaving this morning for Holten. Add the rifle and the ammo to my bill.

The clerk figured out the bill and Jess paid the man. The clerk informed Jess about the general store in Holten and that they would carry a lot more ammo for his new rifle. The clerk also told him what direction to head in to get to Holten. Jess also purchased a nice leather scabbard for the rifle. When he met Carl and Murry at the livery, they were sitting around the front of the livery with the man who ran it.

"What the hell you got there?" asked Carl.

"A new Sharps long gun that buffalo hunters use for long shots."

"You going to start buffalo hunting?" asked Murry.

"No."

"Then what are you going to use it for?" asked Carl.

"To shoot men." replied Jess, as he tied it down to his packhorse. As he was doing so, a thought came to him. "I got it," he said to himself out loud.

"Got what?" asked Murry.

"The name for my packhorse. I've been trying to think of a name for him and I've decided to call him Sharps." Neither Carl nor Murry understood why there was any need to name a horse but they simply nodded and walked their horses out of the livery. Jess had fixed a long line to his packhorse with a fairly heavy rope. As they mounted their horses, Jess asked Carl and Murry which way to head out for Holten. Carl and Murry looked at each other and then at Jess with a dumb look on their faces. Jess simply shook his head and grinned. He gave Gray a little prod and headed out into the street.

"Come on you two bounty hunters," Jess said, sarcastically. "Holten is this way." Carl and Murry fell in behind Jess quietly arguing about who should have found out how to get to Holten.

It took about two days for them to get to Holten. On the first day, Jess stopped at noon and tried out his new Sharps rifle. They were in a large flat area and Jess fired off about a dozen rounds straight out and he was surprised to see how far off the round hit in the dusty ground. Then, he tried a few rounds with the barrel raised up about six inches and again, he was surprised. He made a decision to begin practicing on long distance shots once he was finished with his business with Carl and Murry.

Holten, while certainly a larger town than Baxter had been, wasn't all that big, but the railroad ran through it, and that made it a busier town than some. There were a couple of hotels, several saloons and a few supply stores. The livery in town was fairly large and the man who met the three of them when they arrived was a large rotund man with a smile that never seemed to leave his face.

"Welcome to Holten, men. My name is Rusty and I'd be glad to take care of your horses for you. They will get the best feed and care right here and I have a man who works the place until the wee hours of the night so there is almost always someone here. That mule with the stinker on it will have to stay outside though." Jess, Carl, and Murry all dismounted and the man led their horses into the livery. He helped the three of them take off the saddles and stable the four horses. Carl went around back and tied up the mule.

"So, what you boys in town for? You cattlemen, or maybe buffalo hunters?" he asked, as he watched Jess remove the new Sharps rifle from its scabbard.

"Actually, we are bounty hunters and looking for a man," replied Carl.

"Really?" the man replied, as he changed his glance from Carl to Murry and then to Jess. "Now that young man looks like a bounty hunter but you two…well…you don't seem like the type to hunt men. You men looking for someone particular?" Carl and Murry both seemed to be too hurt by Rusty's comment so Jess took over the conversation.

"I'm...we're looking for a man by the name of Lloyd Akers. He's wanted for several crimes but mostly for murdering some woman on a train that he robbed." Jess showed Rusty the poster with the sketch of Aker on it. Rusty looked at it.

"I wouldn't know his face because I never saw him before, but I sure know the son of a bitch. The woman he murdered was Lee Connor. She was one of the nicest women I ever met. She lived in the house down at the end of the street with Mr. Heath Connor. He is part owner of the train that comes through town here. He hasn't been out much since it happened. He took it real hard when she was killed. He put up most of the reward for Aker. He wants him dead real bad. Says that if someone brings him in alive, he will personally pay any man another thousand dollars to hang him. That man really loved that woman. It's a hard thing to lose something that you love that much."

Jess hung his head a little. "I know exactly how he feels. If you see him, tell him that we will try to make it right for him."

"The only way to make it right for Mr. Connor is to bring that murderer in strapped over a mule just like this one," replied Rusty, nodding at Curley Simms' corpse.

Jess looked Rusty straight in the eyes. "You tell him for me that if we find him, we will bring him in exactly like this one."

"What is your name so that I can tell him who said that?"

"You tell him that Jess Williams said it."

Rusty looked at Jess and then looked down to his pistol and then back up to Jess. "So you are that young man people are beginning to talk about. I should've known by that fancy pistol you got there. You're the one who put down Nevada Jackson and Blake Taggert and a few more. I'll be damned. I thought you were just a made up story and didn't really exist."

"I'm real, I can promise you that."

"You have to go and see Mr. Connor yourself. I know that he would want to talk to you personally about finding Lloyd Aker."

"We heard from someone in Baxter that he was last seen here around Holten."

"That was partially true. They figured that he hid out in the hills for a few days or so but they never found him even though they had thirty men combing those hills. They found one campsite but never saw so much as a shadow of Aker. He robbed the train just a few miles out of town to the east and that's when he killed Mrs. Connor. The train came back to town and Mr. Connor sent out the posse immediately, but they never found him." Murry and Carl had been listening to all of this in silence.

"Show me where Mr. Connor lives," said Jess.

"Well, if you go down the main street, it's the third house on the left after the barber shop. It's a big white house with a large porch. Most likely Mr. Connor will be sitting on the porch." Jess thanked Rusty and motioned to Carl and Murry to follow him.

"We going to see Mr. Connor?" asked Murry.

"You're pretty sharp for an easterner."

"We didn't know you was famous and all," added Carl.

"That comes as much of a surprise to me as you two. I guess talk travels pretty fast, especially when it's about one man killing another."

"So, all those men you killed, they were all pretty fast?"

"Not fast enough," Jess replied.

They walked down the street until they came to the big white house. No one was sitting on the porch so Jess walked up the three steps and knocked on the door. He heard some rustling around in the house and then a tall lanky man dressed in a light blue suit came to the door.

"I've already told everyone in town that I'm not hiring any men right now."

"We're not looking for a job."

"Then what are you here for?"

"We are here to talk to you about Lloyd Aker. Rusty over at the livery told us we should speak to you," replied Jess. Connor's attitude changed at once and he opened the door and let the three men in. Connor motioned for them to sit down in the dining area and he got out a bottle of brandy and placed four glasses on the table and filled them. Then he sat down.

"I want Aker dead and I will pay good money to any man who does the job. There is already a five thousand-dollar reward out for him. I put up three of that and the train company put up the other two. I will personally pay another thousand dollars to the man who brings me his body—dead so that I can personally see the deed is done."

"That's a lot of money for one man," said Carl.

"I got a lot of hate for that man. He took the one thing that meant the world to me. I'm a rich man in the sense of money and power but none of that matters each day when I get up in the morning knowing that murderer is still breathing the same air I am. I will not rest until he is dead."

"We will try to see that you get your wish, Mr. Connor," Jess replied.

"I hope you men are good. Aker is fast with a pistol and meaner than a rattler who's been cornered. He doesn't play by any rules either. If he don't like you, he'll plug you and without so much as a warning. You sure you can take him?"

Jess looked him square in the eyes with a look that made you believe. "If I can find him, I can kill him."

Connor looked into Jess' eyes and saw something there. It was something that you couldn't put a finger on but something that you could feel. It was a feeling of confidence and a complete lack of fear. He also saw the dark side to Jess and that made him wonder about this young man and who he was.

"What is your name?" asked Connor.

"My name is Jess Williams and this is Carl and…"

Connor cut Jess off in mid-sentence. "Did you say Jess Williams?"

"Yes."

"I know of you. You were that kid who had his family murdered. You hunted the men down and killed all three of them. They say you can't be beat on the draw and that you give no quarter in a fight. They say you are the bounty hunter who never brings his man in alive."

"Most of that is true. If a man tries to kill me, I put him down. If he is wanted for murder, I bring him in dead." Heath Connor felt as though destiny had thrown him a miracle when he needed it the most. The only thing he wanted in life anymore was to see the killer of his beloved wife brought to justice and that didn't mean a trial. Now, here he was, sitting in his dining room with the one bounty hunter that could make sure his wish came true. Finally, a spark of hope engulfed him.

"Mr. Williams, if you can bring me the dead body of Lloyd Aker right here to my front door, I will be indebted to you for life. I would give you everything I own if you could do that for me."

"Mr. Connor, that won't be necessary. The reward and the bonus you offered is enough payment for one man. The truth is I would do it even if there weren't a reward for him. This Aker is just like the men who killed my family and I have made a vow to myself that I would hunt down and kill such men, reward or not."

"You'll get the reward and as a matter-of-fact, I'm going to throw in an extra thousand dollars bonus just for you."

"That is mighty generous of you, but you don't have to do that." Carl and Murry shot a look over at Jess and Jess shot a look back at them and they both picked up their glasses and took another sip of the fine brandy.

"I know, but I want to give you every incentive to find Aker and kill him."

"Finding him will be the only problem. Any idea of where he might be?"

"I've had men searching for him since it happened. I keep trying to think of where he might be hiding. That's what I do for most of my day now; sit on my front porch and try to think of where he might be hiding. I don't think he will be in any town around here since he knows I will have men in every town watching for him. I have a hunch he's still hiding in the hills not far from where it happened."

"Seems like you know a lot about the man."

Connor took another sip of his brandy. "I should; he worked for me for over a year." Jess looked surprised as Connor continued. "That's why I know he's fast with a pistol. That's why I hired him. He used to work security on the train when I was transferring money back East. That's how he figured out how to rob the train and when I would have the most money on it."

"Did he do the robbery alone?"

# Brother's Keeper

"No. He had one of the other men who worked for me help him. A man by the name of Adair Kemp. We found his dead body about two miles from the tracks where the robbery occurred. Aker must have figured he didn't want to share the money and gold."

"Well, we've taken enough of your time. I'd like to speak with the sheriff in town. Maybe he could take us out to where the robbery happened. We might as well start there. Maybe we might spot something that everyone else missed."

"I hope so. Anyway, Sheriff Mathers' office is right down the street. He can take you out to where the robbery and murder happened." Carl and Murry shook Mr. Connor's hand and thanked him. Connor shook Jess' hand and held it for a moment as he looked into Jess' eyes. "Please find him and kill him for me…please."

"Like I said, Mr. Connor, if I find him, I will put him down for sure."

The three of them headed for the sheriff's office. As they got close to the sheriff's office Jess spotted an older gentleman with a full head of gray hair sitting on the porch of the jail. As they approached, the man stood up and he was wearing a sheriff's badge. Then, the sheriff's smile turned to a frown.

"I thought you left town for good, Sloan. What in the hell are you doing back here so soon?"

Jess stopped in his tracks. Carl and Murry, who had been following right behind Jess, saw the change in Jess immediately, and Murry almost bumped into Jess. Jess looked as though someone had slammed him in the stomach with a ten-pound hammer. Jess looked at the sheriff with a growing look of confusion.

"Did you call me—Sloan?"

Sheriff Mathers walked down the two steps and looked at Jess a little closer. "I'll be damned. I thought you were that Sloan fellow. You look an awful lot like him but now I can see that you ain't him. These damned old eyes are gettin' worse every day. You sure could pass for his brother, that's for sure."

Jess' brain began to churn out all kinds of thoughts. What should he do now? He had just promised a man who had lost his wife to a killer that he would hunt the man down and kill him. Further, he had two newly acquired friends that he knew would most certainly get killed if they were to go after Aker by themselves. Yet, here he was, talking to the sheriff of this town that he had come to as a result of unknown circumstances, and the sheriff obviously knew his brother, the man he was searching for. His brother had been here in this town recently and yet Jess had been drawn to it by accident, or so it seemed. Then again, was it really an accident or was it destiny playing a role in his life again, like it had with the pistol and holster?

"You all right, son?" Sheriff Mathers asked, after Jess didn't respond for a moment. Jess got a hold of himself.

"Yes. I'm fine. Sheriff, we came to ask you to take us out to the site of the robbery where Mrs. Connor was murdered."

"Have you talked to Heath Connor yet?"

"We just came from there and we told him that we would try to find the man who murdered his wife."

"Good luck. Every man in town and a few dozen more have been trying to do the same thing. Nobody's had any luck so far. I think Aker dug himself a hole and buried himself with all that money and gold and he's simply waiting it out."

"Maybe a few new sets of eyes might make a difference."

"Well, I'll be glad to show you where it happened. By the way, I noticed a mule at the livery with a stinker strapped onto it. Is that your work?"

"Yes sir, it is. The body is that of Curley Simms. He has a reward of five hundred on him and these two men were taking him to Abilene for the reward."

"That won't be necessary. I know Mr. Connor is willing to do anything to make sure Mr. Aker pays for what he done. You can turn the body over to me and I'll take care of everything and make sure you get the reward money."

"Thank you, Sheriff," said Carl. "We appreciate that."

"Sheriff," added Jess, "what can you tell me about Tim Sloan?" The sheriff cocked his head with a quizzical look.

"I never mentioned his first name. How do you know Sloan?"

"You said I look a lot like him?"

"At first glance, I thought you were him."

"I'm his brother and I've been looking for him."

"I guess that explains the likeness between the two of you. You only missed him by a few days. A man came to town and paid him five hundred dollars to read a letter."

"What did the letter say?"

"Don't have any idea. The only thing I know is that he left at daylight and he looked like he was in a hurry."

"Who sent him the letter?"

"The letter came from a man in Black Creek, Kansas." Jess felt another punch in the stomach. "A man by the name of Dick Carter wired me and asked me to ask Sloan to wait for a rider who was bringing him the letter and five hundred dollars in cash to read it. The only reason I know that much is that I had supper with the man who brought Sloan the letter. I think his name was Hanley or something like that. Nice man though. Bought my supper for me. Can you imagine? What kind of man would pay someone five hundred dollars just to read a letter?"

"A dead man," replied Jess. "Sheriff, where do you think Sloan was in a hurry to go to?"

"I don't know for sure, but my guess would be he was heading to Black Creek." Another slam to the stomach. "That's where the letter came from and that's where the rider who delivered it came from and he worked for the man who sent the letter. It would only make sense that he would head there and Sloan did ride out in that direction." A worried look came over Jess as he thought about it.

"Sheriff, what kind of man is my brother?" The sheriff looked at Jess as if he was wondering why Jess would ask.

"You don't know?"

"I've never met him. I just found out recently that I had a brother."

"You're about to find out something else. Sloan was running a poker game with his father Eddie Sloan. So, if Tim Sloan is your brother, Eddie Sloan is your father, I would guess." Jess' stomach felt another blow. He didn't know what to think. His thoughts were spinning around in his head so fast he couldn't grab hold of any of them.

"Sheriff, do you know where Eddie Sloan headed off to?" Jess couldn't bring himself to call Eddie Sloan his father.

"Don't know for sure but he headed out southwest of here. Rumor has it that he runs off to a small town in Mexico to hide out for a while when things get too hot for him. That man has a lot of enemies who would like nothing better than to plug him. He's one mean curse of a man, that's for sure. Your brother ain't any better. He's a gambler, a liar, a thief, a killer, and not much else."

# Brother's Keeper

Another punch to his stomach as Jess hung his head a little. He had hoped that his brother might be someone he could call family, but based on the fact that he had been seen with one of the killers of Jess' family and what Sheriff Mathers had just told him, that was probably not going to happen. And if the sheriff was telling the truth, and Jess had no reason to doubt him, his father was rotten to the core, too. He felt somewhat sad, as if he had just lost the one piece of hope for something normal in his life to happen.

"Thanks, Sheriff. I guess we are ready to take a little ride with you out to the site of the robbery and murder," said Jess.

The sheriff nodded as they all walked to the livery in silence. Murry and Carl could see the pain on Jess' face as they walked. Jess wanted in the worst way to head straight back to Black Creek but he had made a commitment to Heath Connor and he had to honor it. They mounted their horses and started to head out of town. The sheriff had been watching Jess and thinking about what he had told Jess. As they turned down the main street out of town the sheriff asked Jess one more question.

"So, what are you going to do when you finally meet up with your brother?"

Jess thought about it for a moment. He didn't look at the sheriff or at Murry or Carl. He kept his look straight away. "Most likely, I will have to kill him. After that, I'll be looking for Eddie Sloan." Carl and Murry exchanged glances at one another but said nothing. They rode out to the site of the robbery and murder in complete silence.

# Chapter Fifteen

SARA BROUGHT JIM SOME MORE bacon to the table. Jim, Tony and Andy had been stuffing their faces for the last half-hour as if this would be their last meal.

"You men will be able to eat again later, you know," she said as she plopped down the plate of bacon.

"A man has to eat when he can," replied Jim.

"Besides," added Tony, "our next meal might be over at Andy's place." Andy had a hurt look on his face.

"What the hell does that mean?" Andy retorted. Tony smiled at him.

"You still serving those big steaks over there?" Andy and Jim knew what Tony was talking about, but they hadn't told Sara about the horse. Andy smiled as if he was proud of something when he responded.

"Just sold the last of my weekly special last night. Them two-pound steaks went right quickly at the price I was charging."

Tony smiled. "I'll just bet they did."

Jim just grunted and kept eating and Sara shook her head at the three of them. "What do you think Tim Sloan is up to today?" asked Sara, a worried tone to her voice.

They stopped eating and looked at each other. Sloan had been in town for three days now. Tony, Andy and Jim had been taking turns watching him as well as a few other men in town that they could trust. Sloan had started up a daily poker game at Andy's Saloon and had emptied more than a few pockets and bank accounts of the local townsfolk. Luckily though, he had not killed anyone yet, although there had been a few shouting matches over his uncanny luck with cards. Sloan always opted to settle the argument with words when he could concerning his poker game. Not because he had any problem killing someone over a card game, it was simply good business. Once you start shooting the losers at your poker table, people quit playing. Sloan had spent some time walking around town and talking to various people but most didn't offer much in the way of useful information. After all, Jess had saved their town from the harsh domination of Dick Carter and his hired guns. He had wandered into Jim and Sara's general store, but he had no idea of their connection to Jess.

"So far, he seems to be satisfied with winning all the money he can at the card table at my place," answered Andy. "He's been down to Dixie's place. I heard he spends most of his afternoons with a gal by the name of Vivian. She's new at Dixie's and no one knows much about her."

"I've heard him ask a few people about Jess but so far, no one has said anything or that they know who he is, but I'm pretty sure that he knows that most people are hiding something," said Tony.

"Why do you say that Tony?" asked Sara.

"It's just a hunch. It's something about his way of asking and his response. I think he knows everyone is lying to him and he is just biding his time and trying to see how many people will lie to him. I'm not positive but that's how I see it."

"He's a slick one and that's a fact," replied Andy. "I think he knew that me and Tony lied to him the first time he asked us and yet he never let on that he knew. I think he's playing with all of us and simply waiting for someone to slip up or to say something, or maybe he's waitin' to see if Jess shows up back in town."

"That might happen," replied Jim, a worried tone in his voice.

"All we can do is keep doing what we have been doing the last few days and hope that he just goes away," said Sara.

"No man walks away from ten thousand dollars just for killing one man. At least not men like Tim Sloan," replied Andy.

"What the hell are you talking about?" asked Jim. "What ten thousand dollars?"

Andy and Tony looked at each other and Tony decided they might as well tell Jim and Sara what they had heard about the money.

"Yeah," Tony said, hanging his head, it seems that Dick Carter agreed to pay Tim Sloan ten thousand dollars to kill Jess."

"We heard a couple of the ranch hands from the Carter 'D' talkin' about it yesterday in the saloon," added Andy

"That damned Dick Carter," retorted Jim, "that son of a bitch is still causing us grief from his grave."

"I say we all go out there and piss on his grave," Andy said, defiantly.

"That won't solve anything," Sara remarked. "Let's all keep our heads and hope for the best." All three men nodded in agreement.

"And you should have told us about the ten thousand dollars before," added Sara, a hurt tone to her voice. Tony and Andy said nothing but simply hung their heads, knowing that they should have told Jim and Sara as soon as they had herd the story about the money.

They finished with their meals and Andy went back to the saloon and Tony went back to the livery. Tony watched as Sloan left his hotel room and headed over to Dixie's place, probably to see Vivian again. He put his hand on the barrel of his Winchester rifle that he always kept near, especially after the Dick Carter affair, as it was now being called. I should just plug him with my rifle and save everyone the trouble that's coming, Tony thought to himself. The only thing that really stopped him from doing so was that human trait most men called civilized. He leaned his Winchester back against his worktable and went back to work.

| | |

"Well, this is where it happened. Not much to tell though. Aker stopped the train here and his partner was waiting by the tracks with three extra horses to carry the money and gold away. I talked to the people on the train after it happened. They said that after Aker had a few of the passengers load all the money and gold onto the horses, Aker came into the passenger car and he looked for Mrs. Connor. He told her to thank her husband for the pay raise. She stood up and called him a traitor and a thief and he shot her. She fell into the aisle between the seats and tried to sit up and he shot her two more times. There just wasn't any good reason to do that except for plain meanness. People couldn't believe a man could do that to a woman. I knew Mrs. Connor and she was a real fine lady. If anyone brings that son of a bitch in alive, I guarantee I will hang his sorry ass the very same day and there won't be any trial before I do it."

# Brother's Keeper

"Sheriff, if I catch him, you won't have to waste any good rope on a hanging," replied Jess, the rising anger beginning to show on his face. "I know this type of man, and I know only one way to deal with him."

"Well, I have to get back to town. Good luck in your hunt."

"Luck doesn't have much to do with it, but thanks anyway, Sheriff," replied Jess.

Sheriff Mathers headed back into town. He hadn't made ten feet when he stopped and turned around. He reached down into one of his saddlebags and pulled out what looked to be a pretty nice telescope. "These might come in handy. If he's hiding out in these hills, you might have a better time finding him with these. He handed them to Murry who had walked over to the sheriff.

"Thanks, Sheriff. I'll return them to you when we come back to town," said Jess. The Sheriff nodded and again turned back to town. Murry handed the telescope to Jess. Jess pulled it open, extending it all the way and looked through them. They made quite a difference. "These work pretty good. I'm going to have to get me one of these after this is over. It brings things up a lot closer than you can see without it," said Jess, as he handed it back to Murry.

Murry looked through them. "Yeah, these make a big difference." Carl tried them and was just as surprised.

"Well," Carl asked Jess, "what's our plan?" Jess looked all around. They were in a small valley area surrounded by hills. Not giant hills or really steep hills but rather rolling hillsides.

"We have to get on high ground. We'll stay on the top of the hills and start in a small circle and work our way out. Murry, your job will be to keep track of which hills we've been on. Mark each hill with a stick and a piece of white cloth so we know which ones we've been on. Carl, your job will be to use that telescope to see down in the valleys and the hillsides." Carl and Murry nodded in agreement.

"What are you going to do?" asked Carl. Jess looked around at the hills again. Then he took the Sharps rifle out of its scabbard and checked it. He took out a box of cartridges and placed some cartridges into a small leather pouch he usually kept tied to the horn on his saddle. Jess had picked up some extra rounds for the Sharps while in Holten.

"I think I'll do some target shooting with my new rifle," replied Jess. Carl and Murry looked at each other somewhat confused.

"We are looking for a killer in these hills and you plan to go target shooting?" Carl asked.

"That's right. Let's start up there," Jess said, as he headed up the first hill.

"You're the boss, Jess. We'll follow your lead," replied Murry.

Jess looked at Carl and Murry and they headed up the first hill, the Sharps rifle across Jess' lap. When they reached the top of the hill, the three of them dismounted. Both Carl and Murry were wondering exactly what Jess had in mind but they had no real idea. Jess sat down on a big rock for a moment and rechecked the rifle and made sure it was loaded. Carl looked around with the telescope and Murry found a stiff branch to tie a white cloth to.

"See anything, Carl?" asked Jess.

"Nothing yet, but what am I looking for? I know we are looking for Aker but everyone has already looked for him all over these hills. Do you think he will be sitting on a rock down in the valley sipping some coffee and waiting for us or something?"

"No, I don't think that, but if the sheriff is right, and if everyone combed these hills since the robbery happened, how could he have gotten out?" asked Jess.

"Maybe he high-tailed out of here before anybody got here," Carl answered.

"Let's think about it. He had three other horses besides his. He had a partner with him. No one said that they saw Aker kill his partner so he had to do it after the train backed up into town. That had to take a little time, even if he shot his partner in the back."

"Yeah?" replied Murry, trying to follow Jess' thought.

"So, after he kills his partner, he still has three horses and a whole lot of gold and money," continued Jess.

"Okay," added Carl, "so he takes his gold and heads straight out."

"How much do you think that gold weighed, Carl?" Jess asked.

"Hell, I don't know. I guess it depends on just how much gold there was."

"According to the sheriff, it was quite a lot, which is why Aker needed a partner and the extra horses. I don't think Aker could have gotten far enough away with all those horses and extra weight. Think about the dust three horses loaded with gold makes. Someone would have spotted him before he could have gotten out of the hills and the area around the hillsides is flat land for miles. Aker also knows how Heath Connor loved his wife since he worked for him for almost a year. He knows that Connor would have him hanged for killing his wife. I might be wrong, but I think he's still here, hiding out in these hills."

Carl and Murry shook their heads in agreement as if what Jess had said made some sense. Then, Murry stopped pounding the branch in the ground and looked up at Jess, the big rock still in his hand. "But...even if he is somewhere in these hills, how are we going to find him? Dozens of men have already looked for him and no one had seen a trace of him except for some of his tracks he left at the railroad tracks. Those ain't worth nothing since everyone else in the area had trodden through here looking for him."

Jess stared down into the valley to his right. "Well, I guess we have to think a little different from all those others," replied Jess, a smile forming on his lips. "Carl, look down in this valley and let me know if you see anything that looks out of place."

Carl looked dumbfounded. "What the hell are you talking about? It's all the same shit, rocks, brush and a few small trees."

"I know that. But look for something different. Something out of the ordinary like too many brushes together or maybe trees lying sideways as if someone put them there to hide themselves."

Carl was getting the idea now and his eyes lit up. "Oh…I get it now. Like maybe he made himself some cover that looks like everything else around him," Carl said, as if he had came to a sudden realization. Jess smiled some more and shook his head, which was becoming an all too often occurrence lately. Murry sat on a rock and just glared at Carl.

"What? What did I say? Don't start on me Murry, I swear."

"Carl, just keep looking and let me know if you spot anything, anything at all," said Jess, before the two of them could start their all too familiar banter.

Carl looked around with the telescope. He saw some clumps of brush and a few extra rocks in piles but nothing that looked suspicious. Then Carl spotted a larger brush that looked like it was two or three brushes put together.

"Jess, down to my left, just above that large boulder with the single piece of wood on top of it, is a large brushpile. It looks bigger than the other brushes in the area."

Jess laid the rifle on a boulder that was about four feet tall and looked down the barrel in the direction Carl was pointing at. "I believe I see it."

Jess took aim at the small piece of wood on the boulder and slowly pulled back the trigger of the Sharps. The Sharps exploded with a loud boom and the shot echoed throughout the hills. He missed the small piece of wood by only a few inches, the fifty caliber round smashing into the hillside, pieces of rocks scattering in all directions.

"See anything moving, Carl?" asked Jess.

Carl stared through the telescope. "Nothing."

"Keep looking," said Jess, inserting another .50 caliber round into the Sharps.

A few minutes later Carl spotted something. "Okay. I spotted an extra large shadow next to a few large boulders over that way." Jess spotted the area and fired off another round as Carl looked through the telescope.

"Nothing Jess," said Carl, still looking through the telescope.

Carl spotted a few other areas that might mean something and Jess threw a round at it but they came up empty. They went to the next hill and did the same. Carl looking for anything that seemed out of the ordinary and Jess firing a round from the Sharps. Jess was getting accurate with the Sharps and whenever Carl couldn't find anything unusual to shoot at, Jess would simply fire off a half dozen rounds into the hills at nothing but rocks and shadows. That's the way the remainder of the day went and they made camp and turned in for the night. The three of them took turns at watch from the top of the hill they planned to start at in the morning. They awoke before daylight and started the entire process again. Five different hillsides and almost a hundred rounds later, they were all getting discouraged.

"Maybe this ain't gonna work, Jess," said Murry.

"Besides, you're going to be out of ammo for the Sharps soon," added Carl. Jess looked at them and they could see that even he was getting discouraged.

"Okay, maybe you two are right, but let's finish out the day and turn in and see how we feel in the morning."

The three agreed and they moved on to the next hill. Carl was spotting and Jess was firing off shots at the hills. Murry was pounding a stick into the ground when he looked off into the direction of one of the hills they had started on the first day. Something was not right but he couldn't put his finger on it immediately. Then it hit him. He couldn't see the stick he had pounded in on the top of the hill. It was gone.

"Hey, Jess."

"Yeah, Murry, did you see something?"

"It's what I don't see that's interesting."

"What does that mean?" asked Carl.

"The first marker I put on the first hill is missing."

"It probably just fell over," said Carl, dismissing it. Jess, however, did not dismiss anything that seemed out of the ordinary.

"Murry, are you sure you pounded it in far enough?" asked Jess.

"Are you kidding? I haven't had anything to do except pound these sticks into the ground and I pounded them in good. And there hasn't been even a hint of a breeze since we started," replied Murry.

Jess sat down and took a few swallows of water from the canteen. "Here's what we are going to do. Let's act like we don't know the stake is missing. Let's make camp tonight and start out in the morning as if we are following our pattern like we have the last few days. When we head over the next hill, let's backtrack back to the first hill and come at it from the south. If it's our man and he took the stake down, he's probably on the other side of the hill from us."

"But why would he take the stake down?" asked Carl. How does he know we wouldn't think that we hadn't checked out that valley and go there later?"

"Because if it is him, he's been watching and he figures that we would forget where the stakes were and that we didn't even start there and probably wouldn't go back. Maybe he's just pissed off and ripped the stake out," replied Jess. "We have an hour before dusk so let's keep on like nothing has changed. That way, if it is Aker, he will think that in the morning, we'll be one more hillside away from him."

"You're the boss," replied Murry. They continued on and then made camp. Supper consisted of two rabbits that Jess had plugged with his Sharps earlier while he was pounding the hillsides with the Sharps. Jess had taken the heads clean off, leaving all the good meat. Murry was cutting up a few sticks to cook the rabbits on and Jess was cutting a large forked stick.

"What are you going to do with that?" asked Carl.

"The man at the general store back in Baxter told me the buffalo hunters use a support stick like this to balance their rifles on when they are long distance shooting."

"After seeing you take the heads off those two rabbits, I don't think you need it," replied Carl.

"I'll take any edge I can get, Carl."

Carl smiled and the three of them ate a pretty good meal and turned in, each taking their turn at watch. At dawn, they ate a simple meal of pan bread and some bacon, along with a pot of coffee. Then, they slowly made their way atop the next hill and then they went down the hill just enough to be out of the line of sight from the first hill that they had started on. They immediately turned south and worked themselves around the area until they got to the bottom of the first hill. They made their way up to the top. They found the spot where Murry had pounded in the stake. The hole was still evident. Someone had removed it. Jess could sense the danger even though the other two men could not.

"Stay low and be careful. I think he's watching us right now," cautioned Jess. "Carl, take a look at that large clump of bushes where we started the other day, remember? That small stick is still sitting on the large boulder just below the clump of bushes."

"Yeah, I see it. That little piece of wood is still there. You missed it the other day."

"Well, let's see if I've gotten better with this thing," said Jess, as he found two bushes with an opening between them. He stuck the forked stick into the ground deeply enough to support the Sharps. He laid down flat and placed the barrel of the Sharps rifle on the forked piece of wood. Then, he found his target, the small piece of wood lying on the boulder. The piece of wood was probably a hundred and fifty yards away and there was no breeze at all.

"Carl, watch those bushes close. I'm going to fire a few shots off. Murry, let us know if you see any movement around that area." Jess took careful aim. The Sharps barked and the piece of wood shattered into splinters.

"I guess you have gotten better with that thing," Carl said, not taking his eyes away from the telescope, which were trained on the large clump of bushes. The Sharps barked a second time and then a third, one shot into the boulder, shattering chips of stone into the bushes and one straight into the bushes. No movement. Jess fired a fourth round into the clump of bushes. Carl leaned forward a little, as if that could somehow let him see better when a bullet ripped through his left arm, causing him to drop the telescope and scream like a cat grabbed by the tail. He spun around and hit the ground behind the large rock he had been propped up on. A volley of shots kept coming at a steady pace. Jess rolled over to the large rock he was next to and Murry laid down flat just behind the edge of the hill, out of sight of the shooter. Jess counted at least fifteen shots, all from a rifle, he was sure.

"Carl, how bad are you hit?" asked Jess.

"It hurts like hell, but it went right through the flesh and missed the bone."

"That's good; wrap it up tight with some cloth. Tear off your sleeve and use that."

"Nothing good about being shot," complained Carl, as he began to tear off his sleeve.

"Quit complaining and give me the telescope," retorted Murry. Carl threw the telescope over to Murry. Murry rose up just slightly to catch it and when he did, a bullet smacked into his forearm.

"Goddamnit!" screamed Murry. "That son of a bitch shot me!" Murry lay back down and ripped off his sleeve and began to wrap his wound. Jess looked back and forth at the two of them and shook his head. Murry looked at him.

"That bastard shot me!" Murry complained.

"What did you think he would do, invite you down to lunch?" answered Jess.

"Yeah, well he shot me first! And mine is worse that yours!" hollered Carl. A dozen more shots pounded the rocks and edge of the hill all around the three of them.

"I told you two to be careful. Now stay down. At least we know where he is and he can't come out because he would be too exposed. There is no other cover for him except for the clump of bushes. Can you two still handle your Winchesters?"

"Hell yes," replied Carl, angrily, "I'll put some lead in that bastard for shooting me."

"Murry, how about you?" asked Jess.

"Just say the word; I'm ready to start shooting."

"Carl, you start first. Murry, you start firing when he's empty and keep a steady but slow firing pattern to give Carl enough time to reload before you're empty. Carl, you start reloading as soon as you're empty and then start firing again as soon as Murry is empty. That should keep him busy while I try to get a shot at him." Carl and Murry nodded as if they understood what Jess wanted.

"Hold on just a minute. I guess we should ask if that really is Aker down there." Jess hollered out as load as he could. "Mister, we're looking for Lloyd Aker. If you're not him, now would be a good time to let us know."

There was a moment of silence, as if the man was deciding what to do. A loud voice boomed back. "You can tell Heath Connor I'll see him in hell with that bitch of a wife of his!"

"Well, I guess we have our answer," said Jess. "If it isn't Aker, the man down there just made his last mistake. Okay boys, start shooting."

"I guess we're really bounty hunters now, huh Murry," exclaimed Carl, as he began firing his Winchester steadily.

"Hell yes, I damn well guess we are," replied Murry.

"Shut up and keep throwing lead," Jess added, as he rolled back over between the bushes and propped his Sharps back into the forked branch. He kept looking at the bushes above the large boulder and he could see some lingering powder smoke rising from the left side of the bushes. Carl's shots were hitting all around the area. As soon as Carl's Winchester emptied, there was a pause that lasted only a few seconds. A few rounds came back at them from the bushes; one hitting the rock that Carl was now crouching behind, feverishly reloading. Jess saw a muzzle flash coming from the left of the bushes. He picked out the spot where he had seen the flash. He figured the man, hopefully Aker, would fire off a few rounds again when Murry finished. Jess figured right. As soon as Murry stopped, Jess spotted the muzzle flash again and at the very same instant, the Sharps barked, aimed directly at the muzzle flash coming from the bushes. Jess heard a howl and saw the bushes move. A few seconds later, he saw a rifle clatter down out of the bushes. He held up his hand to stop Carl from shooting. They waited for a few minutes.

"I think I might have hit him. I'm going to go down there and I need you two to cover me. Split up a little more so you both have a sharper angle at the bushes. That way there will be less of a chance of hitting me with a stray bullet if you boys have to open up. Murry, take my spare Winchester and make sure both of yours are loaded. If he opens up again, I want both of you to open up at the same time from both angles."

Jess left the Sharps on the hill. He grabbed his Winchester and slowly worked his way down the hill towards the other side. The bushes where the shots had come from were on the other side about twenty feet above the valley. Jess approached cautiously and used whatever cover he could find, which wasn't much at all. He finally made his way to the boulder and stopped there for a moment.

"Aker, you in there?" asked Jess. No answer.

"I have two men with Winchesters on the hill across from you. If you so much as make a move, they will open up on you." No answer. Then, Jess heard a horse. He worked his way around the large boulder, which was the size of a small cabin and then he saw it. Aker lay dead at the mouth of a cave. He had a few wounds from the Winchesters, but it was the Sharps .50 caliber that obviously put the large hole in his chest. He was in a sitting position against the wall of the cave. Jess made sure he was dead and then he waved for Carl and Murry.

"Leave the horses up there and come on down."

Jess walked into the cave, which really opened up after the first twenty feet or so. It was a steep drop and it opened up into a large cavern with a small waterfall pouring down from one side of the cavern into a large deep pool of pristine water. There were four horses tied up to a small log that was lying by the pool of water. There were remnants of a few piles of hay by the pool. Jess heard Murry holler loudly outside the cave opening.

"Son of a bitch!"

"I told you to be careful," Carl yelled.

"Goddamned rocks!" exclaimed Murry. The two of them came into the cave, Murry limping and Carl looking in amazement at the cavern.

"What happened?" Jess asked. Murry just groaned.

"Clumsy idiot tripped over a rock and sprained his ankle," replied Carl, smiling because it wasn't him this time.

"Sprained hell, I think it's broken!"

"Aw, quit your complaining. Hey, we got Aker and now we have enough money to open our place back East," said Carl. Murry smiled at that and then went back to moaning. Carl looked around and spotted a large pile of gold bars with some saddlebags next to them. He walked

# Brother's Keeper

over to the saddlebags and sure enough, they were stuffed plumb full of cash. There were empty saddlebags lying by the gold bars.

"Guess he had to keep handling it," said Carl.

"I've heard that gold will do strange things to a man. I hear it can make a man go crazy. He probably had to handle it every night before turning in," added Jess.

"Looks like they planned this thing pretty well," added Murry.

"I think so," replied Jess. "They hauled enough hay in here for the horses and they stashed enough food for a month in here. They placed enough extra bushes around the opening that no one would have seen it unless they walked right up to it. Pretty slick."

"He almost got away with it," replied Carl, looking out at Akers dead body.

"Yeah, but he didn't know he was going to be hunted by the best bounty hunters in the business," said Murry, proudly.

"Let's get the gold loaded up into the saddlebags and get these horses out of here. We have a bounty to collect and a pretty good one at that."

Both Carl and Murry agreed with that. They loaded up the horses and Carl and Jess walked them up the hill. Murry had to ride because of his ankle. They collected their stuff and headed back into town. Akers dead body was tied down to his horse.

# Chapter Sixteen

THEY ARRIVED BACK IN HOLTEN in the late afternoon. Sheriff Mathers had seen them come in from the east end of town where the livery was. He noticed it because there were three men and a string of horses following, and one of the horses had a body strapped across it. He walked into the livery as Jess was handing Gray over to the liveryman.

"I'll be damned. How the hell did you find him?" Mathers asked.

"I thought about what you said about him having dug himself a hole and buried himself, so I took a guess that he must have had a cave that he was hiding in," answered Jess.

"Yeah, but how did you ever find it? We combed those damned hills pretty good."

"You would've never found it, even if you passed within ten feet of it. It was hidden real well behind some bushes."

"Jess here decided to do some practice shooting with that new Sharps rifle of his," added Carl. "He kept pounding those hills until we finally got a response from Aker."

Mathers chuckled as he turned to Jess. "You mean you kept shooting at the hillsides waiting to see if you'd get a response?"

"I figured we had to do something different," replied Jess. "No one had any luck any other way. Besides, I needed the practice with the Sharps and I got pretty good with it. Sheriff, let's go over to Heath Connor's house and personally deliver this piece of crap along with his gold and money."

The sheriff grabbed the reins of the horse carrying Aker's body and Carl and Murry held the reins of the horses carrying the gold and the cash. They headed down the street towards the Connor house. Heath Connor was waiting on the front porch of his house. He had heard already that some bounty hunters with a dead body had come into town and the truth was Heath Connor pretty much knew whatever happened in town as soon as it happened. He stood as he watched Jess, Sheriff Mathers, and two more men walking horses towards his house. He looked Jess straight in the eyes and Jess could see tears in Heath Connor's eyes.

"Is…is it Aker?" Connor asked, his voice breaking up with raw hatred.

"Yes it is," replied Jess, grabbing Aker's hair and lifting his head so that Connor could see it was Aker. "I told you if we found him, I would kill him. I wanted to deliver his carcass to you personally." Connor hung his head in silence for a moment as if in deep thought. His head rose slowly.

"Mr. Williams. I don't know how I can thank you. I will be indebted forever for what you have done for me. You sir, can have anything from me that you wish, anytime."

"Thank you, Mr. Connor, but the reward will do just fine for us."

"Sheriff," Connor shifted his gaze to Sheriff Mathers, "I want you to take this piece of crap out to the edge of town and place his body spread eagle and face up. I want to be able to watch the vultures and coyotes pick his bones clean."

Mathers shook his head. "Man, that's pretty cold, Mr. Connor. You sure you don't want me to just bury him?"

"There is no way that bastard will ever get a decent burial. He doesn't deserve it or anything else meant for a decent human being."

Mathers had long ago learned better than to argue with Heath Connor when his mind was made up. "If that's what you want, that is exactly what you'll get, Mr. Connor." The sheriff headed back towards the east end of town towing Aker's body behind him.

"Mr. Connor, we got all your gold and money here in these saddlebags," said Carl. "It took us damn near an hour to load it all up."

Connor nodded, and that's when he noticed that the two men had been wounded. "You men should see the doctor and tend to those wounds."

"We will as soon as we get your money in the house. Besides, we ain't hurt all that bad," said Murry, almost proud of his flesh wound.

"Bring all of it into the house," said Connor. Jess followed Mr. Connor into the house and Carl and Murry started carrying the saddlebags into the house. It took them several trips, especially with Murry limping with every step.

"That's all of it," Carl said, as he dropped the last of the saddlebags. "Jess, we're going over to see the doctor and then get cleaned up at the hotel. How about we meet for some supper in the hotel café at five?"

"That sounds real good to me, boys. You two did real good out there, by the way," Jess added.

"Well, we did have you to lead us, that's for sure," replied Murry.

"Yeah, but you still did good. Some men would have got on their horse and ran for the hills at the first shot. You two stayed at it, even after you were wounded. That counts for something."

"I guess that we really are bounty hunters then?" asked Carl.

"Yeah, retired bounty hunters," said Jess, with finality in his voice that both Carl and Murry understood. Both of them headed out to see the doctor and get a good hot bath. Connor motioned for Jess to take a seat.

"Would you like a brandy, Mr. Williams?"

"I don't drink much of the hard stuff, but yes, I think I will."

"So, are you retiring after this job?"

"Oh no, those two are, not me. It was the deal I made with them. I would help them get the reward for Aker and they promised me they would go back East before they ended up dead." Jess explained the story about how they were going to make enough money to open up their establishment and how they had come out here to make quick money at bounty hunting to do it.

Connor laughed at that. It was the first time he had laughed in quite a while. Then, he looked at Jess with a serious look. "I have a business suggestion for you Mr. Williams." He told Jess what he was thinking about and Jess did in fact, like the idea. Jess finished his drink and as he stood up, he told Connor he needed one more favor.

# Brother's Keeper

"Anything, all you have to do is ask," replied Connor with a smile.

Jess went back to the livery and took care of Gray and got a few of his belongings. He went to the hotel and got a nice hot bath and headed down to the café to meet with Carl and Murry. The two of them were already seated and sharing a fine bottle of whiskey. Jess joined them.

"I figured we could afford the good stuff now," exclaimed Carl.

"Well, this isn't what I would call the finest whiskey, but it sure is better than that rot-gut we drank before," added Murry. "Jess, you want a shot of this?"

"No, but I will have a beer." Murry motioned over to the barkeep and he brought Jess a beer.

"This has been an exciting day for me," said Carl. "I can't believe we actually did it."

"Of course, we couldn't have done it without you, Jess," added Murry. "I don't think we can thank you enough."

"The good thing is that you have enough to start your business back in New York and better yet, you're both still alive to see it happen." Carl and Murry both looked at each other and back at Jess.

"Well," Murry said, somewhat sheepishly, "we are a little short of what we had planned. We wondered if we might try one more job before we go back." Carl said nothing; he just kept his head down.

"Not a chance in hell," Jess said firmly, "you boys made a deal with me and you're going to keep it."

"But Jess…we…"

Jess cut Carl off in mid-sentence. "No. We made a deal and that is the end of it. I won't hear any of it. You two are going back to New York or I swear I'll shoot the both of you myself and get it over with."

"We did make a deal," Murry said, "and we'll stick by it. We just thought…"

"I have another deal for you," said Jess, cutting Murry off in mid-sentence.

"Oh yeah, what might that be?" Carl asked, getting excited.

"I want you two to take the entire six thousand dollars of the reward money. I'll keep the five hundred reward from Curley Simms."

"Now who is backing out of a deal? We were supposed to share the money," said Murry.

"We are, but I want to invest my share in your business. I figure it should buy me a ten-percent share of the profits since you two will be doing all the work. Sound like an okay deal with you boys?" asked Jess.

"Consider it done, my friend," said Carl.

"Yeah," added Murry, both men shaking hands with Jess to seal the deal.

"Maybe we can get those padded leather chairs right away after all," said Murry.

"And maybe the carpeting. I think we can cut back on the crystal glasses and some of the fancy woodwork," added Carl. Jess shook his head as he spent the rest of his meal listening to the two of them bantering back and forth about their business.

"I guess all we have to do next is collect our money and get some tickets for the train," said Carl, as he sat back in his chair with another shot of whiskey in his hand.

Jess smiled as he reached into his back pocket. "No need for that. I already have you two booked on the train to New York. I also have your bank draft for the six thousand dollars and I will personally put the two of you on the train leaving out tomorrow."

"I heard the train to New York didn't leave until the day after tomorrow," Carl said, confused.

"Mr. Connor was nice enough to change the schedule for me. It leaves tomorrow and your two sorry butts will be on it," Jess responded, with that same finality in his voice.

"Sounds like our friend here has been busy," Murry said to Carl.

"I didn't know you wanted to get rid of us so fast," added Carl.

"The faster, the better," replied Jess. "I need to protect my investment." They all laughed at that.

# Chapter Seventeen

**C**ARL, MURRY AND JESS HAD their morning meal at Heath Connor's house. He had left a message at the hotel for them. As they arrived at the Connor residence, Heath Connor was sitting on his porch with his chair turned towards the end of the main street. They could see why. Just as instructed, the sheriff had placed Aker's corpse spread eagle just outside the end of town. Far enough to keep the smell from bothering anybody and yet close enough to allow Heath Connor to watch the vultures and coyotes pick his bones clean. Connor was actually looking through the telescope when the three of them walked up to the porch. Carl and Murry had a strange look on their faces but Jess smiled as if he understood in some strange way. As soon as Connor noticed them he put the telescope down and stood up to greet them.

"Good morning, gentlemen. I'm so glad you agreed to accept my invitation to join me for breakfast. I have the best cook in town in my house and she has whipped up some mighty fine food. The dining table is already set and I believe she is ready to serve it up anytime we're ready." The four men went inside and sat down at the dining room table and they had no sooner taken off their hats when a woman with a smile as wide as the Mississippi waltzed into the room with a hot pot of coffee.

"Good morning men," she said in a somewhat melodious tone. "Anyone want coffee?" They all nodded in the affirmative and she went about pouring the coffee. "There's cream and sugar as well as some honey on the table if you want it," she added as she swept back into the kitchen.

"That is Wanda Dopkowski," said Connor, "and she is probably the best cook in town. She is a polish immigrant who showed up here about five years ago and has been working at a little café just around the corner from the hotel. You are going to love her cooking."

"It sure smells mighty fine," Carl chimed in.

Before Jess or Murry could add their two cents worth she came bustling back into the dining room with a huge plate of flapjacks in one hand and a heaping pile of bacon in the other. She plopped those down and returned a few seconds later with a pot full of scrambled eggs and a large platter of freshly baked biscuits and cornbread. That was followed by a large plate of ham along with a platter of eggs done over easy and one of her polish dishes called potato pancakes. The butter, syrup and all the other fixings were already on the table. Murry, Carl and Jess were so overwhelmed by all of the wonderful food they simply stared at it. Wanda put both of her hands on her hips and looked at them as if trying to break the spell.

"I cooked it, but I ain't gonna put it on your plates, gentlemen. Now, dig in, I have a nice chocolate cake waiting its turn on the table for dessert. They all dug in as they were instructed. They were passing around the plates to one another and they ate more than their share of the food. As soon as they finished and each one of them made the claim that they couldn't eat one more bite, Wanda came in with four plates, each with a large slab of chocolate cake with some type of chocolate syrup on it and it was absolutely delicious.

"I have never had cake this good before," said Carl.

Murry stopped cramming the cake in his mouth and lifted his head, which was about two inches from the plate. "This is one time I have to agree with my partner, this is wonderful. Wanda, you want to go back East with us? We can set up a little shop and you can make cakes and whatever you make. We can sell them to all the restaurants in the area around where our establishment will be." Wanda put her hands back on her hips, which was what she always did when she was trying to make a point.

"That's a nice offer, gents, but there are too many people back there in the East. I like it fine out here. Some of the people out East are a little too fussy for me. I want people to appreciate the food I cook and out here, they really appreciate a fine meal, when they can get one."

"Well, that is exactly what we had here," said Jess, as he finished his last morsel of cake off the plate. "I hate to admit it Wanda, but this was every bit as good as my ma used to cook." Heath Connor had told Wanda about Jess and how he had lost his family so Wanda understood how meaningful the comment was. She gave Jess her best smile and looked him in the eyes with a motherly look.

"That's about the best compliment any woman could get, Mr. Williams. I'm glad you enjoyed it. It's too bad you gentlemen can't stay for supper. I could make you some of my polish dishes. You would love them I'm sure."

Heath Connor broke in. "Thank you Wanda for another fine meal. As for the supper offer, that would be wonderful but these men have to leave this morning. Okay men, the trains waiting for you. It was scheduled to leave an hour ago, but I told them to sit still until we get there."

The four men got up and headed out towards the north end of town and arrived at the train station. Jess was almost laughing at the sight of Carl and Murry. Both of them had bandages wrapped around their arms and Murry was still limping from his sprained ankle. They loaded up what few things that Carl and Murry had to take back to New York. The most important thing was the large bank draft from Mr. Connor. Murry had that in his shirt pocket. He wasn't about to let it out of his sight.

"Well, I guess this is it," said Murry, as he shook hands with Jess and Mr. Connor. "I appreciate everything you did for us, Jess, and we won't forget it. You will have to come out East and see your investment sometime. We discussed it last night and we are going to have a wooden J hand carved out of the finest wood and hang it over the door of Murry and Carl's. When people ask what it stands for, we'll tell them all about you. And, once a week, everybody in the place will get a free drink and we'll tell them it's from our silent partner, Jess Williams."

"That's right, Jess," Carl added, as he too shook hands with both men. "Everyone who comes into Carl and Murry's will know all about you and what you did for us. We were lucky to have run into you and that's a fact." The train whistle blew loudly.

"Time to board the train you two," Connor said. Carl was helping Murry step up into the train and Murry was moaning about the pain in his ankle.

"Quit pushing me," exclaimed Murry.

"Well get you ass up the step before the train leaves without us," Carl replied.

"It ain't leaving without us, and I thought we had agreed to call our place Murry and Carl's?"

"I never agreed to that, you just kept saying it. Besides, Carl and Murry's sound real nice to me. It kind of rolls off the tongue right nice, don't you think?"

"I'll roll your sorry ass off this train once it gets going a little faster and you can walk back to New York!"

"If I get off this train that bank draft is going with me!" yelled Carl.

Murry finally got on the top step and they entered the train. Jess and Connor watched as they walked back and sat down at a table by the window facing them. The window was open and Connor and Jess could hear the argument still going on. As the train pulled out all Jess could see was Murry and Carl locked in another heated debate with each other.

Jess shook his head. "I'm damn glad we got them on the train. I don't think I could've taken much more of that. I think I would've had to shoot at least one of them." They both laughed.

"They damn sure do argue a lot, that's a fact," replied Connor. The two men walked in silence back towards the livery. Jess retrieved Gray and the newly named packhorse, Sharps and then they walked back to Connor's house.

"Thanks again, Mr. Connor," said Jess, as he shook Connor's hand one last time.

"No, I'm the one doing the thanking here," said Connor, as he looked out at the now half eaten body of Lloyd Akers. "You gave me what I needed and I will never forget it. You have a friend for life, Mr. Williams. You ever need anything, you let me know." Jess got up in the saddle and tipped his hat at Connor.

"You think those two will make it to New York alive?" asked Connor.

"Yeah, but not before they drive a few people to jump off your train though," replied Jess as he turned Gray towards the end of the town. Connor watched as Jess headed out and then turned north, heading back in the direction of Black Creek, Kansas. He watched as a few vultures flew off when Jess went by. He smiled as they returned to continue picking at Aker's body again. "Keep eating till it's all gone," he said, to no one but himself. He sat back down in the chair on his porch and continued watching the vultures with what could only be described as a look of satisfaction on his face.

| | |

Jess headed a little west first, looking for the trail he had come south on since he knew there were a few good creeks along the way. He found a nice spot to take a break around the middle of the afternoon. He made some coffee and was chewing on one of the biscuits that he had willingly taken from Wanda when he left the Connor house. He saw a dust cloud off to the north, probably a mile away or so. He got out the telescope he had bought in Holten and opened it up. He saw a single rider coming at a pretty good pace and a spare horse behind him with a saddle on it. Someone's in a hurry to get somewhere, he thought to himself. He removed his shotgun from his sling and sat it down on the boulder next to him. He didn't know if the man meant trouble or not but he would be prepared for it anyway. Jess was only about twenty feet off the trail so unless the rider took a turn east or west, he would ride right by Jess. He stood as the rider approached and slowed after seeing Jess. He waved as if to let Jess know he was friendly but that did not make Jess relax yet. The rider

# Brother's Keeper

dismounted about fifty yards from Jess and walked his horses the rest of the way.

"Howdy Mister, mind if I sit a spell and take a break?"

"Not at all, help yourself to some coffee and a biscuit if you like."

"That sounds damn good and mighty nice of you." Hanley went about tying his horses to a branch on a tree and got out his coffee cup. He walked to the fire and filled his cup and grabbed one of the large biscuits. He noticed the double-barrel on the boulder next to Jess.

"You expecting trouble?" asked Hanley.

"Not really, but if it shows up, I'll be here to greet it."

"Well, just so you know, I ain't it."

"I figured as much, once I got a look at you." Hanley was about to take a large bite out of the biscuit when he finally noticed it. He took one look at the pistol Jess was wearing and that caused Hanley to look at Jess a little more closely.

"I'll be damned. I was hoping to get lucky but not this lucky," said Hanley. Jess looked at him curiously, wondering what he meant.

"Might your name be Jess Williams?" Jess stiffened a little at the question. He had gained a reputation as a fast draw and he knew that men would begin to seek him out simply to try to outdraw him and prove that they were faster. For all he knew, this man was one of them. Jess slowly rose up and stood. It was then that Hanley noticed that the hammer strap was off Jess' pistol.

"Who might you be and why are you asking?" Hanley could sense the danger.

"Hold on Mister, I ain't no threat to you. I'm not a gunfighter looking to call you out. If you are who I think you are, I've been sent to find you and bring you a message."

Jess relaxed and took another sip of coffee. He looked Hanley over for a moment. "Who sent you to find me?"

"So you are Jess Williams?"

"Yes."

"Well, I'm Terrence Hanley and it's an honor to share a cup of coffee with you."

"It's a pleasure to meet you too, but let's get back to that part about who sent you to find me and bring me a message."

Hanley filled his cup again and sat back down. "Cal Hardin, back in Black Creek, sent me to find you. He wants me to tell you that your brother, Tim Sloan, is back in Black Creek waiting for you." Jess did not respond; he calmly listened as Hanley continued.

"It seems that Dick Carter, before his untimely death by your hands, sent a message to your brother. In the message was the offer to pay your brother the sum of ten thousand dollars to kill you. Carter gave the money to Cal Hardin to hold. Hardin promised Carter that he would pay the money to your brother once he brought your dead body to Hardin to identify."

"I thought the bounty Carter had on my head was three thousand dollars," replied Jess.

"There's still that too, but Carter must've figured that hiring your own brother to kill you was worth a whole lot more money. Hell, Carter was crazy with hate for you. He probably would have paid anything to see you dead by your own brother's hand."

Jess thought for a moment about what Hanley had said before responding. "So, if Hardin is supposed to pay off my brother for killing me, why did Hardin send you to find me and warn me?"

"Because Hardin don't like any of this one bit. He figured he owed Carter and he made a promise, but he will only keep the promise he made to Carter and he never promised not to warn you."

"Why did he pick you to find me? I've never met you before. How would you even know what I look like?"

Hanley went silent for a moment and swallowed hard. "I'll tell you, if you promise to keep that pistol holstered." Jess grinned and nodded in agreement.

"I work, well…did work for Carter. Now I work for his widow, at least I did when I left. I'm not sure I'll be working for her by the time I get back, but that don't matter none since Hardin offered me a job. Anyway, I was the one that Carter sent to find your brother. Since you and your brother look a lot alike, Hardin figured I might be able to pick you out. I want you to know that I never read the letter that I delivered to your brother but I knew that it involved money and that your brother would collect it back in Black Creek. By the time I got back to the Carter ranch, you had already killed Carter so I kind of figured the whole mess was done with. When I accepted this job with Hardin, he told me the whole story. I guess that's the whole of it, in a nutshell."

Jess didn't respond right away. He sat there and thought about what Hanley had told him. He thought about the evilness of Dick Carter's plan to have his own brother attempt to kill him. Again, destiny seemed to be playing a role in Jess' life. It was almost too much to take in and grab hold of. Here he was, looking for his brother when his brother was looking for him. He wondered if there was some unknown force that was working to bring the two of them together or was it just the way things were supposed to work out. Less than six months ago he learned about the brother he never knew he had and then he found out that his brother had been spotted with one of the killers of his family, Blake Taggert. Now, his brother was being paid to kill Jess and for no other reason than money. Then he remembered the lesson that his pa had taught him. You have to play the cards life deals you. You can't change it and you can't run away from it.

Hanley watched as Jess was thinking about all that Hanley had told him. He had watched the expressions on Jess' face as it went from puzzlement to anger and finally to a look of determination. He could see darkness in Jess' eyes. It was a darkness that he had not seen in a man before. It was something that you could actually feel if that was at all possible. It sent a chill down Hanley's spine. Then, in an instant, Hanley could see calmness come over Jess as Jess got up to fill his coffee cup again.

"Well, it seems that my brother and I finally have something in common."

"What would that be?"

"It seems that we are both out to do the same thing, except he's being paid a lot of money to do it."

"Ten thousand dollars is a whole lot of money," said Hanley.

"Yeah," agreed Jess, "but he won't be collecting it, you can be sure of that."

"I saw your brother kill a man back over in Holten over a card game. He's pretty fast with that left hand of his."

"He'll need all the speed he can muster when he faces me," replied Jess.

"I'm thinking' you might be right about that, and thanks by the way."

"Thanks for what?"

"For not shooting me like you did Deke Moore."

"Deke Moore got exactly what he deserved. Besides, you're just the messenger. And I guess Cal Hardin is trying to make something wrong a little more right, I have to give him that much and I'll tell him so when I see him."

"He'll appreciate that and I know it for a fact. He ain't like Carter, I can tell you that."

"Well, seems like you will have some company on your ride back to Black Creek, Mr. Hanley," said Jess.

"Terrence will do just fine, Jess," replied Hanley, "and I can't think of any man I'd rather have riding next to me."

They broke camp and mounted up and started their ride back to Black Creek. It was a quiet trip, neither man talking. Terrence Hanley was thinking about what was going to happen when they got back to town. He would glance over at Jess once in a while. He felt sorry for the horrible turn of events that had changed this young man's life so dramatically. And yet, he seemed to have taken it all in stride, dealt with it, and survived to be a honed mankiller and he was young enough to be Hanley's son. Jess' thoughts were on something else though. He was asking himself one question over and over in his head—Why had Tim Sloan been riding with Blake Taggert?

# Chapter Eighteen

"**J**ESUS CHRIST! HOW DAMN lucky can one man get!" exclaimed Trent Holt. "You ain't lost a hand in over an hour."

"I guess I'm just lucky today," replied Tim Sloan.

"Yeah, you've been lucky every day since you came to town," added Tom Otto, who had been locked in a poker game with Trent Holt and Tim Sloan. Sloan had been taking their money winning pot after pot the last few hours. He had cheated on a few hands when he needed to win but in most of the hands, he simply had outplayed the two men. Trent Holt went to the bar and got another bottle of whiskey. Andy handed him the bottle. "Why don't ya quit while you still have a few dollars left, Trent?" asked Andy.

"Hell no, I'm gonna win all my money back from that snake. I know he's cheating, but I can't spot it. He's one slick player for sure."

"Well, don't go pissin' him off and get yourself a dirt blanket."

"Yeah, yeah, yeah," Trent said, as he sauntered back over to the table and poured himself another drink. It was Otto's turn to deal and he dealt all three of them another hand.

"Them boys ain't got sense enough to quit," Tony said, shaking his head. He had been sitting at the bar drinking some coffee with Andy for the last few hours. He was doing what he was supposed to do, keep an eye on Tim Sloan.

"Nope," Andy added, "and they both been drinkin' too much. I got a bad feelin' that one of 'em is gonna do somethin' stupid sooner or later."

"That's what usually happens when you mix whiskey, poker and one man winning too much money hand after hand," added Tony. Just then, Jim Smythe came into the saloon and walked up to the bar next to Tony.

"I got some bad news, boys," Jim said.

"I was wondering when it would happen," replied Andy.

"I just talked to one of the ranch hands from the Hardin spread. He told me that Cal Hardin sent a rider out to find Jess and tell him about his brother being here and looking for him."

"Damn," said Tony, "I was hoping Jess wouldn't come back for a while and this brother of his would get tired of waiting and leave town. Guess that was hoping for a little too much, huh?"

"Hell, he ain't goin' anywhere 'cept right here," replied Andy. "Ten thousand dollars will plant roots on a man. Besides, he's been making a pretty good living at the table the last few days. Damn kid is as good at the card game as any I've seen."

"Well, what the hell are we going to do now?" asked Jim.

"What the hell can we do?" asked Andy.

Tony looked back and forth between Andy and Jim. "Well, maybe we should just plug him out in the middle of the street with no warning, like Jess did to that Deke fellow."

"We can't do that Tony," replied Jim. "That would be considered murder and we ain't like that."

"Maybe not, but I'll tell you this. If that snake Sloan doesn't face Jess in a fair fight, I will put a few chunks of lead in him with my Winchester and I won't warn him before I do it, I promise you both that." They all nodded in agreement.

"I've got to get back to the store. Tony, keep an eye on Sloan and we will just have to wait it out and see what happens." Jim walked out of Andy's and back to the general store. Tony was about get up and go out back to take a leak when the argument flared up again. Trent Holt was standing up now and weaving back and forth, the effects of the liquor working on him pretty hard now.

"I know you've been cheating' but I can't figure out how!" exclaimed Trent. Tom Otto was trying to grab Trent's left hand and pull him back down in his seat but Trent kept pulling his arm away, which caused him to weave even more. While that was going on, Sloan's left hand dropped below the table.

"Come on, Trent. Let's just quit and go get something to eat and sober up before you do something stupid."

"I ain't hungry and I ain't going nowhere till this cheating' snake tells me how he's doing it."

"I told you I don't need to cheat you boys," replied Sloan, sarcastically. "You boys just ain't good enough at the game."

"I've been playing poker longer than you been breathing air, boy. I could win you any day in a fair game. If you ain't telling me how you're cheating, I want my money back from the last dozen hands."

"Now, don't get yourself into something you can't get out of, Mister," warned Sloan. "If you handle that side iron as well as you play poker, your losing streak is about to get worse."

Otto had given up trying to get Holt back down in his seat and could only watch now. Holt stood there, weaving back and forth and glaring at Sloan. The whiskey had clouded his brain as well as his judgment. Then he did it. He reached for his pistol and before he got it out of his holster, Sloan's gun barked loud from under the table. The slug ripped into Holt's right thigh knocking him down to the floor. Sloan stood up slowly, his pistol still pointed at Trent Holt lying on the floor. Holt was still holding onto his pistol, which was yet another bad decision for Holt. If he had been thinking clearly, he would have dropped the gun right then and there but he wasn't able to think clearly. Too many shots of whiskey and too many poker hands lost were all too common ways for a man to get killed and this was no exception. Holt tried what he normally knew he shouldn't. He tried to take another shot at Sloan who was all too happy to finish what Holt had started by putting another slug square in the middle of Holt's chest, ending the game along with Holt's life. Andy had reached for his double-barrel under the counter but Tony spotted his move and grabbed Andy by the arm with a grip that made Andy's mouth tighten up like a mans ass on a prison farm.

"Don't you even try that Andy," Tony said quietly, "that boy will plug you before you'd get that thing above the counter." Andy grunted to himself, knowing that Tony was right and had probably saved his life.

Tom Otto hadn't moved an inch during all of this. He sat right there at the table with both hands on the table. Sloan, seeing no other threats in the saloon whirled his gun and dropped it ever so gently back in the holster. He sat

# Brother's Keeper

back down at the table and started collecting the cards. He looked over at Tom Otto who had that same look Sloan had seen before after taking a player out of a poker game...permanently.

"I suppose you don't want to be dealt back into the game, huh?"

Otto nervously looked over at Sloan. "Well, uh...I suppose I best be gettin' back to the missus, if you don't mind, Mr. Sloan."

"Go on and get on home to your woman," replied Sloan, a look of disgust on his face. Otto wasted no time in leaving.

Andy walked around the bar and over to Trent Holt's body. "You didn't have to do that, you already had him wounded and on the floor," said Andy.

Sloan glared at Andy. "Man pulls on me, I kill him. It's that simple. You all saw it. I tried to get him to give it up but he wouldn't let it go."

Andy sent Tony out to get the Doc and the Undertaker. "I saw it, just like everyone saw it, but you didn't have to plug him that second time," replied Andy. "You coulda shot him in the arm and just wounded him again; you're good enough with that side iron to have done that."

"I don't see it that way. Man should've walked away and went home to his woman like the other man did."

Andy shook his head. "I don't think I want you playin' in my saloon anymore. It's bad for business."

Sloan glared at Andy with a hateful look. "No man is going to tell me where I can or can't go. If you want to go back and try for that double-barrel again, I'll let you get it above the counter before I put a slug or two in you."

"You saw that, did ya?" Andy was almost smiling.

"I saw you go for it and I saw your friend save your life. You were one second away from blazing a trail straight to hell."

Andy stopped smiling and Tony returned with the Doc and the Undertaker. Two men helped the Undertaker haul the body off and Doc Johnson and Tony had a drink with Andy at the bar. Sloan, true to his word, sat back down at the table and kept shuffling the cards and folding them one handed. Doc Johnson finished his drink and turned to head out of the saloon. He stopped momentarily at Sloan's table. He looked Sloan straight in the eyes.

"Trent Holt was a friend of mine, Mr. Sloan. You best hope you don't get shot in this town 'cause if you do, you'll have to ride to the next town to find a doctor to fix you." Doc Johnson walked out.

"You tell him Doc," added Andy, not one to leave well enough alone.

"Shut-up old man before I come over there and yank that pile of fur you call a beard right off your face," said Sloan. Andy gave Sloan one of his looks and turned back to Tony who said, "You're going to get yourself shot for sure."

Sloan hung around the saloon for another half-hour hoping to get another game going but no one showed up, at least to play poker anyway. He asked a few of the men who had come in for a drink or a meal did they want to play, but none of them would sit at his table. They had already heard about Trent Holt's demise and no one wanted to follow in his footsteps. Sloan finally got bored and walked out and headed down to Dixie's place. He was probably going to see Vivian again. She was his favorite and they had become more comfortable with each other with each visit.

# Brother's Keeper

Sloan walked into Dixie's and was met by Dixie herself. She had no last name; none of the women working there used last names. Dixie was older than she looked but she had long ago stopped peddling her flesh in a cathouse in Dodge City, Kansas. She had saved all her money and several years ago she moved to Black Creek, Kansas and purchased a nice little boarding house with four rooms upstairs. She hung out a sign and opened her establishment. She started out with two of the girls she used to work with in Dodge City and she was now a businesswoman, and quite a successful one at that.

"Where is my my little woman, Vivian?" Sloan asked.

Dixie smiled. "She's right upstairs in room four, like always. She's been whining about you not showing up yet today. I think she has taken a liking to you."

"Most women do once they find out about my wonderful personality," Sloan said, as he patted Dixie on the rear.

"I don't think it's your personality she is fond of."

Sloan smiled and headed up the stairs. He knocked on the door of room four and he heard footsteps heading for the door quickly. His hand was on the butt of his pistol with the hammer strap off. It was just something he did without even thinking about it.

Vivian opened the door and smiled at Sloan. "I thought maybe you weren't coming by to see me today."

"I've been a little busy."

Vivian frowned. "I heard the gunshots over at Andy's Saloon. I heard about Trent Holt."

Sloan took off his gun belt and carefully placed it on a chair, which was next to the bed. It was within easy reach if he were to need it. "He shouldn't have called me a cheat. I tried to warn him, but he decided to do something stupid when he shouldn't have."

Vivian started undressing. "I heard one of the other girls just this morning say something about you looking for your brother, Jess Williams. You know, he was just here not too long ago."

Sloan stopped all movement. "What, you know about Jess?" Why didn't you tell me?"

Vivian blushed. "I just found out about it this morning. I was waiting for you to come to visit me so that I could tell you."

"Tell me what?"

"A lot of people in town know about Jess. Jim and Sara Smythe over at the general store know your brother very well. He stays there when he comes to visit. That's all I know."

Sloan picked his gun belt back up and began strapping it on again and Vivian was now stark naked. She could tell Sloan was furious.

"You're not leaving yet, are you? We haven't even kissed yet. Don't you want a little of this before you rush off."

"Not right now. There is something I have to do and it can't wait. Thanks for the information." Sloan threw ten dollars on the bed and headed out the door.

"Where are you going in such a hurry?" asked Vivian, that whine in here voice again.

"To pay a visit on the Smythe's, and it won't be a pleasant one, I promise you that."

Sloan headed down the stairs and straight out the front door of Dixie's. He looked straight down at Smythe's General Store. He walked off the boardwalk and headed straight for the general store. Tony was sitting in his chair just inside the livery and watched as Sloan headed straight towards Smythe's General Store. What really caught

Tony's attention was the way Sloan was acting. He looked mad and hell-bent for trouble.

As soon as Sloan walked into the store and found no one behind the counter, he banged his fist down on the counter. "Doesn't anyone work in this damn store?" Jim came running out of the back room to see what all the commotion was about. Sara was one step behind him.

"I'm going to ask you a question," said Sloan, "and I better get the right answer the first time because there won't be a second time. Do you two know who Jess Williams is and where he is?" Jim and Sara exchanged glances.

"Don't be looking at your whore, just answer the question!"

"Now see here, Mister, you can't call my wife…."

Sloan cut him off before he could finish. "I can damn well say whatever I want!"

Jim reached down to where he kept his double-barrel but the cocking back of a hammer stopped him. Sloan had slicked his pistol out before Jim's hand had moved one inch.

"Yeah, you go ahead and grab that scattergun and see how fast you can get a glimpse of your next life."

Jim stopped and put his hands on the counter. "Sara, go into the back room." Sara didn't move, mostly because she was frozen in fear. She knew this young man would not hesitate to pull the trigger. She began to think about what Jess had told her about how ruthless some men could be.

"She ain't going anywhere," Sloan said with a sneer. "I want her right where I can see her. Now, you've got about one second to answer my question and then I'm going put a bullet right through you skull. Then, I'm going to ask your whore there the same question and if she don't answer, I've got no problem with putting a bullet in her head and if you doubt me, you will surely be sorry Mister. I've about had it with this two-bit town. Now, what's it going to be?"

Sara was even more terrified now and she could not move or hardly even breathe. Jim, knowing he had no choice now, answered the question. "Yes, we know him," answered Jim.

"That's a start. Now where the hell is he?"

"I don't know for sure, but he is on his way back here now."

"Really? How did you find that out?"

"One of the men who work out at the Hardin ranch told me that Cal Hardin had sent a man to find your brother and tell him that you were here."

Sloan looked a little puzzled. "Now, why do you suppose he went and did that?"

"You'd have to ask Cal Hardin 'bout that."

"I think I might, but not before I finish what I came here to do."

"And just what did you come here to do?" asked Jim, afraid of the answer.

"Why, to make ten thousand dollars—and kill my brother," Sloan answered, speaking as if what he had said was nothing more that going down to the creek for an afternoon of fishing. He holstered his pistol in his customary fashion and turned to walk out when Jim said, "You didn't ask me why your brother left town."

Sloan stopped and turned back to Jim. "All right, I'll ask. Why did he leave town."

Jim smiled what could've only been considered an evil grin when he answered, "He's looking for you."

# Chapter Nineteen

TIM SLOAN WALKED OUT OF Jim and Sara's place and headed for the saloon again. He never knew that Tony had the sights of his Winchester square in the middle of Sloan's back all the while he was talking to Jim and Sara. Tony kept the Winchester on him as he walked to the saloon and he wanted in the worst way to simply pull the trigger but something inside him, something that he could not understand, refused to let him do it. "Damn it" he said to himself as he put the Winchester down. As soon as Sloan was inside the saloon, he walked over to Jim and Sara Smythe's. When he walked in, Jim was holding Sara who was sobbing in his arms.

"I had my Winchester aimed square in the middle of his back all the time he was here. If he'd of shot either of you, I would've plugged him," said Tony.

Jim was angrier than he had ever been in his life before. "Hell, you should've plugged him anyway."

"He had that pistol trained on you. How was I to know it wouldn't go off and kill you anyway? I figured to wait it out and see. What the hell did he want?"

"He wanted to know if we knew Jess and where he was."

"You didn't tell him, did you?"

"Hell yes, I had to tell him. He threatened to kill me and then Sara after that. I had no idea you had him covered. I swear, if I had known, I would've refused and let him shoot me just so you could kill him. It would've been worth it."

Sara lifted her head from his chest. "No, I wouldn't want that and Jess wouldn't either and you know it. Besides, Jess wants to face his brother and it's going to happen sooner or later and if it's later, someone else will die by that young man's hands."

Tony grunted and looked at Jim. "You know what? She's right. We've all been trying to keep Jess' brother from finding Jess when that's what Jess wants in the worst way. We should've told Sloan about it when he first hit town. Maybe Trent Holt would still be alive."

"I doubt it," replied Jim, "that boy has a lot more killing inside of him."

"I reckon you're right about that. Let's hope he can keep that smoke wagon of his in the holster until Jess gets back to town. I'll go over and fill Andy in. Sloan is over there again, probably trying to get up another poker game." Tony headed over to the saloon. Sara placed her head back on Jim's chest again and sobbed some more.

"Jim, I was never so scared in my life before. I was sure he was going to kill the both of us," she sobbed. "I think I understand now."

"Understand what, Sara?"

Sara's head rose up, "I think I understand what Jess is doing by hunting down men like that. I've been having a hard time trying to justify it, but when I felt for that one moment that I was going to lose you for no reason and maybe lose my life, too…well…I think it finally hit home with me. Jess is right. Men like that don't deserve to walk the same streets as the rest of us. Men like that don't deserve to live. I think that if I had the courage to do it, I would kill that young man myself. I would shoot him down in the street like the dog he is."

Jim put her head back on his chest and held her firmly. "Now, now, calm down. We're not like that, but we sure know someone who is...and he's on his way back, I hope."

Tony walked into Andy's Saloon and sauntered up to the bar. Andy was wiping off some glasses and exchanging glares with Sloan, who was sitting at a table, shuffling cards. "Well, the secret's out," said Tony.

"What do ya mean by that?" asked Andy. Tony told him about all that had just taken place over at Jim and Sara's.

"That little bastard needs killin'," said Andy in a low enough voice so that Sloan couldn't hear him. "I say we grab my double-barrel and blow his sorry ass outta that chair the first time he ain't lookin'. Maybe you should distract him somehow so I could get the drop on him."

Tony shook his head. "In case you've forgotten, we ain't a professional gunman like him. I don't think he misses much. He'd probably get at least one of us before it was over. I say we let our boy Jess handle it. I think he would want it that way."

"You're probably right 'bout that." Just then, LeAnn walked out of the back but Andy stopped her in her tracks. "Get yer ass back in that kitchen woman!" LeAnn huffed and spun around and went back in the kitchen. Andy wanted to keep her out of sight from Sloan figuring that nothing good could come from it. "That damn woman's got a memory shorter than my pecker," Andy complained.

"I thought you wanted to marry her off?"

"Not to that piece of crap."

There was a moment of silence and then Tony said, "That short, huh?"

"Kiss my ass," replied Andy as he looked over at Sloan who now looked agitated.

"Jesus Christ," exclaimed Sloan, "a man can't think with you hollering like some old woman."

"What you gonna do, shoot me like you did Trent?" exclaimed Andy.

"You know the only reason I don't you old cuss?"

"No, why don't ya tell me?"

"Cause you look like the ass end of a mule I once had," retorted Sloan, smiling at Andy. Andy almost replied but common sense finally got a grip on him and he kept his mouth shut and went back to wiping up.

| | |

Terrence Hanley woke up to what he thought was a cannon exploding. He jumped up from his bedroll trying to shake the cobwebs from his head and was reaching for his pistol when he saw Jess lying flat on his stomach; the Sharps Big Fifty lay across his saddle. Smoke was still coming from the end of the barrel and the smell of gunpowder still lingered heavily in the air. Hanley then realized that he was making himself quite a nice target and now that his brain was starting to come out of the fog, he dropped back down on the ground behind his saddle.

"What the hell is going on? Are we being shot at or what?"

Jess smiled and stood up, propping the Big Fifty against his saddle. "No, I don't think that rabbit's got a gun or a head anymore. Figured we could use some fresh meat for today and when I woke up, I spotted that rabbit out about one hundred and fifty yards and decided there was no sense in missing out on the opportunity for a good meal later on."

"You hit that rabbit a hundred and fifty out?"

"Yep, that Sharps is one fine long gun. I like it more every time I shoot it."

"You might want to warn a man who's in a sleep before you fire up that thing."

"Sorry about that. I'm so used to being alone on the trail I guess I didn't think much about it."

Jess walked out to pick up the rabbit. He gutted it and tied it on the packhorse. It would make a good meal later in the day. They made some coffee; bacon and pan bread and broke camp but not before Jess cleaned the Sharps rifle. He always kept his weapons in good order. They had been riding for a few hours when Hanley broke the silence.

"You don't talk much."

Jess glanced over at him and smiled. "I do when I have something to say."

"Mind if I asked you a question?"

"Don't mind at all," replied Jess.

"When you finally meet up with your brother and face him, do you think you will actually be able to…well…kill him?"

Jess thought about it but only for a few seconds. "If he is what I think he is, yes, I'll kill him for sure, brother or not. I still have some hope that maybe he's nothing more than a liar, thief and a man who cheats other men out of their money at the poker table. I can live with that although I wouldn't want any part of him. If he turns out to be a killer of innocent men and women, then he's no better than the men who murdered my family and that puts him on my bad list. I only know one way to deal with people on my bad list." Hanley didn't have to wonder what that meant.

"Remind me not to ever get on your bad list," replied Hanley.

Jess smiled. "You know, I was looking over your horses this morning. They are two of the finest horses I've seen in a long while. You wouldn't want to part with one of them, would you?"

"Not mine to part with," replied Hanley. "Cal Hardin loaned them both to me to catch up with you. They are mighty fine animals and they can run long and hard too. Maybe Hardin will sell you one if you ask him."

"I might do that. Gray here has been a great horse but he's getting a little tired. He's going to deserve a long rest pretty soon."

Hanley looked at Gray and then at the packhorse.

"Where'd you pick the packhorse up at?"

"I bought him from some rancher along the trail. I ran into two men who had been robbed and stranded and needed a ride."

"How'd they get robbed?"

Jess thought about the whole thing with Carl and Murry for a moment. He shook his head and laughed. "I don't think I want to tell you."

"Why not? Hell, we ain't doing nothing else but riding."

"It's too long of a story."

"Come on, the way you're smiling it must be a good one."

"It is."

"Then tell me."

Jess smiled. "Remember that thing about reminding you not to get on my bad list," said Jess, still smiling.

Hanley frowned. "I think I just lost all interest in that. I'll be shuttin' up now."

They rode in silence for the next several hours. They decided they wouldn't make it to Black Creek until the next day so they made camp and fixed a nice meal with the rabbit. They picked the bones clean and they both finished off a good plate of beans and that was followed by a few pots of hot coffee and some casual conversation before they finally turned in.

| | |

Randolph Jackson had been on the trail for months now. He was hell-bent on finding and killing the man who shot his brother Nevada Jackson. He knew who shot his brother; he just didn't know where the young man was, at least, not until recently. He had started his search in Red Rock, Texas after he heard the news that his brother had been killed in a gunfight. By the time he had heard the news, he made arrangements to hit the trail and make it to Red Rock, Texas, Jess Williams was long gone.

Randolph traveled from one small town to another, asking questions about this young man, Jess Williams. He finally ended up in a small town called Baxter and it was there that he found out that Jess Williams was from Black Creek, Kansas. He had also come to the realization from the information he had gathered about Jess Williams, that he was mighty fast with a pistol. When he had first learned of the demise of his brother, his first thought was that there must have been some trickery involved or that his brother had no warning and was murdered, even though he was told that it was a fair fight. He thought that because he knew how fast his brother Nevada was with a pistol. He knew because he had taught him how to draw. The only one who could beat Nevada Jackson in a fair showdown was Randolph himself, or so he thought.

But now, he had finally come to the realization that it probably had been a fair fight between his brother and Jess Williams. Of course, it didn't matter to him now. He was hell-bent on finding the man who killed his brother and, as usual, reason or common sense would have nothing to do with the matter. That was the way it was as far as he was concerned. He would avenge his brother's death and that was that. It was his sworn duty to do so.

He rode into Black Creek in the later part of the afternoon. He stopped the first place most men did, the first saloon he could find. He tied his horse and walked into Andy's Saloon. Randolph dressed much like his brother Nevada. Mostly black, with a black leather holster with some silver studs and a very nice Colt .45 Peacemaker in the holster. The holster was tied down low and tight to his thigh. Randolph could sense the tension in the saloon immediately and he could sense where most of the tension was coming from. It was emanating from a young man sitting alone at a table, shuffling and dealing cards to himself and an imaginary player that wasn't there. Randolph walked up to the bar.

"What can I get ya?" asked Andy.

"Whiskey, and make it the good stuff."

Andy grabbed a bottle of his good whiskey from under the bar. He poured him a shot, which he downed with one quick motion and motioned for Andy to pour him another one. "Where ya from, Mister?"

"Hell, I'm not sure anymore. I've hit every damn shit-hole of a town over the last several weeks. Can't remember half the names and don't want to anyway," answered Randolph, downing the second shot and asking for the third.

"Lookin' for work or just riding the trail?" asked Andy.

"Naw, I'm hunting for the young man who killed my brother."

# Brother's Keeper

Andy had a smile on his face and an idea in his brain, which didn't happen all that often. "Might the young man who killed yer brother go by the name of Tim Sloan?"

"No, why do you ask?"

"Cause that's Tim Sloan sittin' right over there at the card table. He's killed his share of men, that's fer sure."

Randolph glanced back at Sloan and then back to Andy. "He fit's the description, but not the name. I guess the only way to find out for sure is to ask," Randolph said, downing his third whiskey. He turned to face Sloan who had already sensed something going on. He decided to see if the man at the bar was interested in a game of cards.

"How 'bout a game, Mister?" asked Sloan.

"I'm not looking to get into a card game; I'm looking for the young man who killed my brother, Nevada Jackson." Andy, who had been leaning on the bar, hoping to see a gunfight ensue between these two, heard the name Nevada Jackson and that made him stand straight up. He remembered about Jess telling him about his gunfight with him. *Jesus Christ*, he thought to himself. He listened intently now at the conversation as it continued.

"You fit the description but the barkeep says your name is Tim Sloan. That right?" Sloan shot a glare at Andy, knowing that Andy obviously had something to do with this.

"That's right, I'm Tim Sloan, but I didn't kill anybody by the name of Nevada Jackson, at least, not that I know of. What's the name of the man you're looking for?"

"They told me his name was Jess Williams."

That got Sloan's attention real fast. Andy, now that what he had feared was now confirmed, shook his head. Here was yet another gunslinger looking for Jess to kill him for revenge. Sloan was thinking hard now about how to continue with the conversation. He didn't want this man to get a crack at his brother before him and lose the ten thousand dollars he had already been spending in his head. He slowly stood up and pushed his chair back, his hammer strap already removed.

"Mister, what is your name?"

"Randolph Jackson, brother of Nevada Jackson," he answered, slowly removing his hammer strap.

"Well, Randolph, it seems that we have a little problem."

"What might that be?"

"Jess Williams is my brother."

Randolph stiffened a little at that. "Is that so? I guess that's why you fit the description so well. You're wrong about that little problem thing, 'cause if you're taking his side in this matter, we have a big problem. Now, if that's the case, let's get this over with right now and then I'll take care of that no good brother of yours as soon as our paths cross."

Sloan was trying to keep some information from coming forth until he could decide how to handle this whole matter, but he couldn't let the threat go unchallenged. It was simply his nature. His mood changed towards a darker side and his words now held a sarcastic tone as he spoke. "Listen, Randolph, I ain't taking my brother's side in this matter or anything else, but if you want to challenge me, I suggest you go meet with the undertaker first to get measured up real nice for the pine box you'll need when this is over."

Randolph smiled so hard he almost laughed. "Hell kid, I've taken down more men already than you will if you live to be an old man, which ain't likely. What makes you think I can't take you? Hell, I've been slinging iron longer than you've been breathing air."

Sloan glared at Randolph, trying to decide whether or not to chance outdrawing this man. Normally, he would have went through with it without a thought, but that ten thousand dollars was nagging at him like a itch that couldn't be scratched, and that altered his way of thinking, temporarily at least. It was then that the idea came to him. "So, you want my brother dead in order to avenge the death of your brother, correct?"

"That's exactly what I want, and I don't care how I get it either."

Sloan smiled an evil grin. "Well, what if I told you that I am here waiting for my brother's return so that I can kill him myself?"

Randolph was taken aback by that. He had such a close relationship with his brother Nevada that he couldn't fathom one brother killing another, yet he had heard of such things. "You're going to kill your own flesh and blood, your own brother?" Randolph asked, not believing what he was hearing.

"Yes sir, that is exactly why I've been sitting here waiting around for the last few days." Randolph was still trying to wrap his brain around this idea. He was thinking about it all when Andy broke the silence.

"The only reason he's here to kill his brother is that he's being paid ten thousand dollars to do it," Andy hollered.

Sloan shot a glare over at Andy. "I swear old man, I'm going to put a bullet square in your ass before this is over," exclaimed Sloan.

"Why my ass and not my head?" Andy asked, sarcastically.

"Because every time you sit down, I want you to think of me."

"Yeah, well…when your brother get's back to town, you won't be gettin' a chance to shoot anyone else," exclaimed Andy.

Randolph interrupted. "Ten thousand dollars, huh? That's a lot of money for killing one man. I suppose if I'm the man who kills your brother, I could collect the money myself?"

Sloan was beginning to lose it when he came up with another angle. He did not want to lose out on the money and even though he thought he could take Randolph, he didn't want to take the chance now. He was a poker player and was always trying to assess the odds. "Okay, I'll make you a proposition."

"I'm listening."

"If you and I go at it right now, one of us is going to die, that we know for sure. If it's you who gets shot, you'll go to your grave never having the satisfaction of knowing that the man who killed your brother is dead. Who knows, he might just beat me to the draw. Unlikely, but you never know. Now, if it's me who dies, you will get your chance at my brother, but he is pretty fast and he might kill you, in which case, you still don't get your revenge."

"That's a whole lot of fancy talk but what the hell are you getting at?" said Randloph, trying to follow Sloan.

"Here is what I propose. You wait here until my brother gets back and let me face him down first. If I kill him, I will give you one thousand dollars just for letting me get the first chance at him. If for some reason, he gets me, then you still have the opportunity to face him and collect the entire ten thousand dollars yourself. Don't you see? You have nothing at all to lose in the venture. Plus, you will have the satisfaction of watching his own brother kill him. What could be better than that?"

Randolph went back to the bar and poured himself another shot of whiskey and downed it. He thought about the proposal for a few minutes. Andy was staring at him the whole time. Randolph slammed his shot glass down on the bar and turned back around to face Sloan. "You know what, kid? I have to agree with you. I wanted to be the one to kill him but to be able to watch you kill him in front of me, well, that's even better. And, I'll make a thousand dollars to watch him die. I couldn't think of a better deal in a hundred years."

Sloan relaxed and sat back down at his table. Andy went back to cleaning up and shaking his head in disgust. Sloan shuffled up the cards again. "Randolph, would you like to play a few hands of poker?"

Randolph grabbed the shot glass and bottle from the bar and walked to the table. "Hell, might as well. I have to keep an eye on you anyway. I don't want to miss the big showdown." Sloan smiled and dealt the cards.

# Chapter Twenty

HANLEY AND JESS WOKE TO A cool breeze and light rain. Jess had to work to get the fire going. He scrounged around some trees to get some kindling that wasn't wet from the light rain yet. They made a nice meal and several cups of hot coffee.

"Damn, it's getting too close to winter for me," said Hanley.

"I agree. I think once this is all over; I'll head south until it gets warm enough."

"Hell, you might have to go into Mexico to do that."

"If that's where it's warm, then that's where I'm going."

Hanley laughed. "If I had a lick of sense, I'd join you."

Jess thought about that for a moment. He liked Hanley okay but he liked to ride alone most of the time. He didn't want to start relying on someone else. He was in a very dangerous business and the only person he could fully trust was himself. He hoped Hanley wasn't serious and didn't think he should say anything unless it came up again. He threw what was left of his coffee into the fire. "I suppose it's time to break camp and head into town. No sense in putting off what is going to happen eventually?"

Hanley nodded in agreement. "I guess not, not that I want this to happen. I wish you would just ride on down to Mexico and enjoy the weather and the women, but I know you ain't going to do that until this thing between you and your brother is finished."

"You are right about that, except for the women part," Jess replied.

"What, you don't like women?"

Jess thought for a moment as he finished saddling Gray. "I guess I probably would but there is no place in my life or line of work for women. They will surely take your mind off other matters and that's when someone will put a bullet in you. That's not going to happen to me. I'll leave the women to you."

"Hell, I like that idea even better."

They mounted up and headed towards the town of Black Creek, Kansas. Hanley was riding to the right side of Jess. He kept looking at the pistol that was firmly held in its holster by a leather strap. Hanley had noticed that the hammer went straight up instead of curving back like most pistols and the strap had to be tight. He had also noticed that Jess, in what he believed to be a somewhat unconscious move, was always testing the strap and making sure it was firmly on the hammer. If not, it would fall out of the holster too easily since the holster didn't hold the gun in like most holsters. Of course, what Hanley had noticed most of all was when Jess would walk away from camp every night and spend some time practicing with the pistol.

"That sure is an unusual pistol and holster, that's for sure," said Hanley.

Jess looked down and checked the leather strap again. "It sure is, and I'm lucky that I have it. I can't explain it, but the gun almost forces you to draw it differently and because of the way it was put together, you can do things with it you couldn't do with any other gun I've seen. I don't know who made this thing but whoever it was sure knew what he was doing."

"I know one thing for sure," said Hanley, "you can snake that thing out of the holster quicker than anything I've ever seen, and I've seen some fast gunmen."

Jess smiled. "So, you've been watching me practice, huh?" asked Jess, knowing all along that Hanley would watch Jess when he spent his practice time, usually right after supper.

"It's hard not to watch a master at his trade."

Jess actually laughed out loud at that. "I don't think anyone has ever called me a master yet. I'm not sure that's true but I am pretty good with it."

"You can call it what you want young Mr. Williams, a shootist, an expert, a gunslinger, or whatever description you want to use to describe your ability with that thing. Maybe unnatural would be the best description for it, but you are most likely the fastest man alive on the draw. And not just that either; that thing you do with thumbing that first shot and then fanning the next few shots is—well, unnatural. I saw it, but if I told someone about it, I believe they would call me a liar right to my face."

"Well, I did once have a preacher say something like that to me. Maybe it is unnatural, but whatever it is, I'm thankful for it. It will help me accomplish what I want to do with my life."

"And that is?"

"Kill as many bad men as I can."

Hanley shook his head but not in a bad way. "Bounty hunting is a dangerous business, but I think you've taken it to a whole different level than most men."

"You are most likely right about that."

"You know what else I'm right about?" asked Hanley.

"What?"

"I think your brother is in a whole heap of trouble."

Jess didn't respond right away. Hanley could see that he was thinking something through in his head. When he did respond, his voice had a tone of determination in it. "I do believe you are right, Mr. Hanley." They rode the rest of the way in silence.

Hanley suggested that since the Hardin ranch was right along their trail that they stop there to freshen up and get any information on what was going on with Sloan. Jess agreed. They rode up to the Hardin ranch and they were greeted by a few of the ranch hands. Cal Hardin walked out of the ranch house and motioned for them to come inside. Both Jess and Hanley walked up on the large porch that surrounded three sides of the house. They all exchanged handshakes and went into the house and sat down at a large wooden table.

Cal Hardin was the first to speak. "Woman, get some coffee poured for these men!"

Cal's wife got busy, not in any mood for another argument with her husband. She kept staring at Jess though, trying to figure out how to feel about this young man. She still feared him and yet she still could not understand why. Maybe it was simply because she knew that he had killed so many men at such an early age or maybe it was because he looked so similar to his brother, Tim Sloan. She did not like Sloan one bit. She could sense that he was an evil man and maybe she figured since they were brothers, that they both had some evil in them. Yet, she could sense no evil in this young man sitting at her table. She could see hardness in Jess' eyes but she also sensed good in him at the same time. She placed some cornbread and some butter on the table and filled the cups with coffee.

"That will do," quipped Cal, "leave us alone for now and if we need anything else, I'll let you know." She walked out of the kitchen and went upstairs. Jess was the first to speak.

"Mr. Hardin, is my brother in town right now?"

Hardin hung his head a little, still somewhat ashamed of his part in this whole thing, although he was trying to make it as right as he could. "Yes. I've had men watching him around the clock. I felt it was the least I could do since I'm the one who agreed to hold the blood money on your head. I hope you can accept my apology for it, but when a man owes another man a favor, I believe in granting it."

"Yet you sent Mr. Hanley out to find me and warn me. Doesn't that kind of go against what you promised Carter you would do?"

"I suppose so, to some degree. I'm trying to justify that myself, but I simply could not stand by and let it happen without trying to warn you. Maybe I was wrong to agree to hold the money in the first place but that's behind us now. I think what's important is what happens next."

"What happens next is I go into town and face my brother. I have a few questions I want to ask him."

"Your brother ain't here to answer any questions. He just wants to kill you and come and collect the ten thousand dollars I'm holding."

"I know that, but first things first. Besides, it's not him who is going to control the event."

"You think you're that good with that pistol you have?" Hardin asked, nodding at Jess' pistol.

It was then that Hanley, who had been silent so far, entered the conversation. "Oh yeah, he's that good and a whole lot more. I've had the pleasure of watching him work with that thing and I can tell you that he can draw faster than anyone I've ever seen and he doesn't miss what he's aiming at either. I watched Sloan draw on a man and he ain't half as fast as Jess here is." Hanley said it as if he was proud to be the one to say it.

"Well, you'll have to be good," said Hardin. "One of my men watched him kill a man in Andy's Saloon. Your brother is pretty good with a gun but the worst thing is that he has no regard for another mans life. In my book, that makes him a very dangerous man."

"Mr. Hardin, I know one thing for sure. If my brother is what I think he is, even if he gets me, he is going to die doing it," Jess replied. Hardin and Hanley both believed him.

Hardin figured this was a good time to give Jess some more bad news. "You have another problem facing you when you get to town."

"What is that?"

"There is a man by the name of Randolph Jackson in town. He's looking for you too."

"He wouldn't happen to be the brother of Nevada Jackson, would he?"

"I don't know."

"I kind of figured that was going to happen sooner or later, but I didn't know when."

"The way I heard it, Jackson is going to let you and your brother go at it, and if your brother doesn't take you, Jackson will step in next."

"Yes, and he ain't forgot who shot his only brother."

"The timing sure could be better but I'll just have to deal with it," said Jess, almost casually. "I do have a question for you though. I'd like to ask you about those two very fine horses you own out there. What is the chance I could buy one of them from you?" asked Jess.

"Not a chance in hell," replied Hardin. "But I will be honored if you would accept them both as a peace offering for my involvement in this matter."

Jess' frown quickly turned to a grin. "I guess that makes us even then, but I only asked for one."

Hardin looked at him with a grin. "Hell, that packhorse would never survive the run either of those two long horses would give him. He'd drop dead in his tracks and either of those two horses would keep on running long and hard. If you plan on staying with a packhorse, you'll need the both of them. I won't change my mind and that's the end of it."

Jess reached out and shook Cal Hardin's hand. "I'll take good care of them, you can be sure of that." Hardin finally began to feel a little better about things.

"Well," said Jess, "no sense putting off what's going to eventually happen anyway." He stood up and shook hands with Cal Hardin and thanked him for the horses again. "I'll come back and get them after this is all over."

"You won't have to. I want Hanley to ride to town with you. That way he can report back to me. He can leave both horses at the livery for you."

"That's mighty nice of you, Mr. Hardin. Hanley was right about you when he told me you were a fair man."

"One more thing," said Hardin, as he handed Jess an envelope filled with money. "Here is the ten thousand dollars from Carter that I've been holding. My deal with the devil is over with. I guess if your brother's good enough, he can take the money from you himself. If not, I believe the money belongs to you."

Jess took the envelope and looked at Hardin with a new look of respect. "I don't figure that I could ask anything more of you, Mr. Hardin, and that's a fact."

Jess and Hanley mounted up and headed into Black Creek. Hanley could sense the change in Jess as they rode. He could feel the impending doom that was about to happen. Two brothers facing one another and one would surely kill the other before it was over. Hanley was pretty sure who was going to be lying in the dirt when it was over.

Tony was working on the front hoof of a horse when he noticed two riders coming into town. He stopped what he was doing and was wiping his hands off when he noticed who one of the riders was. It was Jess. He felt good and bad all at the same time. Jess and Hanley rode up to Tony and dismounted. Tony gave Jess a firm handshake.

"I'm usually glad to see you come back to town, but I'm not so sure this time."

"Under the circumstances, I can understand why," replied Jess.

"So, you know your brother is here and looking to put a bullet in you for money?"

"Yes, I know the whole story now, even the part about Nevada Jackson's brother being in town also."

"You just seem to draw the worst of the lot, don't you?"

"I think it's my wonderful personality that does it."

Tony laughed and looked at Jess' pistol. "I think it's that thing you got strapped around your waist that does most of it," Tony said, as he looked at the two fine horses that Hanley had brought to town. "Damn fine animals," exclaimed Tony as he looked them over, running his hands up and down the two horses, checking their teeth and hoofs. Must be long horses I suspect?"

"They belonged to Cal Hardin until today," said Hanley. "He gave the both of them to Jess here as a peace offering."

Tony frowned at the mention of Cal Hardin's name and looked over at Jess. "Is that his way of saying he's sorry?"

"Maybe," Jess replied, "but he really didn't cause this, Carter did. I don't have any problems with Hardin. My problem is with my brother and I'm about to deal with that shortly. Tony, I trust you will take care of my two new fine horses?"

"I'll be glad to. What are you going to do with Gray? He's still a good horse although he ain't getting any younger."

"I was hoping that you would take him for me. Ride him once in a while to work him but mostly just let him relax. I trust you won't sell him to anyone?"

"I'll keep him right here. Anytime you come back to town, he'll be here waiting for a visit. What about the packhorse?" Jess looked at the packhorse. He was a good horse but nothing compared to the two that Hardin had given him. "You can sell him and put it towards my livery fees, which you seem to keep forgetting to collect from me."

Tony grinned. "I guess that's fair enough."

Jess nodded as if they had an unwritten agreement. Then Jess' mood changed as he gave Tony the look that Tony had seen all too often before. "Tony, I suppose my brother is over at Andy's?"

Tony frowned, knowing that something was about to happen and he knew from experience that it would not be something good. "Yep, and I'm going over there with you. Andy and I will make sure things go fairly for you, I promise you that."

Jess checked both his pistol and his pa's Peacemaker. "How are Jim and Sara, Tony?"

"Fine, but scared clean out of their wits. They ain't been outside the store since yesterday."

"Why, what happened?"

"That damn brother of yours pulled a gun on Jim and threatened to shoot him and then Sara next if they didn't tell him what he wanted to know about you. I damn near plugged him with my Winchester but I didn't."

Tony could see Jess' face harden some more. "He shouldn't have done that."

"Don't I know that for sure," replied Tony, knowing what that meant. Jim and Sara was the closest thing to family that Jess had and he would not allow anyone to harm them in any way and if someone did, they would answer to Jess for it. Everyone in town still remembered the Sheriff Newcomb event.

"Well, let's go over and visit with Andy and have a little talk with my brother," said Jess, as he removed the hammer strap from his pistol. Tony and Hanley walked about two steps back from Jess as they headed for Andy's. They hadn't gotten more than a hundred feet when Tim Sloan walked out of Andy's Saloon and stood on the porch, watching as Jess and the other two men approached. Their eyes locked on one another. Life was ironic sometimes. Two brothers separated at birth and never knowing one another and now they were going to engage in a gunfight where one was sure to kill the other.

"Well, well, well, I finally get to meet my brother, the great Jess Williams. They say you are pretty fast with that side iron of yours."

"I've heard the same about you."

"I guess it runs in the family."

"Speaking of family, where is my so-called father who abandoned our mother?"

Tim Sloan slowly walked down the few steps and into the street. "My guess would be that he is already down in Mexico somewhere where it's warm. Then again, you never know with him. He's a wanderer for sure. Why do you care, he ain't having anything to do with you anyway."

"You are wrong about that. I intend to find him just like I found you and face him."

"What makes you think you'll get the chance?"

"Oh, I'll get the chance, you can count on that."

"That would mean that I would be dead."

"You might be able to count on that too," said Jess, a hardness forming on his lips.

"You sure are a cocky little bastard, I'll give you that. I like confidence in a man."

"I have another question for you."

"Go ahead. I believe in granting a man his last wishes; especially my own kin."

"What were you doing riding with Blake Taggert?"

"Why would you want to know that?" asked Sloan, puzzled by the question.

"I'm asking because he was one of the three men who murdered my family, including your real mother."

"What do you mean was?"

"Yeah, he seemed to have gotten himself killed?"

"Taggert was pretty fast with a pistol, who took him down."

"That would be me."

"Taggert was a good friend of mine. We worked together on a few card games and shared some whores. I didn't know he was involved in your family's demise but why the hell should that matter to me anyway? I ain't got a mother, just a father."

"You have a mother who gave birth to you. She is buried out at the ranch right beside my pa and my little sister Samantha. She would have raised you and taken care of you if you hadn't been taken away from her by your father. Now you tell me that one of the men who did it was a good friend of yours?"

"Hey, I don't give two shits about your mama or your little sister. I'm only here for one reason. I'm getting paid ten thousand dollars to put a slug in your chest. What do you think about that?"

"I'll tell you what I know for sure. Cal Hardin gave me the ten thousand dollars and I have it on me right now. If you want it, you'll have to take it from me."

Sloan sneered at Jess. "I don't think that will be a problem."

"I hope you haven't spent any of the money yet."

"Not yet, but I'm thinking about buying Dixie's. I like the women there and I wouldn't mind coming back to town from time to time and causing all your friends here in town a little grief."

Jess realized now that his brother was no better than the Blake Taggerts of the world. He was just one more man that needed to be put down, brother or not. Tim Sloan would go through life causing innocent people nothing but grief. He would continue to kill, rape, lie, cheat and steal. Maybe it wasn't ultimately his fault and he was simply a product of his environment; but that didn't matter. In the end, no matter how you try to reason it out, Tim Sloan was a bad man and had to suffer the same fate that many others already had and many more to come, if Jess had his way.

Just then, Randolph Jackson walked out of Andy's and stopped on the porch. He had a shot of whiskey in his left hand, leaving his right hand free. "I just want you to know that I'm here to finish things if your brother can't."

Jess spoke to Randolph without taking his eyes off Tim Sloan. "You must be Nevada Jackson's brother I take it?"

"That's right, and you're the little bastard who killed him."

"You know it was a fair fight. I didn't want to draw on your brother. The truth is; he forced it."

"That don't mean squat now. He's still dead and as his only brother it's my job to avenge his death."

"That'll be your choice but I'm going to warn you not to make even the slightest move until this is over. If you do, Andy, who is right behind you with that scattergun pointed at your back will blow you off the porch. If that don't kill you, I'll put a bullet in you without even thinking about it, understand?"

"I don't mind waiting my turn. I've been looking forward to it," replied Randolph, finishing his whiskey and throwing the shot glass out in the street. Jess' eyes turned to ice and Tim Sloan saw something that he hadn't noticed until now. There was a sense of seething rage in Jess. It made Sloan wonder for just a second or two, but nothing mattered now except the ten thousand dollars. He sneered at Jess.

"Time to find out which one of us is faster," said Sloan.

"I wouldn't have it any other way…" Jess had barely finished his last few words when Sloan went for his gun. Sloan got it partially out of the holster when Jess' first slug hit him square in the chest. He staggered back a few steps and dropped his gun, his hands trying to stop the flow of blood that was now making a large red spot on the front of his shirt. He stood there wobbling back and forth with a look of amazement on his face. He coughed; a little spittle of blood on his lips. He wheezed when he spoke.

"I guess we found out who was faster, huh?"

Jess still had his gun trained on his brother. "I guess so."

"I suppose there's no sense in getting the Doc either, huh?"

"Nope," replied Jess, the hardness showing in his voice. "I wouldn't let him save you anyway, even if he could. I will do you one last favor though. I like your idea about granting a dying man his last wish."

"And what might that be?"

"I can put you out of your misery right now."

Sloan's knees were beginning to buckle a little now and he knew he didn't have much more than a minute left and it just didn't matter anymore. "Go ahead and finish it now and let me die in the street standing with my boots on," Sloan replied, only a second away from collapsing.

Jess did not hesitate. No sooner than Sloan had gotten the words out of his mouth, Jess fanned two shots. The first blew out Sloan's heart and the second hit him just above his eyes. He flew back and hit the dirt flat with a thud. Jess stood there for what was probably a whole minute looking at what he had just done. He had killed his own kin, his own brother. He had taken a big step over that imaginary line that most men won't cross under any circumstances, and he was okay with it. He searched his heart to find some remorse for killing Sloan, but he could only find pity. He felt sorrow for the fact that his brother never got the chance to turn out to be something other than what he had turned out to be but that was not Jess' doing. He had kept an eye on Randolph who seemed to act somewhat different now. He hadn't moved during all of this and probably some of the reason for it was that Andy was aiming his scattergun at his back and Tony had his Winchester trained on him at the same time so Jess knew he was covered. Of course, the main reason he hadn't moved a muscle was that he had just witnessed the incredible hand speed that Jess had just demonstrated. Jess began to empty the three spent cartridges from his pistol and reload it. He looked up at Randolph with a look that could make most men shudder.

"Well...Mr. Jackson, I guess it's your turn now," said Jess, his voice low but firm. Jess could see that Randolph was visibly shaken and still wouldn't move.

"I...I think I might have changed my mind about it. I mean...well...my brother is dead and this won't bring him back or nothing...so...I'd be willing to call it off if that's okay with you." Jess holstered his pistol and looked at Tony. Tony saw the look, he had seen it before and he knew it wasn't anything good for Randolph.

"I don't think so," said Jess, almost nonchalantly.

Randolph looked puzzled, as if he hadn't expected quite that answer. "So, you don't agree with me getting on my horse and riding out of town and forgetting this whole matter?"

"No, I don't," replied Jess.

"I don't understand. You know I can't beat you. Hell, even I know it now after I saw you draw."

"Let me explain it to you so you do understand," replied Jess. "You came here to kill me because I killed your brother, even though you knew it was a fair fight between Nevada and me. Now, you've seen me draw and you don't want to face me now. What you will do for sure though, is wait to see me somewhere in another little town or maybe follow my trail and shoot me in the back like a coward. I know men like you. You won't give up until you kill me and since you know you can't do it fair, you'll do it any way you can, but you will try to do it, of that I'm sure.

So, you're going to do it right here and right now. Get down off that porch and face me."

"What if I refuse?" exclaimed Randolph, still nervous but now agitated.

"Then I'll just plug you right there on the porch where you stand. If you don't want to draw, that will be your choice and I won't take any blame in it, but don't make the mistake of thinking I won't do it because I surely will." Jess heard Andy's voice holler out from inside the Saloon.

"He'll damn sure do it, I saw him do it before myself," hollered Andy.

Randolph was beside himself now but he was smart enough to know he had run out of time. He had just watched this young man kill his own brother and that made him a man who would do the unthinkable. He knew he was doomed but there was no way out of it now. And, he had his pride to think of. He would rather go out in a blaze of glory than be known as a coward who wouldn't draw. He walked down the steps and into the street.

"Well, at least I'll be remembered as one of the many men who braced Jess Williams," said Randolph, mustering all the courage he could.

"Yes you will, and you will have something in common with your brother Nevada."

"Yeah, both murdered by the same man," replied Randolph, a hint of defiance in his voice.

Randolph went for his gun and when he did, Jess hesitated for a fraction of a second. Randolph saw it but he didn't stop his motion, hoping he might have a chance. He didn't. Jess had given him that fraction of a second but no more. Jess drew and fired two rounds into Randolph's chest and he staggered back and fell right next to Sloan's body. He was dead as he hit the ground. Jess holstered his pistol after reloading it and Tony walked up next to him.

"Jess, why did you hesitate like that?" asked Tony.

Jess looked at him. "You know, I'm not really sure. Maybe since I didn't give him any choice, I felt I owed it to him, but I don't quite know for sure. It just seemed to happen. Maybe something in the back of my brain was trying to stop me from killing Randolph and let him ride out of town and that made me hesitate. I'm not sure I'll ever know for certain."

"Maybe there's hope for you yet."

Jess looked at Tony, not quite sure of what he meant. "I do know one thing for certain."

"What's that?"

"I figure I'm always going to have a long list of men to watch for over my shoulder, but these two won't be on it." Andy came out of the saloon, his double-barrel slung over his shoulder. He looked at Jess with a frustrated look. The onlookers all started to go back to their shops and homes.

"Are ya finished fer jest a little while now?" exclaimed Andy. "I'd like ta have a little peace and quiet for maybe a day or two."

Jess put his hand on Andy's shoulder. "I think that's a great idea, Andy."

"Might as well, you done killed everybody what needed killin', 'cept for that man, Randolph," said Andy. "I'm not sure you shoulda done that."

"Yeah, but it wouldn't have been you he would have been looking for tomorrow or the next day, it would have been me."

"I can't argue with ya on that one."

The Undertaker came and took the bodies away, but not before Jess removed his brother's gun belt from him. He took Randolph's pistol and holster. He kept his brother's but gave Randolph's to Tony.

Tony took it and smiled at Jess. "I suppose this is your way of building up some credit at the livery?"

Jess smiled back at him. "You could say that."

"Let's go have a drink and relax for a bit," said Tony.

"Damn good idea," exclaimed Andy, "and I'm a buyin'."

"You sure are getting generous lately, Andy," replied Jess.

"Well, I figure I gotta stay on your good side, I seen what you do to people on yer bad side," Andy replied with a grin.

Jess grabbed the envelope that Hardin had given him and showed it to both Andy and Tony. "I have a better idea, Andy. I think it's only fair that Tim Sloan pay for the drinks since he won't be having any use for this money now." Both Andy and Tony nodded in silent agreement. Both also noticed that Jess had not referred to Tim Sloan as his brother.

# Epilogue

ANDY, JESS AND TONY HEADED over to Andy's and were met by Jim Smythe along the way. The four of them shared a table and a bottle of Andy's best whiskey and shared their thoughts about all that happened over the last several months. They talked about how Carter had taken over the town and how Jess had come back to Black Creek to take care of it, along with Carter and his bunch of hired killers. They talked about Jess's brother and how that all played out. Jim, Andy and Tony did most of the talking, Jess adding a comment now and then.

"Well, Jess, what now for you?" asked Tony. "You want to reconsider that sheriff's badge again?"

"No thanks, Tony. I've got to move on in a few days. I think I'll head south towards Mexico and warmer weather."

"Might that have a little something to do with your father?" Jim asked.

"I suppose so."

"Well, ya don't need to be in no hurry," said Andy. "You should stay in town a few days and relax."

"Actually, I'm going to do that, believe it or not. I need to take care of a few things. As a matter of fact, you boys can help me with some of it. Tony, I need you to make me a new leather sling for my scattergun and knife."

"I'll make it look real nice for you," replied Tony.

"Jim," said Jess, turning to him, "I need that new double-barrel I saw behind your counter. I'm going to have Tony here cut it down a little more and then shave off the stock some to make it more like a pistol handle like this," Jess said, as he took Andy's scattergun and showed Tony how he wanted it cut down and the handle shaved.

"Consider it done, my friend," replied Tony, still looking over the scattergun and mentally making notes as to how he would do it. The four of them all raised their glasses and tapped them together in friendship.

Over the next few days, Jess relaxed and wandered around town, spending time with Jim and Sara and with Tony and Andy. Most of the townsfolk were friendly to Jess although some would not even exchange glances with him. Jess sensed it wasn't because they didn't like Jess, it was more that they were fearful of him. The preacher in town tried to give him a spiritual lesson on the evils of killing but Jess politely told him to work his words on someone who was listening. He knew there was no way he could make any preacher understand what he was doing. "You do your work, and I'll do mine," Jess had told him.

Jess paid a visit to the gunsmith in town and had him load some ammo for him. He asked the gunsmith to make some special loads for his Sharps Big Fifty. He wanted the slug a little lighter and the cartridge loaded with a little more powder so it would shoot a little flatter on a long shot. He had him make some special loads for his pistol. He had the gunsmith reduce the powder load slightly as well as the slug. That would reduce the kick a little and yet still with deadly results. Jess figured it would help when fanning the pistol. He switched out Gray and the packhorse for the two long horses and he supplied up for his trip south. He purchased extra stock ammo from Jim along with the best telescope Jim had in stock.

He stayed with Jim and Sara, in the same spare room upstairs where he had stayed the day his family was murdered. He remembered that day as if it were yesterday and mostly because he made sure to remember it every day. It was those thoughts that gave him the strength and drive that made him the man that he was. It was the rage he felt for the men who had murdered his family and other men like them that allowed him to do things most men couldn't. Like shooting Deke Moore who was wounded and sitting in the middle of the street unarmed or forcing Randolph Jackson to brace him in the middle of the street.

He knew that most people couldn't see it the way Jess saw it. Maybe that was because they couldn't feel the rage that Jess felt. It did not matter to him that some people would never accept his way of dealing with bad men. All that really mattered is that he believed in what he was doing and that was that.

He was looking at himself in the same mirror he had looked into that very day that his life had changed from a normal one to a very different and dangerous one. He could see it in his own face. The loneliness, the sadness, and the coldness underneath his eyes, hidden deep until someone made the fatal mistake of bringing it forward. He finished washing up and went down for breakfast with Jim and Sara.

Jess was leaving today and Jim and Sara were sad about that, but they were grateful that they had at least been able to keep him with them for a few days. They talked and ate and simply enjoyed each other's conversation, but it was time to say goodbye, for now.

"Are you certain you won't stay for just one more day?" Sara asked.

"I'd like to, but I have to get moving. It's going to get real cold soon and I have discovered that I don't like it that cold, especially for one who rides the trail most of the time," replied Jess.

"Well, it was sure nice to have you around for a little, especially when you ain't shooting someone," laughed Jim. "Hell, it's been almost three days now since you shot someone."

Jess grinned. "I guess you're about right there. I don't really take much joy in shooting someone, but if it needs doing, I don't mind it much either."

Sara gave Jess a long hug and kissed him on his cheek. Jim did the same but left out the kissing part. Jess turned and walked out and headed for the livery where he knew Tony had been getting his horses and his things ready. He had told Tony he would be pulling out today.

As he walked into the livery Tony was sitting with Andy, waiting for Jess.

"Morning, you two," Jess said, "time to move on for me." Tony and Andy stood up and both shook his hand.

"You going lookin' for yer father, huh," asked Andy. Jess looked at Andy and then over to Tony.

"Tony, I think Andy might just be getting a little smarter each day."

"Yeah," said Tony, "but still not smart enough to keep his yap shut when he should." They all laughed at that.

"You sure you don't want to take LeAnn with ya?" asked Andy, his hopes dangling on a string.

"Not a chance in hell, Andy. But you knew that already," replied Jess, smiling.

"Well, ya can't blame a man for tryin'," replied Andy.

"That's exactly what I was talking about," Tony said, laughing. "The man can't keep his yap shut."

Jess walked his horses out of the livery and mounted up. He had decided to call his new horses the same names, Gray and Sharps. He liked to keep things simple. He nodded his head to Tony and Andy and turned his horse toward the end of the street.

As he walked his horse out of town some of the townsfolk waved at him as if to say thank you. He felt good about that. As he got to the end of the street there was an old lady sitting on her porch in a rocking chair. She stood up as he passed her place. It was the old lady who had spoken to him back in Carter's Hardware store the day he chased all the customers out and over to Jim's store.

"You take good care of yourself, young Mr. Williams. Some of the people in town won't say it, but most of them are grateful for what you did. And for me, you keep doing it. There are a lot of people out there who need someone like you even though they might not know it."

He smiled at her and removed his hat in respect. "Why ma'am, I think that's probably the nicest thing anyone has ever said to me," replied Jess, stopping momentarily. "Thank you and I promise you that I will continue doing what seems to have turned out to be my life's work. You take care of yourself, ma'am," he said and he began again on the road leaving town.

As he rode that first day, he thought a lot about what had happened. He thought about his father and where he might find him and when. It didn't matter, just so long as he finally did. When that day arrived, he would deal with it in the same manner as he had with his brother. He smiled at the irony of being the one to finally collect the blood bounty that Carter had place on his head.

It was a cold but sunny day with just a slight hint of a breeze. He shuddered a little. Not from the cold though. It was because he remembered about Andy asking him to take LeAnn with him.

# COLLECT THE ENTIRE JESS WILLIAMS SERIES

The series of Jess Williams novels continues with the third novel, titles **"JESS WILLIAMS—SINS OF THE FATHER."** This third novel is due out in 2006. It will be the third novel in a series based on the same fascinating character.

Follow Jess Williams' life story as he travels throughout the West working as a bounty hunter and being truly the fastest man alive in the Old West with a pistol.

On the next several pages you will find an excerpt from **"JESS WILLIAMS—SINS OF THE FATHER."** In the back of this book, you will find how you can order your copy today along with other books available by the author and bojibooks.

Read on...

# Sin's Of The Father

The saloon was no different than any other saloon that one would find in many of the small towns scattered throughout the west. It reeked of cheap whiskey, and cigar smoke lingered heavily in the air. There was one bartender behind the bar and a few women sitting around waiting for one of the men to take them upstairs for a little attention. One of the women was sitting next to a man who was playing poker at a table with three other men. They had been playing for several hours now, and it was obvious to everyone in the game who was in control. Eddie Sloan always liked to have a whore sitting next to him when he was playing cards and he always liked to control the game. Most of the time he could control it simply through his well-honed skill at the game and when that didn't work, he could always fall back on his cheating skills. Sloan had honed his cheating skills over the years to a level of perfection that most men would never acquire. He could palm cards, hide them and make them disappear without anyone else noticing it. He would practice those skills in his hotel room every day so that he could always keep sharp and way ahead of the best of players.

He would often ride out of whatever town he was staying in and practice his pistol skills for hours. It was another skill that went along with his profession as an expert poker player, especially when someone at the table would finally get fed up with losing every hand and make the mistake of calling Eddie Sloan a cheat or a liar. That was the mistake Brad Tillman was making at this moment.

"Jesus Christ!" exclaimed Tillman. "How in the hell did you get another two pair? Hell, I've never had that many good hands in a row in any game and I've played a lot of poker. You just can't be that lucky, it ain't natural."

Sloan leaned back in his chair and picked up his cigar and took a long pull on it and let it out slowly, savoring the flavor. He enjoyed a good cigar much like he enjoyed a good whore once in a while. He looked completely relaxed and completely within his environment. He looked at the other two men as if to see if they were going to start complaining. Sloan could see in their faces that they wanted to say something, but they would not. They knew all too well that Eddie Sloan was not a man to cross or especially call a cheat. They would be no problem for Sloan. They would simply lose all their money to Sloan and walk away, which is exactly what most of the men who played poker against Sloan always did. Poker was a little like being a gunslinger. Even though you knew the man you were up against was a better player, you just had to try your luck to see if you could be the one who could brag that you beat the best poker player in the west—Eddie Sloan. To this day, no one had ever beaten Sloan at poker and this day would be no different. The pot on the table had grown to almost two hundred dollars before Tillman called Sloan's hand. Tillman thought he finally had a winning hand with a pair of kings and a pair of fours. His smile had quickly faded when Sloan laid his pair of aces and a pair of eights on the table. This was the hand that had quickly become known as *the dead man's hand*. It was the very same hand that Wild Bill Hickok was holding when Jack McCall shot him in the back while Hickok was playing in a poker game in Deadwood, South Dakota on August 2, 1876.

Sloan looked squarely into Brad Tillman's eyes and found what he was looking for. "So, what are you saying, Tillman? Are you saying that I'm unnaturally lucky?"

Tillman leaned forward in his chair. "I'm saying anyone who can win that many hands and have that many good hands in that short of a time has got to be cheating."

It was the one thing that Brad Tillman shouldn't have said, but he had said it now and there was no taking the comment back. Sloan motioned for his whore to go to the bar. She knew what that meant and she did not linger. She had seen this before and knew that it would not be long before lead flew and someone died. She walked up to the bar next to a tall man who had a full head of golden hair along with a beard and a mustache. He was sipping whiskey and watching the event unfold as if he had bought a ticket for it. When she placed herself to the left of the man, she partially blocked his view of the poker table and the man politely asked her if she could move to his right.

She looked up at him curiously. "You've never seen a gunfight before?" she asked, somewhat nonchalantly.

Frank Reedy looked her over. She was prettier than most of the women who worked in her profession. "Normally, I don't much care to watch one man shoot it out with another for no good reason, but I have a vested interest in this one."

Her curiosity grew a little more. "What do you mean? Do you know those men?"

"I know one of them. Eddie Sloan. The man you were sitting with. You know the one who keeps winning hand after hand."

She laughed. "I don't know what you'd call it. He is either the luckiest man I've ever met or the best poker player anywhere in the west, but he never loses a game. What is your interest in him? If you're looking to get into the game, I believe there will be an empty seat real soon," she said, looking past Reedy's shoulder at the unfolding argument.

Eddie Sloan had put down his cigar. He was now glaring at Brad Tillman. "Mister, did I hear you correctly. Did you just call me a cheat?"

Tillman pushed back his chair and slowly stood up. "I do believe that's what I called you—a cheat. I heard about you before and that's why I got into this game. I wanted to know if the great Eddie Sloan was really the best poker player in the west or if he was a cheat. Now I know the answer. I've played a lot of poker and no one is that lucky for that long of a time."

Frank Reedy watched intently as Eddie Sloan slowly stood up to face Brad Tillman. "I'm going to do you a favor," said Sloan. "I'm going to give you a chance to apologize for your remarks and then ask you to leave the game and the saloon. Also, don't ever sit at a game that I'm playing in, ever. If you do, I will plug you before your ass hits the chair."

"And what If I don't?" replied Tillman, a growing defiance in his voice.

Sloan sneered at Tillman. "Then we will have to see if you can handle that side iron better than a deck of cards."

"I can play just fine, when everyone at the table is playing fair and with the same deck of cards."

Sloan lowered his head a little. "Now, there you go again, saying something that you ought not to. I warned you once; I'm not going to warn you again."

"You can kiss my ass, Sloan. I can beat you in a fair card game and I think I can beat you on the draw, too."

"You might be making a big mistake thinking that, Tillman. You ain't got a chance in hell of beating me. I'm telling you, if you snake that thing out, I'll plug you before you clear leather."

"Yeah…let's just see about that."

Brad Tillman went for his Colt .45. His hand reached the butt of his pistol and he had barely started to get it out of the holster when Sloan's Colt .45 barked loudly, punching a hole right through the middle of Tillman's chest. Tillman stumbled backwards and Sloan put another slug into Tillman's chest as he was falling over, making sure he would not get back up from the floor. Sloan looked around the room to see if anyone else was going to challenge him and when he saw none, he simply whirled his Colt .45 back into his holster and began to sit back down and collect his pot of money when Frank Reedy spoke.

"Mr. Sloan, that was mighty impressive. I've seen some fast guns but you are one of the fastest men on the draw I've seen in a long time," said Reedy, keeping both hands on the bar so as not to give Sloan the wrong idea.

Sloan had stopped his movement toward his seat and stood back up and looked Frank Reedy over for a moment. "You look like you might be one of them bounty hunters. Are you planning on trying my hand too?"

Reedy shook his head. "No sir, not me. I know my limitations and I know I can't beat you on the draw, that's for sure."

"Well, good, you're a smart man to admit it. It's too bad Tillman there wasn't as smart," remarked Sloan, glancing over at the now dead body of Brad Tillman. Sloan again started the movement of sitting back down in his chair and was stopped by Frank Reedy's next statement.

"I do, however, know someone who *is* faster than you."

That got Sloan's attention right away and he stood straight back up. Then he smiled. "You must be talking about my boy, Tim. He's about the only one I know that might have a chance against me and that's because I taught him everything I know about drawing and shooting a pistol."

"Evidently, you didn't teach him enough."

Sloan's demeanor turned somewhat darker. "What the hell does that mean?"

"Tim Sloan seems to have managed to get himself killed." replied Reedy, still keeping his hands on the bar so as not to give Eddie Sloan any reason to think that Reedy was going to challenge him.

Sloan looked down at the table, thinking out loud for a moment. "I wondered why I hadn't seen him. Hell, I thought he went out East to play poker and was having too much fun and hadn't made it back yet..." Then Sloan looked up at Reedy with a glare. "Are you the one who killed my boy?"

Reedy shook his head no as he answered. "No, I didn't kill your boy, but I know who did."

"Who?" demanded Sloan.

"Your only living son," answered Reedy, a mischievous grin on his face.

Sloan was thoroughly confused, which wasn't something he was used to. "What the hell are you talking about? I only had one son, and now you're telling me he was killed by my only *living* son? That doesn't make any sense to me." Sloan thought again for a minute and then it finally came to him. He remembered about leaving Tim's brother back with the woman who had bore him his two sons. He had taken the one son who looked to be the stronger of the two. "I'll be damned. I haven't seen or heard from my other boy since he was a baby. And now you tell me that he's gone and killed his own brother, Tim?"

Reedy looked at Sloan with that same strange grin. "I know it sounds kind of crazy but yes, that's what I'm telling you."

"Well, why the hell do you suppose he went and did that?"

"You'll be able to ask him that yourself in a moment or so. He is probably walking up the street as we speak."

"What the hell is he doing here?"

"He's looking for you."

# ACKNOWLEDGEMENTS

Thanks to **Dave Hile** from Hile Illustrations for the magnificent artwork on the cover and **Barb Gunia** from Sans Serif. They are both spectacular people who have this innate ability to capture just what I am looking for on the covers of my books.

Thanks to my dearest friend, **Michael J. Reddy Sr.,** from Immortal Investments Publishing has published many famous sports celebrity books including Gordie Howe, Bill Gadsby, Willie Horton, Otto Graham, Eddie Feigner and Billy Taylor. He will also be publishing books for Lem Barney, Johnny Bower, and many more. Michael will also be depicted on the cover of "Sin's of the Father," which will be the third book in the series. Thanks for always lending an ear and your continued support. Michael will be depicted in this series of books as Frank Reedy and he will be on the cover of the third book, SINS OF THE FATHER.

My wonderful, beautiful and talented wife, **Jill**. She is responsible for the typesetting and formatting of everything between the covers. In other words, she makes it all look good.

**Michael J. Reddy Jr.,** another fantastic person and true friend. He is depicted on the cover as Tim Sloan, Jess Williams' brother.

**Mark Neal** who is depicted as Eddie Sloan on the cover. Thanks for your friendship and making Eddie Sloan come to life. You can see him ghosted in the clouds. He will also be on the cover of "Sin's of the Father."

# Acknowledgements

**Murry Kalinsky** who is depicted as a bounty hunter named Murry in this book. Murry is from New York and we became friends when we met in Cancun, Mexico. Murry recently lost his beautiful wife Judy and we will all miss her. She was a great lady.

**Carl DiCono** who is depicted as a bounty hunter named Carl and the partner of Murry. Carl is from Atlanta, Georgia, and if you were to ever meet Carl and Murry, you would understand why I used them as characters in this novel. Carl was also from New York and now lives in Atlanta with his wonderful wife, Anita.

Thanks to all of my rough draft reviewers **Tim and Paul Oneill, Aimee Reddy, Bill Gabriel, Tammy Harder,** and my grandson, **Eric Lockhart**. They all helped in making the book better. If you find any typos in this novel, I'm sure it's their fault.

A special thank you once again to **Ted Williams Jr.,** who depicts Jess Williams on the cover. When I asked him if he would pose for the cover on the first book, he did so enthusiastically and with a flare that only he could pull off. The illustrator and photographers were amazed at how well he responded to the camera and how well the photos turned out. So when I asked him to pose for the second and third book covers, he never hesitated, and once again captured just what we were looking for. He's a perfect model able to slide right into character and a great friend.

From Left to Right: Bob Mernickle (Custom Holster Designer), Shandrianna, Sherrie (Wife), Stormie

I want to once again thank Bob Mernickle of MERNICKLE CUSTOM HOLSTERS for his craftsmanship in designing the holsters you see on the covers of the Jess Williams novels. This holsters were custom built for me by Bob and were designed for fast draw use. Bob has been designing and building custom holsters of all kinds for over twenty-five years. He can build almost anything you need and designs a large line of custom leather goods for weapons old and new. If you want the best in quality and design, he is the man to call.

Mernickle Custom Holsters
1875 View Court
Fernley, NV 89408
www.mernickleholsters.com
Phone: 775-575-3166
Monday through Thursday 9:00 a.m. to 5:00 p.m. (PT)
Fax: 604-826-0518 ▪ Toll Free: 800-497-3166

# Immortal Investments Publishing

Michael J. Reddy, Publisher
35122 W. Michigan Avenue
Wayne, Michigan 48184
Phone 800 475-2066
Fax 734 467-6312
www.immortalinvestments.com

## Presents...

**"Mr. & Mrs. Hockey®"**
Gordie & Colleen Howe

■

**"The Grateful Gadsby"**
Bill Gadsby

■

**"The People's Champion"**
Willie Horton

■

**"Get Back Up"**
Billy Taylor

■

**"From an Orphan to a King"**
Eddie Feigner

■

**"OttoMatic"**
Otto Graham

Visit **www.immortalinvestments.com** to view more books available.

Robert J. Thomas began his writing career after serving as Mayor of the City of Westland, Michigan, for three consecutive four-year terms. His first work was a non-fiction book titled HOW TO RUN FOR LOCAL OFFICE, which has been sold worldwide and is used by college professors around the country as a teaching manual. This book has since been followed up with HOW TO STAY IN PUBLIC OFFICE, which is proving to be another success.

His love for western books and movies has turned his attention to a series of western novels based on the character Jess Williams. THE RECKONING is the first in a series of western novels by the author and BROTHER'S KEEPER is the second in the series.

Robert currently resides in the City of Westland where he is working on the third book in the Jess Williams series titled SINS OF THE FATHER.